ELVIS LIVES ON PLANET FOOTBALL

Windsor Holden

For Tracy, with all my love

ABOUT THE AUTHOR

Windsor Holden was born in Newport, Monmouthshire, in 1970. He studied at the universities of Southampton, Rutgers (New Jersey) and Leeds, before embarking on a career as a telecoms analyst. *Elvis Lives on Planet Football* is his first novel.

He is married with two sons, two stepdaughters and lives in West Sussex.

He has always been very, very bad at football.

Cover design by John Amy.

CHAPTER ONE

I

Macko, dirty bastard, hadn't cleaned the pan. Gerry was not surprised: the thick black etchings on the porcelain were Macko's trademark after a night on the Guinness. And last night, after all, Macko had drunk one hell of a lot of Guinness.

Gerry winced, pulled down his boxers and gingerly rested his behind upon the throne. He stared, bleary-eyed, at the dog-eared pile of magazines – *FHM*s, *Loaded*s - tucked just inside the door, before gingerly selecting a copy. He settled back, the evacuation a sudden explosion before he got halfway through the first sentence of a randomly selected article on the joys of group sex.

Gerry reached out absently for the toilet roll that was perched on top of the stone-cold radiator. There was a toilet roll-holder jutting out from the wall, but the roll encompassing it had not seen any paper since the house's last female inhabitant, a sales assistant at Asda, had left in disgust - at the house in general and Macko in particular – some three months ago. In the interim, successive rolls had simply been located within arm's reach, and their cardboard skeletons now formed an abstract sculpture at Gerry's feet.

No paper. No fucking paper.

Save for a wispy, apologetic shred, the latest roll, too, had run its course. Macko, as the previous incumbent of the bathroom, should have observed the proper etiquette and fetched a new one from the airing cupboard on the landing. But had he hell.

Well, he could fucking get one now. Gerry glared at the back of the bathroom door. "Macko!"

The Irish twat had not sunk back into torpor just yet

5

- there had been noises off during Gerry's brief sojourn in the bathroom, shufflings and coughings suggesting that Macko was probably rummaging through his pockets in the hope of finding a cigarette. At Gerry's cry – hoarse, broken-voiced – the noises ceased abruptly.

A muffled "What?" Then a volley of coughs, descending into a rasping retch.

"You Irish bastard!"

"Would there be a problem?"

"You've used all the bastard paper, you bastard!"

There was a brief pause. "Then there would be a problem, wouldn't there?"

"Yes there bastard would!"

"There's some paper in the airing cupboard."

The back of the bathroom door got the Gerry glare treatment again. "Macko, my keks are round my ankles and there's shit dripping from my ring."

"I appreciate your predicament."

"Roddy McCall, could you alleviate it by fetching the paper? If you would be so kind."

"You just called me a bastard."

"Bearing in mind you're the bastard that used all the paper, then you're still a bastard."

"Say please."

"Please you Irish bastard will you bring me the bastard bog-roll."

Gerry heard Macko make his way through the obstacle course of dirty laundry that was his bedroom floor, heard the airing cupboard door creak open and shut. Macko knocked delicately on the bathroom door, and Gerry levered himself (equally delicately) from the throne, stretching out to the door handle while still half-squatting. He opened the door just far enough to permit Macko to thrust a pristine roll into his hand, before settling back, appeased, to swab up.

"Don't use it all at once", called Macko, as he ambled down the stairs.

II

Their house was part of a redbrick terrace, late-Victorian or early-Edwardian, vying with its neighbours to be the most drab and wretched in the street. As Africa, *fin de siecle*, the houses had been divided up amongst a small number of regional powers: only here the Salisburys and the Bismarcks were the Hardwickes and the Patels, whose similarity to the great imperialists ended with a shared indifference to their tenants' welfare. Gradually, as the incumbent occupiers died or moved away, Hardwicke and Patel moved in, augmenting their dismal suzerainties property by property across the suburban sprawl north of Leeds.

Arshad Patel now owned seventeen such properties, five in this street alone; Norman Hardwicke's tally was thirteen (a fourteenth pending), and he, too, had a significant presence here (here being Birch Lane), with four houses. They assured would-be tenants, both in the small ads in the *Evening Post* and when unctuously showing off the properties, that all were "mixed professional" houses. Should any interested party enquire as to the state of the cooker/curtains/carpet/etcetera, then Mr Patel would tut vigorously, or Mr Hardwicke would mutter into his beard, and dark tales of good-for-nothing (and frequently bone-idle) students would be trotted out: on a lighter note, such wastrels would never darken the door of these houses again, as these days Mr Patel (and of course Mr Hardwicke) took a keen interest in all their charges. Meanwhile, the matter of the cooker/curtains/carpet/etcetera was "in hand" and the offending item would probably be cleaned/replaced within the next few weeks.

Both Gerry and Macko were agreed that Norman Hardwicke's tenants were mixed, if not all professional: in with the twentysomething teachers, trainee accountants, bank clerks, telesales staff and blue-collar boys came an assortment of petty criminals, drug addicts, DSS claimants, students (good-for-nothing or otherwise, who had presumably slipped through the net on days when the keen anti-student radar of Mr Hardwicke had been deactivated), and the occasional illegal immigrant. They were rarely told of impending arrivals: on several occasions, they had returned home to find complete strangers in the house, leaving them unsure whether to call the landlord, the police, or both.

Indeed, that was how Gerry and Macko had first met. Gerry, returning from a traumatic weekend away at his then girlfriend's home in Wimbledon, had discovered a scrawny, unshaven man – late twenties at a guess - sitting cross-legged on the lumpen sofa, steadily working his way through Gerry's chocolate hobnobs, the phone jammed between ear and shoulder as he brooded over a TV listings magazine while engaging a telesales rep in earnest but chaotic conversation over the relative costs of the various adult channels. He looked up with a grin as Gerry thought, *Oh no, what have we got this time?*

"If we go halves, d'ya fancy TVX?" he had asked hopefully. And to Macko's great delight, Gerry, after contemplating the matter for around two seconds (*What would Emma think – oh, fuck her*) had said, *yeah, OK; besides, it's better than the crap on the other filth channels.*

And thus, over a mutual appreciation of satellite pornography, was a lasting friendship born.

III

Gerry Angel worked in a sprawling further education college on the outskirts of Leeds, low in repute but high in self-importance. While Gerry recognised its limitations, he was at the same time profoundly grateful that it had given him the opportunity of a first post in academia, albeit one that obliged him to perform the more menial tasks eschewed by his superiors in the Department of Sociology, such as developing, maintaining and interrogating a research database and teaching first-year undergraduates about post-modernism first thing on a Monday morning. It was, he hoped, a stepping stone to greatness, or – failing that – a senior fellowship at a University that people had vaguely heard of, a publishing deal and maybe the odd appearance as a talking head on *Newsnight*.

However, it was not an employment that particularly taxed or indeed interested him. Or, just as worrying for Gerry, one that was likely to excite the interest of anyone beyond the confines of Scrimpton College. Nothing had emerged in the course of his research that was likely to win him that first publishing deal. It was a pity, he often thought to himself, that he couldn't simply make Macko the subject of any future thesis. The how, why, what – and, some nights, where - of Macko, he firmly believed, would be enough to fill a small encyclopaedia, although one best kept out of reach of children and those of a nervous disposition. Like Gerry, Macko worked at (or at least, was paid by) the college; he had been employed there in an administrative capacity for several months before his appearance on Gerry's sofa, but since Gerry had little call or desire to visit the stolid, gloomy building which housed the college's administrative heart, and since

Macko spent most of his time on the premises conscientiously seeking to avoid anything which approximated to gainful activity, it was hardly surprising that their paths had not previously crossed. Unlike Gerry, Macko had no career plan, unless it were to shift still greater quantities of Guinness while simultaneously engaging in the vague but hopeful pursuit of every female that caught his eye.

However, to say that Macko had no ambitions was not strictly true. He had several, worthy enough in their own way.

"I'd like to fuck the alphabet", he had said one morning, à propos of nothing.

Gerry had to know more, and said so.

"You know, work my way through from A-Z. Although not necessarily in alphabetical order. And if you limited yourself to one of each you might miss out."

Gerry was impressed by the scale of the task facing his housemate, but felt obliged to point out some of the obvious difficulties facing him. (Obvious to Gerry, but perhaps not to Macko.)

"What about X?"

"Xena," said Macko, stoutly.

"How many bloody women are you going to come across called Xena in Yorkshire?"

Macko became somewhat defensive. "Cross that bridge when I come to it."

"How many bridges you crossed so far?"

Fingers and thumbs came into operation as Macko did some impromptu calculations.

"Twelve down, fourteen to go. Pity I can't swap some of the As and Ls for Xs and Zs, but there you go."

Suddenly Macko's challenge had assumed a rule structure all of its own, where multiple couplings with ladies of the same initial were permissible but tradeoffs of those ladies were not. Gerry accepted those rules, and with that acceptance became the *de facto* arbiter of the contest, subjecting them to minute scrutiny.

"What letters have we got then?"

"A, B, C, F…"

"F?"

"Fiona Graham. Lass at sixth form college. Good shag, wanted kids at seventeen, fuck that."

"Fair enough. Next?"

"H, J, K?"

"K?"

"Katherine whatsit. Ritzy's Katherine. Tits Katherine."

"Hang on, are we counting actual penetrative sex here?"

"Oh, definitively."

"Well, I seem to recall the only time you got Katherine into the sack you told me you were too pissed to get it up." Macko looked sheepish. "Down to eleven then, mate?"

Wandering over to the sink, Macko brightened up.

"Well, you know what they say, a job half done is a job begun. I'll get there sooner or later."

At his current rate of progress, it would be later rather than sooner, thought Gerry. It had been a fallow period for Macko since Gerry had glimpsed a slim blonde hastily traversing the landing a couple of months ago. That was not for want of trying: Gerry had observed at close hand – not without a touch of *schadenfreude* – a succession of knock-backs in the pubs, nightclubs, bus stations and taxi ranks of Leeds and its suburbs, knock-backs couched in varying degrees of delicacy and emotion, knock-backs that more than once ventured into the physical arena leaving Macko nursing a bruised eye, cheek or – on one occasion – testicles. Still, none of these failures had dimmed Macko's apparently inexhaustible, Panglossian optimism that tonight would be the night.

Not that I can talk. Gerry had been single for nearly six months now. He had met Emma at a party shortly after the start of his Master's degree at Scrimpton; she had been in the final year of a media studies course. Over the course of a evening fuelled by copious quantities of Sauvignon Blanc, she had declaimed extensively on structuralism and post-structuralism, modernism and post-modernism, the conversation seguing exotically across the theories of Barthes, Cixous and Lyotard as filtered by the mind of Emma Mayhew; Gerry had nodded sagely, and through an alcoholic fugue, thought that: *well, she's a bit chubby, but she's got nice tits. I wonder...*

They had woken up the next morning in Gerry's bed and spent the next three years together.

It had been a disjointed togetherness. Within a few months, she had sat her finals, achieved a decent result, and decamped back to her parents' home in Wimbledon for a brief spell; she had found a job as an account manager with a West End advertising agency, rented a room in an Ealing flat and bought a golden hamster, upon which (or so it seemed to Gerry) she lavished far more attention than she ever had upon him. For his part, Gerry had – to his surprise and delight – achieved a distinction in his Master's, on the back of which the college had offered him a research post, an offer accepted with alacrity.

It was never going to go down well with Emma. Even before she found the agency job, Emma had been trying to sell him the idea of his moving down to London; of his moving in with her, doing some temping. Once she had started work, she had steadily upped the tempo, sometimes wheedling, sometimes aggressive; sometimes expatiating on the delights of the capital, sometimes bombarding him with selective grim recollections of her student days in Yorkshire.

Rather than tell Emma of his decision over the phone, he had taken the train down to King's Cross that evening and paid her a visit at the Ealing flat, where effusive congratulations on his achievement (or effusive thanks for the bouquet he had bought for her at the train station) were conspicuous by their absence: instead, she imbued the evening with a calm, considered coolness at the news that Gerry Angel would, in effect, be continuing to live the student lifestyle at a northern college while she was doing a proper job in the heart of the metropolis.

No sex tonight, Gerry thought gloomily; and he was right.

He was introduced to the hamster, which bit him on the thumb.

That was the beginning of the end, although the dénouement would be prolonged and desolate. Even during their brief period of proximity in Scrimpton, it had rapidly become apparent that they had little in common and yet neither was willing to admit it, preferring to soldier gamely on than sever the tenuous romantic link; perhaps some kind of relationship, however ill-starred, was better than none at all. Despite the geographical separation necessitated by Emma's relocation and Gerry's entrenchment at the college, they grimly endured, although the weekly migrations from north to south – and vice versa – soon became fortnightly, then monthly, while the nightly telephone conversations petered out into curt calls occurring twice weekly, then once, as they increasingly realised that there was less and less to say to one another.

Gerry had finished it in the end, delivering the announcement over the phone in a monotone. She had not demurred: maybe this was a mercy killing for their relationship; maybe she was grateful; maybe she hadn't cried afterwards. That was how he tried to justify and console himself, as he set down the receiver and wept.

He had wept for the remainder of that evening, and intermittently for much of the following day, breaking into uncontrollable bouts of sobbing as memories forced their way cruelly into everyday activities: watching *Supermarket Sweep*, watching *Neighbours*, watching the preamble to the Merseyside derby on *Monday Night Football*. He had dissolved into tears yet again, attempting to force down a few mouthfuls of toast for dinner as the game kicked off, when he had become aware that Macko was watching him from the doorway, expressionless, having materialised in the shadows. Gerry looked up, beginning a stumbling apology for not having shouted to Macko that the game had started, and besides he hadn't thought that Macko would want to watch it because Liverpool were playing and he was always calling them a shower of Scouse shite, and then the tears caught up with him again.

Macko considered him for a moment, his mouth creasing into a frown.

"I'm not having this," he said at length. "Be back with ya in a mo."

Six mos, in fact. Bringing with him two fourpacks of lager and a quarter bottle of cheap whisky. All of which – together with half a bottle of Thunderbird that Macko found at the back of a cupboard when the whisky was running low – disappeared over the course of the next five hours. During this period Gerry underwent a Damascene conversion, prompted by a comment that Macko dropped, à propos of nothing, into the conversation.

"I mean, let's be honest Jez. At the end of the day she treated you like a piece of shit and she was fat and ugly."

A shaft of enlightenment. She had, realised Gerry with a vengeance, treated me like a piece of shit. And she was fat and ugly. What the fuck had he seen in her?

The following morning, Gerry had woken up with a hangover that told him in no uncertain terms he should not even consider raising his head from the pillow for the foreseeable future. He had bowed to the hangover's greater knowledge and remained huddled under the duvet for much of the day, head throbbing and body aching, until a call of nature obliged him to stagger across the landing to the toilet. But the lager, whisky and Thunderbird had had the desired purgative effect: his feelings for Emma had been expunged as fully as his sobriety the previous evening. As the sun sank and he shuffled down to breakfast cum dinner in his dressing gown, he realised with a sense of release that he was free: to fart in bed; to go out on the lash; to buy pornographic magazines; to watch football; to cast a discerning eye at the multitude of pretty young undergraduates that coursed through his department. At that moment he cast off the burdenings of guilt and shame and rejoiced in the glorious, carefree sense of indulgence that he had rediscovered. And promptly got dressed and went down the pub.

Besides, he had never liked Barthes.

IV

"He was a weird fucker last night," said Macko, sipping his coffee. The contretemps over toilet rolls forgotten, the pair now breakfasted on the remnants of the previous evening's pizza.

"Who?" Gerry stared at him across the table, briefly uncomprehending, before realisation dawned as to the identity of the weird fucker in question. "Oh, him."

15

Him. Sixty-five, maybe seventy; lean, pock-marked face; greying hair that had been slicked and greased backwards, forwards, everywhere; sideburns that seemed to merge into the profuse curly growths that poured from his substantial ears; dry, dry lips.

They had stumbled across him in a bar off the Headrow, a former spit n' sawdust pub that had recently been renovated and reimagined in the hope of attracting a younger, more cash-rich demographic. To an extent it had succeeded: all around them was new Leeds, brash, besuited, excessive, vociferous, bellowing over a thudding bass backdrop for chilled lager or a white wine spritzer. Yet dotted amongst these newcomers were a few remnants of the old guard, singly and in twos and threes, still sitting at the same old tables (or to be precise, in the same locations where those old, grizzled tables had stood prior to being shipped out to the amenities' tip and replaced by pristine, black square-topped items stained with a veneer finish) and resolutely supping their bitter. For Gerry and Macko, the bar was not a regular haunt by any means: it was the tail end of a long session that had embraced many pubs in the city centre, and they had entered simply because Macko had been following a lady's derriere down the Headrow, a small, round *fecking perfect* lady's derriere wearing lurid and limited lycra, a derriere that had talked to Macko as it passed him atop a pair of supple thighs and had begged him to keep up. So he had followed it and Gerry, sighing inwardly, had followed Macko: and no sooner had they entered the bar than the derriere had been swallowed up amidst a heaving mass of suits and noise. And instead, they had found *him*, sitting alone with his pint.

It being just about the only table in the place with unclaimed seats, Gerry and Macko had immediately laid claim to them, Gerry flinging his jacket across one while braving the melee at the bar and emerging ten minutes later with a Guinness and a pint of bitter. In his absence, Macko had fretfully scanned the area for any sign of the derriere, but to no avail. His older companion had said nothing, nor did he do so until well after Gerry's return, simply staring into space; Gerry and Macko were essentially oblivious to his presence, engaged in a vigorous discussion over the relative charms of female TV presenters, until Gerry became aware that his sleeve was being tugged by a mottled, scrawny hand. He looked across to see that the old soak was staring intently at him.

"He's still alive, mate. Don't believe that 'he died on the bog' bollocks. Wasn't his body. Did you see the body? Wax dummy, mate. Wax dummy."

Gerry and Macko exchanged glances.

"Oh yes," said Gerry, a trifle hesitantly. The grip on his sleeve was released and their companion leaned back into the faux leather sofa.

"That coffin weighed 900 bleeding pounds. Nearly sixty-five stone. And do you know why? 'Cause there was a friggin' air conditioning unit in there to stop the wax from melting."

"Right," said Gerry. He thought, *I'm not sure where this is going but I'll roll with it for the moment. I'm sure we can take him if he turns nasty.*

"Think about the headstone. Whassit say? Elvis Aaron Presley. Not his name. One A. Alpha Romeo Oscar November, not Alpha Alpha. Now his dad: if that was really his boy in the ground, there'd've been one 'a', no doubt."

Oh, he's talking about Elvis! Why wouldn't he? And they had nodded sagely in response, and Gerry, though alcohol had kicked most cognitive processes out the window, had thought*: I don't care if Macko sees six birds with their tits hanging out heading this way, we'll* *skip this fucking pub from now on.*

"Now Elvis had loads of books: his bibles, his Book of Numbers, an Autobiography of Yogi" (the image of a cartoon bear at a book-signing session flashed irresistibly before Gerry's eyes, and he had to bite his lips to stop himself from giggling) "all that stuff he picked up from Larry Geller. And where did all these go to? Nobody knows. They just disappeared."

The storyteller sucked at his pint, temporarily moistening those dry lips. Gerry watched, transfixed, uneasy, as the froth and moisture disappeared into the parched crevices.

"This was a guy with loads of enemies. The Mafia wanted Elvis dead. He kept getting death threats – to himself, his wife, his family. The game wasn't worth the candle anymore, mate. Time to jack it all in."

"And?" said Macko, in spite of himself.

The lips parted to reveal a triumphal smile in all its decaying glory. "Two hours after Presley was reported dead, some guy looking just like him bought a ticket for Buenos Aires. The ticket was in the name of John Burrows. Which was a regular Presley pseudonym."

"So Presley fucked off to Argie-land?" asked Gerry.

"Nah, that's bollocks."

So it was a joke, thought Gerry. *Nice one, oddball.*

"You wouldn't go to fucking Argentina if you were Presley, would you? He had a good laugh when I told him about that one."

Macko half-laughed but the sound dried in his throat. Gerry looked sharply at their companion.

"'That would have been a comedown,' he said to me. 'Besides, the guys sorted things out real great.'" The storyteller's eyelids fluttered, and he rubbed his forehead with a bony forefinger and thumb. "Nah, he's got it good now, although he doesn't sing anymore. He said these days he gets to watch the footie. Got a season ticket. I mean, he told me he'd just been to the Leicester game at Elland Road. Said we should have pissed it."

The last dregs of his pint were drained, and dimly, above the raucous yells and the whirring of his own mind Gerry heard bar staff asking for glasses. The storyteller rose, and for the first time Gerry noticed how tall he was, and how painfully, pitiably thin.

"I'll be seeing you, then. Night, lads."

"Night," replied Macko, faintly, to the storyteller's back as he stooped in the doorway, then was swallowed up by the departing throng. Macko drummed his fingers on the table and turned to Gerry.

"Fuck me. Elland bloody Road."

"What a load of bollocks." Gerry enunciated each word slowly, meticulously: and yet as they both dissolved into laughter, Gerry felt a brief, inexplicable chill dart its way up his spine.

V

Him. He laughed again at the memory, not a good idea with a mouth full of cold pizza. He laughed, but: that chill again. *Stop it,* he told himself: *your man was a care in the community case.*

"Reckon it'd be worth goin' to the next Leeds game then?" asked Macko.

"You go to a Leeds match?"

"Well, obviously I'd take a piss outside the main gates as a mark of disrespect, and I wouldn't wear me little Roy Keane number, but Jesus, if Elvis is gonna show? After all, Elvis at sixty in the stand's gotta be better entertainment than the shower on the pitch."

Gerry nodded vaguely and smiled. Macko was the footie nut, although he predominantly surveyed matches from the sofa, occasional visits to Old Trafford notwithstanding: Sky Sports had followed TVX almost immediately, so that Macko could enjoy Premiership action, Spanish football and the Bundesliga more or less on tap. Gerry enjoyed football, appreciated a good game, but did not crave wall-to-wall matches to fill his every waking hour in the way that Macko did, or at least those waking hours which were not spent watching pornography and in the largely fruitless pursuit of tail. For Gerry, it had been an obsession, pretty much, in his pre-adolescence: a Liverpool fan from the Welsh valleys, he had endured delicious agonies listening to countless commentaries on his portable radio, desperate for Kenny Dalglish or David Johnson to win it at the death, or for David Fairclough, Super Sub, to come on and clinch it. In those days, one or other of them nearly always did, and on Monday mornings he and his mates could taunt the minority of kids who had opted for Forest or United or Arsenal.

But even before the titles dried up, even before King Kenny hung up his boots, other challengers were emerging for his affections: as Liverpool sank behind first Everton, then Arsenal, Gerry was already devoting more time to other interests: sci-fi, music, birdwatching. Faced with the choice of an afternoon following the scores on Sport on 2 and Ceefax, or an afternoon in a cold, damp hide at the reservoir squinting through binoculars at an array of dun-coloured waders, he would usually opt for the latter. He was a nerd, but what the hell, he had just clocked a black-tailed godwit.

In turn, black-tailed godwits would be pushed down the pecking order as Gerry became a goth, or more accurately a demi-goth: he liked the music, liked some of the clothes, but didn't have the inclination to embrace the lifestyle as wholeheartedly as many who wound up on the Scrimpton campus: an assortment of silk black shirts, skinny black jeans and demonic jewelry would be donned when the occasion demanded it – such as a gig or a night out down the Cockpit – but deep down, he was never able to escape from the impression that, all dolled up in his gear, he did look a bit of a tit. So by the time the Master's came along, the silk shirts had been at the back of the wardrobe for many months.

When Macko had moved in, Gerry's football intake had naturally increased dramatically once more, although – despite Macko's best efforts – it never again achieved the obsessive heights of nearly twenty years before.

Partly because, these days, Liverpool were fucking awful.

VI

It was a poky, one-bedroomed flat, sparsely and plainly furnished: but it suited his needs admirably. Located less than ten minutes' brisk walk from the ground, it was also relatively secluded, the upper floor of a semi-detached property near Holbeck cemetery. The other flats in the building had, unsurprisingly, been vacated before he moved in: occasionally one or other would be occupied by an agent sent from Upper Lupton to check on him, but for the most part they remained empty and silent: perfect.

Just across from the cemetery was a small corner shop where he could buy his groceries: nothing fancy, nothing extravagant, but then his tastes didn't run in that direction. Besides, the modest allowance that he had been allocated wouldn't have allowed it, particularly when the cost of a season ticket and a Sky Sports subscription had been taken into account. He was content with a bowl of cereal for breakfast and a ham sarnie for lunch; with Fray Bentos pies for dinner, accompanied by mash and frozen veg; with cut-price ready meals; with sausage, egg and chips; with chicken bhuna once a fortnight from the Indian at the far end of Elland Road; with instant coffee and a few cans of discount lager. That did him fine.

In season, the football was all that really mattered. He would attend all the home games, catch the away games that were televised on Sky, and listen to the remainder on local radio. During the games, he tried to avoid more than the occasional interaction with fans in neighbouring seats - Hartshorn had impressed upon him the need to keep such contact to a minimum if their arrangement were to be maintained, and to reduce the risk of exposure: fortunately, the fans that occupied the seats next to his own were far more interested in the activity on the field than in the appearance of the man who had turned up at the start of the '78-79 season and had been an everpresent since; a man whose features and physique, so bloated and flabby at that first game, had become steadily leaner over the years (Fray Bentos pies notwithstanding); the close-cropped hair had shifted gradually, imperceptibly, from chestnut to grey. His attire was inevitably the same – replica shirt, tracksuit bottoms, topped off by a parka when the local weather grew particularly inclement.

Hardly stylish attire, but all Leeds.

The pie, the mash and the veg were history; the washing up was done, and he was watching the video highlights of the '92 championship winning team: watching it for maybe the fiftieth time. But tonight he was distracted, disturbed: that old guy had recognised him as he left the Indian, or recognised who he used to be: had come up to him, talking about seeing him at the Hayride, before getting on to the stuff about John Burrows and Argentina. That was close to the bone; he had passed it off as a joke, rolled his eyes in mock despair at a couple of thickset, heavily-tattooed young men drinking on the street nearby, had made his excuses and left. That could have been awkward; could still be awkward, if he ran into the guy again.

There was another matter, more pressing, more exciting: more exhilarating. Earlier in the day he had felt the signal for the first time, faint but insistent: for the first time in twenty-one years, others were on their way. The signal was getting stronger by the hour; soon – in no more than a couple of days – they would make landfall.

For him, exhilarating; for them, dangerous. Because Hartshorn would send his men out to look for them.

CHAPTER TWO

I

In the last years of the twentieth century, the Air Staff 2 offices could be found on the fifth floor of the unimaginatively named Main Building in Whitehall. They comprised a handful of small, drab, unprepossessing rooms, indistinguishable from those elsewhere in that vast, soulless edifice. Indeed, their doleful uniformity had long been a cause of despair to the civil servants that passed their days engaged in the task, as grim and hopeless as that of Sisyphus, of administering the bureaucracy of the United Kingdom's defence. Even those employees that had worked in Air Staff 2 for several years would on occasion amble past their intended destination and finish up in Defence Intelligence 3 or Air Staff 4 or some equally colourless division or agency. They would then proffer their apologies for disturbing their counterparts in Defence Intelligence 3 or Air Staff 4 and retrace their steps along the fifth floor's labyrinthine corridors, sometimes arriving back at Air Staff 2 to discover a similarly confused individual in search of Logistics and Supply.

The main purpose of Air Staff 2 was to provide a point of contact between the public and the government *viz-a-viz* what might be broadly described as mysterious alien phenomena. And the desk officer of Air Staff 2 was its public face.

At present, that public face wore a pained, tired expression.

Graham Mayhew was fifty-five. For more of those years than he cared to remember he had been a desk officer with Air Staff 2: logging calls, answering routine enquiries pertaining to events witnessed for which those calling were unable to deduce any logical explanation. Usually, there *was* a logical explanation and he was able to provide it: freak meteorological conditions, low-flying aircraft. But occasionally there were calls pertaining to sightings for which Mayhew could provide no such explanation. And for these calls he would, with a heavy heart, be obliged to inform Blackwater, the department's link man with MI13. With a heavy heart, because later that week Blackwater would burst into the office, give Mayhew a cheeky, patronising wink, gather up the files relating to those sightings and depart, but usually only after he'd given Mayhew the lowdown on his latest sexual conquest.

Mayhew stared wearily at the orange folder on his desk. *Sod you*, he said to the folder. *I've had to call Blackwater because of you. I've had to get MI13 involved. I've had to involve a department that doesn't exist, and an absolute asshole who works for that department.*

Until comparatively recently, the British government had not formally acknowledged the existence of either MI5 or MI6, despite the former having a fairly obvious set of offices on the bank of the Thames. It was certainly not going to acknowledge the existence of MI13. The first military intelligence agency had been set up under the aegis of the War Office during the First World War, with the initial task of breaking codes used by the German armies. In the interwar years, the number of agencies had grown steadily in number, partly, it was alleged, to accommodate the growing number of Cambridge undergraduates needing comfortable sinecures; there were agencies for Russian intelligence (MI2), for Eastern European intelligence (MI3), for aerial reconnaissance (MI4), all the way along to MI19, which was charged with obtaining information from enemy prisoners. Gradually, most of the departments were merged into one another or else shut down, usually when someone belatedly realised that the majority of staff had been double agents for years.

According to the pseudo-histories of these various shadowy agencies, two MI numbers were never assigned: MI13 and MI18. This was only partly true. MI18 was never assigned simply because of a clerical error; such was the proliferation of agencies during the Second World War that the army officer charged with the creation of what became MI19 had been misinformed that MI18 actually existed, somewhere near Bletchley Park. MI13, by contrast, most certainly *did* exist, although its location and role was highly secret, known only to its thirty or so employees, a similar number of high-ranking MoD officials and military personnel, and the regulars of the Horse and Groom, a small pub outside Ascot, who would listen with interest on a Saturday night to Blackwater's high-volume descriptions of which aliens had been witnessed buzzing the planet over the previous seven days. The aforementioned regulars would then listen with an even greater interest as Blackwater briefed them on the latest developments in his love life, and indeed those in the love lives of every other civil servant in the department.

Once Blackwater's personal involvement in an enquiry had been confirmed – typically via a brief but expletive-laden telephone conversation – that enquiry would follow one of two well-established procedures. Under the first of these, Mayhew would be obliged to translate Blackwater's responses into print. Thus, "Thank you for your information: the Ministry does not yet have any explanation for the events you describe" was a stock if somewhat formal transliteration of "Fucked if I know, old son, and quite frankly we couldn't give a monkey's". However, if Blackwater said, "Leave it to me, old son" then it meant that Air Staff 2's involvement in the case was at an end, and that the big boys were taking over.

"Gray-ham! How we doin' me old son?"

Fine until you showed up, thought Mayhew, world weariness descending upon his shoulders. *Busy, even interesting, but fine. Now I have to brief you. But of course, you've been briefed already.*

"A mixed bag", he began cautiously, "but fairly lively. We had three separate sightings of irregular light patterns in Norfolk which were simply a few low-flying jets, one chap from Kent claiming to have seen a ball of purple fire above his house" – Blackwater snorted – "and (we haven't had one of these for a while) another chap from Scotland claims to have returned having been abducted by aliens." Another snort. Mayhew paused. *He knows, but let's continue the little charade.*

"And then there's this little lot."

Mayhew handed him the orange folder. Blackwater opened it, glanced carelessly at the first page and skimmed in a desultory fashion through the remainder.

"How were they submitted?"

"Two direct to us, four through the police."

"No other sightings outside West or North Yorkshire?" (*You know there aren't, Blackwater; you know.*)

"No, nothing."

Blackwater drummed his fingers on Mayhew's desk, cast his eyes to the ceiling, muttered to himself – "No landfall, yet, then" – and then picked up the folder.

"Look, I'll deal with this little lot, matey, if you don't mind", he said patronisingly, tucked the folder under his arm, and turned to leave. Then, almost as an afterthought:

"Can you deal with Purple Fire Ball Man and the others?"

Mayhew nodded. Even before Blackwater left the room, he had begun typing out the standard letter of reply.

Thirty yards up the corridor, Blackwater was already setting wheels in motion, mobile phone clamped to his ear.

"Alan? Alan! Good, matey boy, good. Look, I'm guessing you've heard already – yes, that's it – six in so far, but it's fairly early doors, so how shall we play this? OK. You reckon? Not sure, could just be the tip of the iceberg... I hear what you're saying, matey, I do, but I think if we get any more – any more – we've got to get the boys in... Oh, I think so, matey, I think very much so... After that bollocks that went down twenty years ago I should coco. Look, can you put me through to Brucey... Is he? How did he... Fuck, that sounds nasty, anyway, who's on instead of Brucey? OK, put Rich on... Rich! It's Adam! Look, no time to chat, got to – you did Elaine up the arse? No! You cunt, I only ever got fingers and tops with her... No she did not say I've got a small dick you lying cunt... no she fucking didn't! Anyway, you're a git, you know that? So how did you, er pop the question? I find it can be difficult to get the timing... oh, she stuck her finger? Yeah, that would be a pointer. Anyway, enough of Elaine's arse for the moment... Ha-bloody ha... I need you to keep your eyes peeled matey boy. Seriously peeled. Any reports of meteorites, straight on the blower. And look, this is gonna sound a bit odd, but... I'm betting that we're gonna start getting some rather scary reports in from hospitals in those areas, and fuck me, those places can be scary enough as it is on a Friday without what's about to start kicking off. Like people fucking off from life support machines, just getting up and fucking off out the door... No shit Sherlock, it is fucking weird, I'll brief you later, but just keep me posted if we get any tales like that. And then you can brief me in full on the lovely Elaine… I'm sure you will. Later matey."

And Blackwater strode out of the Main Building's front entrance, climbed into his azure blue Audi TT, and drove off towards a government office that existed on no map, but which any and all of Doug, Phil, Norman or Scotch Joe, regulars at the Horse and Groom, could have told you lay just off the A11, not far from the ghost village of Upper Lupton, matey boy.

II

Fourteen hours later, there was landfall.

III

The Cow and Calf Rocks, aka the Hangingstone Rocks, are (respectively) a stony outcrop and large boulder obtruding from the moorland a few hundred yards above the market town of Ilkley in West Yorkshire. In summer the rocks, and the paths leading to and beyond the rocks, are crowded with tourists; as the days shorten, and the skies grow grey and heavy, and the biting rain sweeps across the moor, the tourist numbers decline: but there are usually a handful of hardy souls clad in windcheaters and walking boots who still brave the moor, maybe pausing for a sandwich or to drink tea from a thermos in the shelter of the rocks.

Not on this day. On this day, the blue lines of a police cordon had been rolled out in the bitter, pre-dawn cold by half-a-dozen local officers, closing off the rocks and the area beyond them. Within an hour, as the sun rose weakly over Ilkley, an army Chinook clattered in; minutes later, a small convoy of military lorries rumbled up the approach road. The police inspector was told politely but firmly that it was no longer a police matter; the inspector replied, tersely, colourfully, that it was, at which point the major with whom he was having the discussion quietly passed him a mobile phone from which Blackwater suggested to the inspector that he should be a good little copper and sign the piece of paper that Major Scott had given him – the major helpfully producing a sheaf of notes at this point – or else he could kiss goodbye to his pension and that would just be the start of it, sunshine. The inspector, a bluff, tenacious individual, was not one to give up quite so easily, but as Blackwater's threats and attendant expletives took on nuclear proportions, invoking successively ministerial interventions, imprisonment, blackmail, violence and finally a combination of all four, the inspector reluctantly signed the forms and retreated to brood at the station.

By the time that Blackwater himself turned up in a second Chinook, it was late morning. Eyes hidden behind mirrored sunglasses and frame wrapped in a heavy black overcoat – "Posing tit", thought the major – he swept over the turf towards a second, inner cordon. This surrounded a circular area of maybe fifty square yards, within which the grass had been completely burned away. At the centre of this circle, half a dozen troops in white NBC suits were poring over something part-buried in the earth: what it was, Blackwater couldn't see, but he had a bloody good idea.

"How many cylinders?" The six men all turned and looked up at Blackwater's question; one stood, rather stiffly, and faced him.

"Mr Blackwater?"

"That's me. So how many cylinders?"

"Only one. Just under a metre in length and thirty centimetres in diameter. How did -"

"I know it would be a cylinder? Educated guess.

30

And I'm talking to?"

"Sergeant Hansen."

"Was it open?"

"Yes, sir."

Shit, thought Blackwater, *shit shit shit shit shit.*

"And have you had a look inside?"

"Well, yes, sir. But somebody's taking the pi- err, mickey, with this, sir."

Blackwater dipped under the inner cordon. One of Hansen's colleagues began to protest, but Blackwater waved him away ("Are radiation levels normal? Yes? Good. Then I don't need to look like a human condom to have a gander at this cylinder") and squatted at the edge of an area of disturbed earth.

The cylinder had been driven deep into the earth, maybe twenty, thirty feet down. Peering down, Blackwater could see the metallic rim of the cylinder, gleaming faintly in the weak sunlight. A number of arc lights had already been installed within the cordon, and Blackwater directed one towards the object.

"It's a joke, it's got to be a bloody joke…" Hansen's voice tailed off.

Oh no it isn't, thought Blackwater, as he stared from high at the internal walls of the cylinder. *Weird it is; shit hitting fan it is; joke it isn't.*

"Get some kind of cover, over this, will you? S'posed to piss it down tonight." He turned to Hansen. "This will have to be excavated. The cylinder's coming with me."

Two hours later, Blackwater was back in the Chinook. In the back of the helicopter, resting within a lead-lined box, sat the cylinder, its inner walls resplendent with a montage of self-adhesive stickers, the photographs worn and fading but instantly recognisable to any aficionado of mid-seventies football: Eddie Gray; Peter Lorimer; Trevor Cherry;

Allan Clarke. Images intended to grace a Panini album now graced an item of rather greater technological sophistication, and had travelled round the universe and back.

IV

The bird had done its job. It had transported the entity across the moor, down the Otley Road, across the University campus, then down towards the Infirmary. It had dutifully followed the road signs, pigeon homing instinct overridden by a much stronger mind which had spent hours studying digitalised pictures of similar signs in preparation for this journey; which knew the significance of those bright red Hs; which was looking out – through a pigeon's eyes – for key words and phrases on those signs; which had, to be on the safe side, done its best to memorise the 3D depictions of the Yorkshire landscape as it entered the approach orbit.

The pigeon had been unlucky. Ten birds had been on their way back to their Ilkley coop, flying in stolid, heavy formation; nine had returned home. The tenth, flying low over the moor at the base of this avian wedge, had plummeted soundlessly to the soil, its senses overwhelmed by the tendrils of consciousness which had enwrapped them.

When the pigeon awoke, moments later, all of the rudimentary universal constructs which defined pigeonness in its brain had been carefully swept away, save one. The entity didn't need birdseed; it didn't need a pigeon coop in Ilkley; but it needed to fly.

And it needed as much of the pigeon's cerebral activity as possible to focus on getting it to its desired location, which meant that for the first time in its life, this pigeon was reading roadsigns.

It was also experiencing emotions for which it was

somewhat unprepared, most notably an insistent, imperative yearning for Leeds United.

These needs and yearnings rapidly became a bit much for the pigeon's brain. Seed and sexual intercourse were one thing; attempting to visualise 1970s footballers was another. Something had to give, and that something was always going to be the brain. The pigeon's descent towards the Infirmary transitioned into a vertical drop as the cerebral cortex gave up the unequal struggle and exploded.

Close enough, though. The entity might not be able to travel far without dissipating into the cold, grey Yorkshire air, but it could manage the remaining sixty or so yards, through double doors, down corridors, homing in on an ebbing life-force. It emerged at last into a small, white room, furnished only with a single bed, armchair and small chest of drawers. Upon the bed lay a human female, slim, dark-haired, maybe twenty-five years of age.

Maybe. It would soon know for sure.

Next to the bed was a bank of electronic machinery which the entity recognised as measuring various signs of life; it provided electronic evidence of what the entity already knew, that the life signs of the female were failing.

She was dying. She was young. She would be perfect.

It reached out for her.

The flatlining digital lines kicked into life.

And as soldiers gathered round the empty cylinder on Ilkley Moor, the body of Lisa Smith sat bolt upright.

V

"Right then", said Blackwater imperiously, "This is where we're at."

The majority of the audience before him exhibited a stony-faced distaste, contemplating Blackwater as if he were a small mongrel terrier that had regrettably forgotten itself and defecated on an antique rug. And, to be fair, that summed up their general perception of Blackwater, although a number of those present were of the more considered opinion that he was on balance a life-form less closely aligned with the terrier and more with the contents of its bowels.

How the hell had Blackwater happened? MI13 may have been secretive, moving in mysterious ways its wonders to perform, but it had performed those wonders at a reassuringly sedentary pace, wholly in keeping with its siblings elsewhere in the machinery of government; this was, besides, the default settings for its inhabitants, a comfortable blend of operatives drawn from other intelligence agencies and unflappable civil servants whose primary concern was to ensure that the shroud of secrecy surrounding their organisation was not lifted lest it reveal the lack of activity underneath. Sure, they negotiated with a host of alien beings – or at least, with what passed for the diverse diplomatic corps of alien beings – but mostly those alien beings were an extremely understanding bunch and only occasionally threatened to engage in behaviour which would either directly or indirectly result in the wholesale slaughter of millions of humans. Thus, such interaction as had occurred had largely been based around informal social gatherings and soirees, albeit with fairly unusual canapés on offer. MI13 was not, it would be fair to say, a department characterised by vigour and dynamism.

And then came Adam Blackwater, a snarling, sharp-suited bundle of energy and invective, demanding that things got done, and right this fucking minute matey, or your poncey Oxbridge arse is on the scrapheap. Brash and cocky, Blackwater bulled his way through the

Upper Lupton corridors. More emollient predecessors had requested (apologetically but firmly) that where it was absolutely essential to have paperwork pertaining to a particular case, then the files in question should be transferred to Upper Lupton for safekeeping, or informally suggested that – in extremis – it might be desirable if witnesses to events which of course had not actually occurred were no longer around to provide an account of said non-events. That was then; now it was: alright, matey, I'll be havin' that, ta; didn't happen on my watch; if he's got video evidence, nab it and kick his balls out through his arsehole, the little toe-rag.

Courtesy was time-consuming, and Blackwater – well, he didn't have time for time. He was far too busy putting the wind up the system and having fun. He had brought in a few of his own kind, seeking to imbue the place with his particular brand of savage, feral enthusiasm for the task in hand. The net result was an atmosphere of mute hostility between Upper Lupton's factions: the bruised but elegantly unflappable patricians and the sneering, boisterous newcomers. Yet within that hostility, work got done – dirty work, unpleasant work, work that laughed in the face of any number of international resolutions and commitments – but it was done with a far greater efficiency than had previously been the case.

"This is where we're at."

He paused for effect, surveying his audience. A smattering of army officers; a few higher-grade civil servants; and, at the head of the table, a slim, silver-haired man of perhaps sixty years of age. His penetrating blue eyes were fixed on Blackwater, his finger tips pressed together.

Their lord and master.

Hartshorn. The guv'nor.

Blackwater continued. "On October 14th, at 0300

hours, RAF Menwith Hill recorded what we now know to be the mother craft: saucer-shaped, flying at no more than two thousand feet, travelling at eighty to ninety miles an hour. Two fighters from Fylingdales were scrambled but the craft accelerated away westwards, travelling over Manchester and Liverpool before veering northeast. It disappeared from our radar shortly afterwards. We suspect that the craft was on a reconnaissance mission: given the time that has elapsed since our last encounter, its occupants may well have wanted to ensure that previous landing sites were still wasteland.

"The craft was also sighted by a number of civilians in the area. Four passed their reports on to West Yorkshire Police, two directly to Air Staff 2. They have already received replies informing them that the RAF were conducting low-level night flights at the time, and apologies for any concerns.

"On October 15th, at between 0200 and 0300, an unknown number of host cylinders were released from the mother craft. The cylinders were released at high-earth orbit, probably simultaneously. Cylinders have been recovered from moorland at Ilkley and Saddleworth; we are currently searching fields in the Wirral peninsula for a third. Given the heading of the mother ship before we lost contact the previous day, we believe that there is a least one further cylinder, probably near Glasgow.

"We have undertaken a preliminary examination of the Ilkley cylinder; we strongly suspect that the all cylinders were steered manually to their respective destinations.

"Given the events of twenty-one years ago, we have set up operatives in each of the landfall sites – and in Glasgow – monitoring emergency radio communications. Specifically, communications regarding missing persons; even more specifically, very ill, hospitalised persons going missing. We already have one strong lead – a male, mid-forties, terminal cancer, has disappeared from a hospice in Kirby. I think it likely that there is a correlation between the Wirral landfall and that disappearance."

A hand went up, tentatively. Blackwater stared contemptuously at its owner, a thin, nervous executive officer. "Yup?"

"You said Wirral landfall. We haven't actually found anything in the Wirral yet."

"They made landfall in the fucking Wirral." Stated with an air of certainty, of finality. "They look for a wide expanse of open ground and in fucking Scouseland outside the fucking Wirral you're fucking struggling, matey boy."

He glared at the officer, who quavered, dropped his eyes and sat sheepishly for the remainder of the briefing, inwardly wishing that aliens hadn't been invented.

"Enough of the fucking, thank you, Adam." The calm, measured tones were those of Hartshorn. "I rather think that Mr Dimmond was querying your certainty that there had been a landfall in that area – the Liverpool area – rather than in which borough of that august city landfall actually took place." Blackwater began to reply, but had managed barely a syllable when Hartshorn held up his hand. "Please, allow me. Adam is absolutely right, though. There will have been a landfall in Liverpool, because, gentlemen, what we are dealing with are football fanatics. The tradition of my youth, when one followed the local team, irrespective of how successful it was, is on the way out; has been, for many years. I have known many young men" – Blackwater giggled inwardly, but remained poker-faced – "who have admitted to me that their penchant for

Arsenal or Manchester United derives not from a geographical proximity to Highbury or Old Trafford but to the fact that, in their formative years, those teams were reaping a respectable harvest of silverware. In the same way, I understand that boys from Bangkok" – (*Poker face, Adam. Poker face*) – "are far more enamoured of the leading lights of England's Premiership than of any local Thai teams."

Hartshorn stood up. "Gentlemen, what we are dealing with, to put it bluntly, is Bangkok in space. They love English football. They love its teams – specifically, the teams that were playing well on their last visit in the mid to late nineteen seventies. And, during their last visit, which team was winning all the trophies, domestic and European? Why, Liverpool. And so, gentlemen, to recap, there will have been landfall in the Wirral.

"Now, Adam, you've done splendidly so far, but I know you're itching to flood the areas with troops: did I see you have some kind of bio-hazard planned as a cover story? Too overt, too garish. There is no evidence that their presence here constitutes a direct threat to us. Furthermore, there are no indications that previous visitations have resulted in any communicable diseases. In fact, judging from their effects on their hosts, quite the opposite. It's not in their interests to be discovered. Think of Mr Pressdee."

(Blackwater thought of Mr Pressdee. A lot. It still blew his mind.)

"So how are the hosts likely to react? They know we will be looking for them. More than likely, they will seek to adopt an alias. They will be unobtrusive.

One of the military officers assigned to MI13, a Major Rendell, spoke up. "You're not just saying we let them carry on – like Pressdee? What happens when the host becomes exhausted?"

"We don't know – there's no precedent. But depending on the age of the host body at point of adoption, I should say that's likely to take many years. Pressdee was looking very well, the last time I saw him. But no, long-term integration is not an option. We don't want any more Pressdees. Adam, you were on the right track when you authorised the communication intercepts. The hosts will have relatives, friends. They will be missed. There is no need to swamp these areas.

"Ensure the operatives continue to monitor the communications, Adam. When we have key suspects, bring them in. They might take a little tracking down but we have time on our hands."

Blackwater coughed. Something was preying on his mind. "Have you received any communication from their home planet?"

"Yes." *Fuck fuck fuck shit fuck fuck fuck fuck*. Across the room, variants on Adam's internal chain of obscenities were echoing through the minds of the assembled officers and agents.

"And?"

"As you can imagine, they're not in the best of moods". A further outpouring of silent invective, steeped in panic, resounded amongst the company.

"And they're on their way." This time Blackwater's "Fuck" was audible. Rendell put his head in his hands.

"As I have said, gentlemen, we have time on our hands. We have a good idea of how fast they can and will travel. I believe that we have two, possibly three months before they arrive. Giving us ample time to identify, capture and restrain any hosts."

The major emerged from the shelter of his hands. "One other thing, sir?"

"Yes, major?"

"When we do find them – given their rather, er, peripatetic nature" (Hartshorn chuckled) "how exactly do we restrain them?"

Hartshorn was still chuckling as he replied. "Well major, we have the cylinders. And in this case, you can put the genie back into the bottle."

Around the table, in a dozen heads, lightbulbs of varying brilliance were suddenly illuminated.

"Peripatetic, oh I do like that. Very good. Right, I think that's about everything, isn't it?"

The meeting had run its course. With a minimum of chatter, the officers dispersed. Blackwater was gathering up his papers when Hartshorn caught his arm.

"Oh and Adam?"

"Yes sir?"

"Softly, softly, catchee alien on this one. Like I said, very low-key. Very."

"Sure, sure" said Blackwater, a hint of petulance entering his voice.

"And Adam – don't be going down the Horse and Groom tonight. I don't mind them knowing about my little liaisons – they don't know who I am from, well, Adam - but I'd like this business kept out of the public bar."

And Hartshorn was gone, leaving Blackwater staring dully at his notes, needing a drink more than ever.

CHAPTER THREE

I

"Roddy,

Can you pop into the office around 2pm. Need a quiet word.

Brian"

Macko stared at the email, perplexed and a little perturbed. Generally, in the colourful history of Roderick James McCall, if someone had wanted a word, quiet or otherwise, then that word had been the prelude to a whole lot more words; disparaging words, despairing words, condemnatory words, words which – depending on which point in that history they had been uttered – almost invariably included "detention", "grounded", "sacked" or "dumped".

There had been that business with the Easter Garden, back at St Patrick's. Twenty-two children had reported for duty on the Monday morning with immaculate tableaux, painstakingly created over the weekend from sand, pebbles, turf, twigs, kitchen foil and earth, providing beautific representations of Our Lord's final resting place on Earth. The twenty-third garden was distinctive to say the least. Its designer had whiled away the weekend over far more pressing activities: watching *Multi-Coloured Swap Shop*; firing his pea-shooter at Mrs McGinty's bull terrier; reading and re-reading *Match Weekly*; playing for Manchester United in the back garden, dribbling with consummate ease round a static defensive wall of Action Men and lofting the ball into a billowing sheet on the washing line that doubled as the back of the net; listening to *Sports Report* on the radio; re-enacting various Second World War battles on the crazy paving with diverse units of 1/72 scale Airfix soldiers, adding a touch of verisimilitude to the proceedings by firing lit matches into the ranks of plastic troops from miniature cannon; scrubbing the patio clean of melted plastic under the supervision of his mother. Having therefore been otherwise engaged while the other twenty-two masterpieces were under construction, the designer of the twenty-third had winged it, as he had winged it in the past and would do so often in the future. Two bulbous, misshapen rocks hastily jammed into an oven tray filled with cat litter. And, in case any viewer should mistake its significance, one rock bore the inscription, "Jesus Was Here" in bright red aerosol paint.

Father O'Connell had had a word, as had Father Xavier, the headmaster. Father Xavier had also had a word with the designer's mother, and the designer's mother had in turn had a word with the designer's father, and then both mother and father had had a word with the designer. And the designer, none other than Roderick James McCall, had been left in no doubt that Our Lord, his representatives on Earth, and Mr and Mrs McCall were less than impressed with his Easter Garden, and that if he didn't want to spend the rest of the school year writing experience lines – or to receive any more clips round the ear from Mr McCall – then he'd better buck his ideas up. Macko had listened dutifully, then ambled off to kick his football against the side of the house, the dire warnings gradually fading from his consciousness, transient as and with no more impact than a gentle April breeze.

And over the years, word succeeded word succeeded word. Detentions, groundings, relationships and jobs came and went, but Macko went happily onwards, amiably progressing through indolent childhood to indolent adolescence and finally to indolent adulthood where he pleasantly accumulated hours in front of the television, punctuated and complimented by drunken binges, one-night stands, takeaway meals, pornography, and a forty a day habit. To Macko's great annoyance, unemployment benefits enabled him to enjoy these activities only in moderation, and so – albeit reluctantly – he found himself obliged to spend several hours, two or three days a week, engaged in the semblance of gainful activity.

Currently, it came in the guise of an administrative role at Scrimpton College. This suited Macko down to the ground. He filled in forms; entered information into databases; carried boxes of paperwork from one room to another, and then back again; directed telephone enquiries to someone else's number; made tea; made more tea. Given that these activities, even if conducted at the pace of an arthritic snail, scarcely filled one-third of the hours for which he was paid, Macko quickly found other tasks to occupy his time, tasks which his superiors might have frowned upon. As he now attempted to deconstruct the hidden meaning of that 'quiet word' which Brian wished to have, the thought struck him that some of these activities might have come to their attention; that, like it or not, Macko might be heading for the job centre once again.

It was therefore with a certain amount of trepidation that he knocked on Brian's door.

"Yes?"

Macko stuck his head cautiously into enemy territory. The enemy in this instance came in the form of a small, slim man in his early forties, clad predominantly in corduroy and facial hair. Brian smiled weakly in greeting.

"Oh, hello, Roddy, have a seat."

Macko sat, and stared at his supervisor with undisguised suspicion.

"You know you're supposed to spend most of the time at the computer, well – doing work for the college?"

"Yes?" countered Macko. It seemed the best thing to say.

"Well, you left your computer on after work the other day." Macko paled. This was bad news. He distinctly remembered spending an enjoyable few hours on www.bigones.com the other day. And, come to think of it, on www.sexybirds.com and www.womeninuniform.com as well.

"And, well, I was passing your desk, and I noticed that your Health and Safety manual had fallen on the floor" (*it hadn't*, thought Macko dully, *it had been taking up half my desk so I threw it there, but better let that one pass*) "so I thought, oh, Roddy's Health and Safety manual has become a Health and Safety Issue, which I thought was rather funny…"

His voice tailed off as he recognised from Macko's demeanour that the humour of the situation, such as it was, had been lost in the telling. Brian sighed, and struggled on.

"Anyway, I put it back on your desk, and then I saw that your monitor was still on, and I happened to look at the screen." (*Bollocks and shite. Here it comes.*) "There was a game on the screen, Roddy. Pinball."

Pinball, thought Macko, *thank fuck! He's talking about* another *other day*! The colour slowly returned to Macko's cheeks as Brian continued with his lecture.

"To be precise, Roddy, it was the high-score table from the game. And there were a lot of scores signed 'Macko' on there. Scores which, judging from the times opposite them, were compiled where you really should have been inputting the information from the student application forms onto the Jeremiah database."

Macko looked contrite. He had become adept at

looking contrite over the past few years. It was a tactic that had never actually prevented any of his dismissals, but it had delayed one or two of them.

"Roddy, you're a good lad, but we really can't have this, can we?"

"Sorry, Brian, I won't do it again." Delivered almost in a whisper, eyes downcast. *That should do it.*

"Good, good." Brian's face, which had become sorrowful in the course of what, for him, counted as a stern rebuke, visibly brightened. "Well, that's all then. And – just keep cracking on with Jeremiah."

"Thanks Brian. Thanks a lot." Macko rose, smiled sheepishly at his manager, and returned to his desk in the corner of the office, where he quietly and assiduously carried on where he had left off before the meeting, playing Minesweeper.

II

At twenty-six years of age, Gideon Nathaniel Kenneth Chubb was short, plump, myopic and odoriferous. He had been short and plump for all of those twenty-six years, and myopic for the overwhelming majority of them. What was now the distinctive G.N.K. Chubb odour - a rank, stale, pervasive odour - had made its presence felt at *chez* Chubb at around the twelve year mark and had not improved with age, becoming progressively more rank and stale (and, unfortunately for his co-habitants, more pervasive) as the adolescent Chubb advanced through his teenage years. Its potency was further enhanced as the days passed since Chubb's last bath, and the intervals between those baths were long. For those co-habitants, far too long. It had to be said that Chubb did not help his cause due to his tendency to change his outer garments only subsequent to each bath, and his undergarments only marginally more frequently. The wardrobe of the twenty-six year old Chubb was modest. Three pullovers in autumnal hues, worn in strict rotation; three cotton shirts, two in a quiet check and the third a faded blue (also rotated); two pairs of beige slacks; a tweed jacket which had seen better years; a duffel coat; and, incongruously, a dinner suit. This item had last graced the Chubb form at his Graduation Ball five years previously, when he had consumed a number of cherry brandies and had vomited, redly, over both himself and a fellow graduand who had responded by hurling Chubb into a nearby pond. Traces of cherry brandy still haunted the suit.

Chubb owed his multitude of initials to a burning desire on the part of his father that his only son should be an international cricketer. Having observed that many of the best cricketers were blessed with three forenames (or, as they appeared in the Widen scorecards, three fore-initials), he reasoned - via a process of deduction not wholly uncommon amongst cricket enthusiasts - that bestowing ample ballast upon his son in this department would provide a suitable launchpad for future sporting greatness.

Dare he hope for a W.E.J. Edrich or a G.A.R. Lock, an L.E.G. Ames or a D.C.S. Compton? Oh he dared, he hoped, but as the years went by, he realised that G.N.K. Chubb would not reach those Olympian heights, nor match the comparatively modest achievements of C.W.J. Athey or an M.C.J. Nicholas, nor even display the Sunday afternoon beer match abilities of a G. Chubb, Snr. Despite myriad coaching sessions, despite hours in the nets, despite plentiful opportunities in those Sunday afternoon beer matches, Chubb resolutely refused to display an iota of aptitude for the game.

Through spectacle lenses of steadily increasing density, Chubb would wait for each delivery in silent terror, hating the game and hating his father's obsession with it; the inevitable rattle of his stumps both a blessed relief (in that it signalled an end to this public humiliation) and the signal for a further cause for concern; not in the slow, heavy trudge back to the pavilion, after his umpteenth duck of the summer, but in the subsequent exasperation of his father. The well-intentioned advice on footwork of his formative matches had long since dissipated into a series of obscenity-ridden tirades; yet still his father persisted, hoping against hope that somewhere within Chubb Jnr lurked a hitherto undiscovered and (except by Chubb Snr) unimagined portfolio of cricketing strokes, to be unveiled in the next innings and provide redemption. Or the innings after that.

So now he would enter the changing room, head bowed, avoiding his father's glance, quietly change back into cotton shirt, autumnal pullover and beige trousers (Chubb's casual attire of choice had become established in his teenage years), pile his kit into a tattered holdall, and make his way homewards; Chubb senior would stare after him, mournfully and think once more, "For fuck's sake". Even vicariously, his dreams would remain unfulfilled.

Eventually, his father relented, to the barely concealed delight of both Chubb and his erstwhile colleagues at Sterner Hill. As his father continued to while away his weekends making moderate scores in village cricket, Chubb retired to his bedroom. This was where Chubb found true happiness: in the novels of Asimov; in *Twilight of the Gods*; in writing computer programmes for his beloved computers; in cyber-conflicts in multi-user dungeons played out via Micronet.

At college, Chubb remained a solitary, reclusive figure. However, the refusal of the college to pander to his wishes and connect a phone line to his room in the Halls of Residence meant that, to get his fix of online computer action, Chubb was obliged to use the departmental machines. Thus, post lectures, Chubb would steadfastly head for the computer rooms and log on for two to three hours, after which time one or other of the technicians would begin to harangue him about hogging the machine, or sometimes about hogging the machine and being a smelly bastard who was stinking the fucking room out. Chubb didn't care; come his final year, he became one of those technicians, and upped his online time significantly.

Much of this time was spent browsing the various online forums that had sprung up during the mid-nineties which were devoted to the unexplained: the paranormal, the mythical, the extra-terrestrial. The extra-terrestrial held a particular fascination for Chubb: the possibility that somewhere, out there, there might be planets inhabited by alien life forms; that some of those life forms might have already been in communication with their human counterparts. This was natural fodder for the embryonic Internet communities, and excitable, textual discussions began to flourish, in part driven by the yearnings and imaginings of Chubb and his ilk; discussions peppered with a host of blurred images of dubious origins.

The Internet brought new experiences. Joy of joys, Chubb had discovered girls. Not flesh and blood, admittedly, but girls in a host of digital formats, girls who would not resist his advances – indeed, gloriously, who did not require any kinds of advances - but who inevitably disrobed through a succession of online images or in the course of a video download. For Chubb, the virtual was the embodiment of perfection: encounters were entirely one-sided, the recipients of his desires wholly oblivious to his social and physical imperfections.

These encounters were naturally brief and furtive when conducted on college premises, but when Chubb finally shuffled out of Halls into a rented room in private accommodation, he immediately hooked up his PC to the phone line, closed the bedroom door and only thereafter emerged on those occasions demanded by work, hunger or calls of nature.

Chubb was already part of the Birch Lane fittings when Gerry moved in. Several years previously, a mass emigration of tenants had left all four bedrooms available for rent, and Chubb - after a careful consideration of their various merits - had selected a modest room on the first floor, partly on cost grounds, partly due to the fact it was opposite a lavatory and thus minimised the distance he would have to go to have a pee, but primarily because there was a phone socket just outside the door, making Internet connectivity that much more straightforward.

Chubb had been at work on the occasions when Hardwicke had showed the properties to its other, current tenants. This was particularly fortuitous for Hardwicke, as Macko worked with Chubb and would most certainly not have signed the tenancy agreement if he had known that Chubb was already well ensconced in the room below that which he would be taking. He discovered the grim truth the evening after moving in: Chubb had inadvertently left his bedroom door marginally ajar after a trip to the lavatory, allowing *l'essence du Chubb* to flood out onto the landing. Gagging, Macko had stumbled into the kitchen, where Gerry was working his way through spaghetti on toast, and demanded to know who had left a fucking dead rat upstairs.

"That'll be Gideon," said Gerry through a mouthful of spaghetti. An awful realisation came over Macko.

"It's that cunt that works in IT for us!"

"Mate of yours, is he?" enquired Gerry innocently.

Macko told him to fuck off and stormed out, slamming the back door behind him. Three minutes later, after the nicotine had kicked in, Macko returned, apologised for telling Gerry to fuck off and asked him if he'd like to go for a pint.

At the George and Dragon – their regular Scrimpton watering hole - Macko vented his spleen. Gideon Chubb, he said, was a fucking health hazard (Gerry would later reflect that, coming from Macko, this was a bit rich); he was a smelly fat fucker; he was an irritating prick; he was a boring cunt. Gerry tried the emollient approach.

"I know he's a smelly bastard, but... well, he keeps himself to himself most of the time. Doesn't bother me much."

This was not strictly true. While he regarded the omnipresent Chubb stench as a low level threat which he regularly sought to combat by rigorous and regular use of powerful air fresheners (and which had sufficiently masked its effects during Macko's initial visit with Hardwicke), he was highly suspicious of Chubb. Someone who spent all that time locked in their bedroom was clearly a bit weird, to say the least. And then there had been that incident with Emma.

Gerry and Emma had been sitting on the sofa, watching a film. A French film, God knows why – it had been late, there had been nothing else on. And, during a particularly frolicsome moment in the film, life had begun to imitate art, hands had started to wander, buttons had become undone, more and more flesh had become exposed.

And Chubb had shuffled in.

Caught up in the joys of the moment, neither Gerry nor Emma had noticed the presence of a third party for

50

some time. Then Gerry had momentarily lifted his eyes from Emma's breasts, and saw Chubb, staring at them with a fixed, intense expression on his face.

"Ahem", said Gerry. Emma yelped and frantically began buttoning up her blouse.

"I was - watching the film", said Chubb, unconvincingly.

"Can you not watch it somewhere else?" said Gerry, aware that his voice was becoming somewhat shrill, and also conscious that he was in his underpants and sporting an erection.

"S'pose", said Chubb, and shuffled in melancholic fashion up the stairs to his room, where he carefully locked the door, lay on the bed and masturbated furiously as his inner eye freeze-framed on the first real, live, naked breasts he had ever seen.

Downstairs, the moment had been lost. Emma had railed at Gerry for not telling Chubb exactly what a dirty pervert he was, Gerry replying with some irritation that it was difficult to find the exact words to use when, err, you know, and Emma had responded by threatening that if Gerry didn't say something later then what kind of man was he? Muttering a few placatory words, Gerry promised her he would have a word with Chubb in the morning.

And so, the following morning, Gerry had reluctantly collared Chubb. This was by no means an easy task, as Chubb ate all his meals in his room. Uneasy about facing Chubb on home ground, primarily due to an understandable unwillingness to bathe in its atmosphere for an extended period, Gerry had instead hovered in the kitchen until Chubb emerged to raid the fridge for milk and butter.

"Gideon, mate…" Chubb stared at him.

"About last night. You can't go creeping up on people like that, fella. Bang out of order." Chubb's mouth opened, but he said nothing.

"Emma was really pissed off about it, mate."

"Oh", said Chubb. He thought for a moment. "Sorry."

"Look, well just be a bit more careful, would you. I mean you knew Emma was coming over…"

"No I didn't," said Chubb, stoutly.

"Okay, well, so you didn't. But if you do come in and we're, well – just leave us to it."

Chubb nodded silently and collected his milk and butter. He turned to leave, then paused and looked up at Gerry. "Should I say sorry to Emma?"

The image of a prostrate Chubb, blood seeping from multiple stab wounds, flashed before Gerry's eyes. "No, no, don't. Just leave it."

Chubb nodded again and left the kitchen.

After that, much to Chubb's annoyance, there were no more fumblings on the sofa. Gerry's relationship with Emma had continued its emotive, inexorable decline.

So Emma was gone; but Chubb, short, plump, myopic, odoriferous Chubb, remained, shut away in his room, happily browsing the Internet for the latest UFO sightings and hard-core pornography.

III

Macko inquired, with far more gusto than pitch, whether, if he faltered, Gerry would open his arms out to him.

And he shoved a pile of half a dozen or plates, swaying dangerously but no longer dangerously filthy, into a cupboard beside the kitchen sink.

Gerry was of the opinion that they should make love, not war, and – while they were about it – that they should be at peace with their hea-ar-ar-arts. While so opining, he continued to work vigorously and with a certain degree of success at a dull brown stain on the lino.

Erasure, they had decided, was a perfect accompaniment to cleaning the common areas of the house. Since the departure of Leanne, aka Disgusted Sales Assistant of Asda, there had been few – if any – nods in the direction of cleanliness. The toilet bowl, so recently besmirched by Macko's behind, was emblematic of the wider picture. Dust gathered on window sills; dirt was ingrained into carpets, and dirt ingrained into that dirt; from the depths of the kitchen bin, from the depths of the kitchen sink and from the depths of Chubb's bedroom came a variety of noxious odours, ripe and pungent, stale and sweaty, intermingling and drenching the atmosphere with their insidious presence.

Then Hardwicke had rung to inform Gerry that a girl would be looking at the house the following afternoon, and suddenly all was activity.

Gerry had insisted that Macko deal with the bathroom, and Macko – after a show of defiance – had busied himself with bleach and bucket, rubber gloves and sponges, and erased all traces of his passing from the toilet bowl. Once the main incriminating evidence had been removed, it was down to work on the tidemarks in the bath – Macko thoughtfully remembering, albeit at the last minute, to use a fresh sponge at this point – and then on the morass of hair and nail clippings from around the sink.

While Macko had been thus engaged, Gerry had been attempting to remember how to change the bag on the hoover. Having sought to consult the manual and failed to find the bloody thing, he'd then sought to consult his Mam on the matter. Mam, he was sure or at least vaguely hopeful, had something similar. Mam, when consulted down the phone line, indeed had something similar, had talked him through most of the process, but then Mr Davies had called with the beans from the allotment and Mam had to go. So Gerry had attempted to put theory into practice; had managed to jam a new bag into place; had turned the hoover on; had started hoovering and found that the dust, rather than remaining in the bag, was escaping through the joints of the hoover. So Gerry had cursed a few times, kicked the hoover, reattached the bag – this time in the manner approved by the manual, and his Mam – and finally set about restoring the lounge to a state more suited to human habitation.

Lounge and bathroom had been ticked off; now, working in tandem, and backed up by Erasure at full blast, they were putting the finishing touches to the kitchen.

Macko blew a kiss at Gerry, who stuck out his tush in return. Macko turned the volume down on the stereo.

"Jesus, this is so fucking gay."

Gerry looked hard at the patch of lino. The stain had given up the ghost.

"She'd better be a looker after all this, Macko."

"Knowing our luck it'll probably be Gideon's twin sister."

They had not sought to involve Chubb in the cleansing of the house; better, they felt, that Gideon remain out of the picture altogether. Besides, as Macko had pointed, put a scrubbing brush near Gideon and the brush would run a fucking mile.

"Time'sit?" Gerry looked at his watch.

"Just gone half twelve."

"I'll go and stick Footie Focus on."

And so they both repaired to the lounge, watching Gary Lineker run the rule over the weekend's forthcoming Premiership matches, adding their own commentary where they felt it appropriate. Busily engaged in mocking the tribulations of Nottingham Forest, they failed to notice the battered Estate car pulling up that signalled the arrival of Mr Norman Hardwicke. Only with the heavy knock on the open back door, followed immediately by a gruff "Afternoon, lads!" did they emerge from their footballing reverie to see a burly figure framed in the lounge doorway.

Norman Hardwicke's complexion was either naturally swarthy, or naturally dirty. If Gerry and Macko had been questioned on this point, neither could have provided any definitive answer, but both inclined to the latter. Certainly, his wardrobe (or at least as far as they were able to judge) was only marginally more varied than Chubb's, and even more shabby; his beard was profuse, unkempt and home to the remnants of many meals long since consumed.

"Hey, there, Norman." Macko looked up insouciantly at the landlord. "Thought you weren't coming 'til two."

"Aye, well, had to change me schedule around. Anyway, this is Rachel, she's having a look at the place."

Hardwicke moved to one side to allow Rachel to view the lounge, simultaneously allowing the boys to view Rachel.

Gerry thought, afterwards, as he reflected on the dreamy vision of beauty framed in the doorway, that perhaps Hardwicke had been talking the while, expatiating on the simple virtues of the battered sofa, the faded flock wallpaper and, beyond the window, the morass of underground masquerading as a front garden. He could not be certain. All he knew for sure was that he had been reduced to a gawking teenager and was desperately resisting the urge to drool. Here, he felt at once, was the most incredible, sensual creature; tall, dark-haired, dark-eyed, rose-lipped, slim-hipped, long-legged – My God, those legs! – and with a perfect bosom accentuated by a tight black T-shirt.

A similar train of thought passed through the mind of Macko, but it was less poetic and involved far more sexual positions.

She was gone, following the chuntering Hardwicke up to the landing.

Gary Lineker and Nottingham Forest were forgotten. Gerry and Macko goggled at one another, mouthing exclamations that occasionally progressed to partial sentences.

"Did you - ?"

"Tits!"

"Legs up to -"

"She'll never -"

"'kin 'Ell!"

"We'll never be -"

"I would!"

Above their heads, Rachel listened patiently as Hardwicke continued his pitch in the spare room. He was just hitting his stride, earnestly eulogising on the room, the property and the suburb in general when -

"I'll take it."

Within the depths of his beard, Hardwicke positively beamed. This room had been vacant for far too long.

"OK then! I thought you'd like it." (He hadn't; he'd vaguely hoped, in the bottom of his heart, that she *might*, but even he was beginning to admit to himself that any house featuring Chubb and Macko as guest stars was a particularly hard sell.)

He fumbled around in a satchel and produced a sheaf of paperwork. "I'll need you to fill these in before you can move in; I'll be needing six weeks rent in advance, and there's a Direct Debit form in there somewhere, and I'll also be needing a reference – usual stuff, you know."

Rachel was already reaching into her purse. "I can give you two hundred now, and the balance of the advance later today, if that's OK – I'll bring it to the office later today with the forms?"

Hardwicke wasn't going to look a gift horse in the mouth. "Oh, that's fine love, absolutely fine. Like I said, fill those forms out, bring the rest of the cash to the office, and you can have the keys then."

Later that afternoon, Rachel Moran, formerly known as Lisa Smith, sat in the corner of a small pub in Rawdon where she carefully filled out the forms which Hardwicke had given her. She paused briefly at the section which obliged her to give a reference; a momentary smile, a few more block capitals and a signature, and the paperwork was completed. Before embarking on the forms, she had ordered a drink – taking her cue from the previous customer at the bar, she had asked for a pint of Black Sheep ale – and to her surprise, she had found that she rather liked it: enough, in fact, to order a second pint half-way through concocting the fiction of her recent past.

To her delight, a TV screen above the bar was showing the latest scores and goalflashes from that afternoon's football matches: she watched attentively, first cursing under her breath as the caption indicated that Manchester United had already stuck four past Wimbledon, then leaping up, punching the air –

"Get in!"

- as *Nottingham Forest 0, Leeds United 1* flashed across the screen.

This was what she had come here for. This was life. All over this wonderful land, from Carlisle to Plymouth, from Swansea to Southend, games were unfolding, ninety minutes of passion, toil, commitment, physicality, skill and – where appropriate - skulduggery, all combining with the single aim of sticking that ball into the back of Their net, and stopping those buggers in the other playing strip sticking it into Yours. That was what mattered. And when it's your boys that had done the sticking, when the ball is in the bottom corner of the Forest net, that's when the tension, that teases you as the minutes tick down, that holds your guts in a vice-like grip as the ball is pinging around your penalty area, that's when you can scream it out in ecstatic release; and when the final whistle goes and you're a goal or more to the good, you can punch the air again and kiss that tension goodbye: until the next time.

She had watched games from more than twenty years ago, grainy offscreen recordings smuggled back to the home world; watched them time and time again. Now she was here, a few miles from her precious Elland Road. OK, Leeds were currently lording it a hundred miles or so to the south, but... A great start to her stay, if it stays that way.

It didn't. Half an hour later, Forest equalised.

Shit. Bastard bastard Steve Stone.

Next game will be different, she promised herself afterwards, trying not to be too disconsolate. *Next game, I'll be there.*

She drained the second pint of Black Sheep and walked the two miles to Hardwicke's office, where the remaining bureaucracy and pecuniary matters were completed, after which Rachel came away with the keys to her new abode.

Hardwicke had scanned the paperwork and pocketed the cash, and deemed that all had been in order. He had frowned when he reached the reference – was she taking the piss or what – but then realised that he'd misread the block capitals, and laughed.

"God, you know, I thought that said…" She was already smiling.

"Oh, I think he gets that a lot."

After she'd gone, Hardwicke shook his head and chuckled again. Fella was asking for it with a name like that.

Ellis Pressdee, indeed.

CHAPTER FOUR

I

Mrs Alice Prior, MD (Cantab), FRCS, had had better weeks.

Monday had been nits; Deborah had come home from school positively jumping with the things, poor love, and she must have got them from one of the other children in Year Two that day because Alice had gone through her hair – and Jonathan's - with the nit comb the previous day and there had been nothing, not so much as an egg, on either of them. So she'd had to give them both an extra dousing with the delousing shampoo that evening, much to both children's annoyance and Alice's inconvenience, and Jonathan had thrown a temper tantrum afterwards that was impressive even by his standards. Anyway, the upshot was that, busy with shampooing and calming children, she'd burnt the dinner and forgotten to record *Coronation Street* on the video.

Tuesday, and the extent of Alfie's illness had become apparent. Alfie was Alice's beloved old Mini, which a few days earlier had begun making painful, grinding noises whenever Alice changed up from second to third. The noises had gradually increased in their intensity, leading Alice to book Alfie in for a check up after she'd dropped the children off at school and nursery. She'd then driven a courtesy car (dinky little Fiat; not bad, but not her Alfie) to the infirmary, only to discover that the lovely, lovely Lisa Smith was now suffering unexpected complications after her hole in the heart operation and that the prognosis was not good. Alice's mood had remained bleak throughout the day – the operation had gone so smoothly, dammit! – and after an afternoon spent in meetings with management consultants it had become bleaker still. Then back to the garage, and a further dose of bleakness in the shape of a large bill for a new gearbox for Alfie; then back home, and the sight of both Deborah and Jonathan scratching away like mad. More shampoo, more combing; did not burn dinner but forgot to tape *Eastenders*.

Wednesday; had been planning to give class teacher a piece of her mind for not keeping children with nits away from school. Plan forgotten after phone call from infirmary informing her that Lisa Smith had signed herself out. Children dropped off in a blur and then straight to infirmary (or at least, as straight as the interminable bloody Otley Road traffic would allow). Heated – incandescent – conversations with duty doctors and sundry nurses unfortunate enough to get in her way. Had managed to get hold of Lisa's number and left a message on her answerphone. Had smoked a cigarette for the first time in six weeks. Had cursed Lisa for making her smoke first bloody cigarette for six weeks. Had smoked another, then another. Had sleepwalked through a minor surgery. Had returned home to find two itching children, both hyperactive after too much chocolate. Had been very abrupt with childminder. Had run out of red wine.

Thursday; Lisa had left her a message on *her* answerphone – *sorry for leaving in a rush like that, many thanks for everything, 'fraid I won't be able to come in for the examination you wanted, need a bit of a break from everything after the op, off to stay with my cousin in Bristol, bye. Bye.* Well that's that settled. Everything fine and dandy. Is it hell – and I'm smoking more cigarettes because of you, you flighty girl. It was a bloody miracle you survived the night; there is no way – no way – you should have been physically able to sit up in bed after that, let alone dance through the ward (singing songs about Leeds United, so the sister said) and sign yourself out. Had spent day in a cigarette haze and had performed another operation somewhere along the line. Had remembered to stop off at Tesco on way home to buy more cigarettes and bottle of Merlot. Had put children to bed. Had been unable to find bottle opener. Had screamed at wall and had to rush upstairs to quell respondent wailings from Jonathan. Had glimpsed bottle opener in trinket box next to Deborah's pillow. Had taken deep breath and calmly asked Deborah what aforementioned bottle opener was doing there. Had received explanation and told Deborah that mummy really wasn't very happy that she had taken it because it was stripy and that Jonathan had said it would look nice next to her Barbie, and that, young lady, she'd better jolly well get to sleep as soon as, or else. Had used bottle opener as Nature intended.

Friday, and had been woken at three by a distressed Jonathan who had wet his bed. Had staggered, wine-addled and sleepy, into the kids' bedroom, stripped bed, taken sodden sheets downstairs to washing machine, had large glass of water, staggered back upstairs, turned mattress over, failed to get fitted sheet to stay in place, told Jonathan he could come in with her. Had slept uneasily for the rest of the night, Jonathan insisting on taking up around four-fifths of the bed.

Had silently thanked the Lord that it was Roger's turn with the kids this weekend.

Had arrived at the infirmary to encounter the human whirlwind that was Laura Gregory.

II

"In Bristol? Bullshit!"

"She called me yesterday to say that she was going to stay with her cousin."

"She hates him! They haven't even spoken since he ran off with her boyfriend two years ago."

After less than four hours sleep and with a bottle of Merlot glugging its way around her system, Alice Prior was in no mood for this. She stared at Laura: plump, red-haired, clad head to toe in black, her figure generously arraigned with Gothic jewellery. It was a figure that had become quite familiar to Alice and her colleagues over the past couple of weeks, first accompanying Lisa on a couple of pre-op visits and then – then it had been Tuesday.

Alice shrugged, tired, helpless.

"Maybe they made up?"

"Did they hell! Just before the op she was slagging him off!"

"Have you been round to her house?"

"Of course I bloody haven't! For Christ's sake, I came straight here, just hoping she was still alive after you fannied up the operation."

Alice bridled. "I did not fanny up the operation," she said stiffly, trying to remain calm, the hangover hammering out an insistent beat within her skull.

"Well, clearly not. So much 'not' that she's done a runner when she's barely been able to walk for the past month. Jesus, why did I have to be in London yesterday?"

Laura thumped Alice's desk in frustration. Alice winced. She got the distinct impression that Laura would be more than happy to thump her instead (or possibly as well). Indeed, she recalled that, the day before the operation, Laura had cheerfully informed her that if she (Alice) fannied this one up, then she (Laura) would stick her tits in a mangle and shove her stethoscope up her arse. And when the complications had set in on Tuesday morning, she'd nervously broken the news to Laura, half-expecting her to carry out her threat. But no, Laura had just stood there, colour ebbing away from that already pale face, blinking away the tears, swearing softly to herself; almost on automatic pilot, she had walked into the ward where Lisa lay, silent and motionless, the digital renditions of her fragile life-signs at the bed-side telling their own sad story. Laura had bent down, kissed Lisa's forehead, then rising, looked straight at Alice. Alice had stared into the void behind the eyes; no rage, no sorrow, all emotion blown away by the enormity of what Laura was witnessing. She had stared into that void on so many faces; faces of children, mothers, fathers, friends, lovers. And every time that void wanted to swallow you up, too, but you couldn't let it, because let the void win and you couldn't do your job. But every time it hurt so much.

Then Laura had turned, mumbling in the doorway that she would call, heedless of the activity around her in the infirmary, still locked within her void. Alice had watched her going, sadly. She knew that soon Laura's void would open its doors – maybe before Lisa died, maybe not – and then the pain would come rushing in. Until that time she had the numbing anaesthetic of nothingness.

"Are you listening to me?"

Yes, the void was gone all right, and Laura was pissed off.

"Sorry, sorry. Look, there was nothing I could do. She'd signed herself out before I got here."

Alice wearily rubbed her eyes. "Look, Laura. Go round there. Maybe she's still there. Maybe she hasn't gone yet."

Laura snorted. "Like she's ever going to go there." But, she thought, Alice was making sense.

"Yeah, I'll go round there."

"Laura – could you do me a favour – if she's there,

64

ask her to come in again? Please?"

"Sure." Laura was already turning, pushing the double doors, her mind busy with a thousand tumbling thoughts.

III

Had watched Laura go. Had sat down for a rest, only to be disturbed by some ridiculous man (MoD, so he claimed) who was poking around looking for confidential patient information. Had given him a piece of her mind.

IV

Chubb, meanwhile, had never been happier. The Internet forums were buzzing with details of the sightings; rumour nestled cheek by jowl with conspiracy theories and wild speculation. Added to that, there was a real live girl in the house again.

He had been safely ensconced in the foetid environs of his lair when Hardwicke had ushered Rachel around, much to the landlord's relief; but Gerry and Macko realised that, sooner or later, Rachel was bound to bump into Chubb. So, acting primarily from a self-interested perspective (as Macko had opined with feeling, "We can't let an arse like that walk out of here"), they had proactively engaged in a form of damage limitation and primed her for First Contact as they sprawled on separate sofas and she leaned on the lounge wall.

"Yeah, like Norman said, there's this other guy who lives here", Gerry muttered, unable to look Rachel in the face.

"He's a cock," offered Macko bluntly. Macko was unable to look Rachel in the face either, primarily because she had changed into a low-cut top and he felt a compunction, an obligation even, to focus his gaze relentlessly and shamelessly on her cleavage.

"He's a cock, he smells, and he's a bloody weirdo. But," he continued, sensing by Rachel's slightly perturbed demeanour that this really wasn't selling the Chubb-as-a-housemate proposition, "he keeps himself to himself, pays his bills, doesn't nick food from our cupboards and doesn't hog the bathroom in the morning. So he's not too bad really."

"Just try not to get into conversation with him," Gerry chimed in. "If his B.O. doesn't kill you, all that balls about bloody aliens and UFOs will."

"Aliens?" asked Rachel, a trace of nervousness entering her voice.

"Yeah, how they're always trying to contact us. God, as soon, as he found out that my ex's dad was like the government spokesman for stuff like that, I couldn't get rid of him for days. It was awful, like having a really smelly puppy dog hanging round your – oh, hang about, here's trouble."

'Trouble' was the muffled thump-thump-thump of a really smelly puppy dog descending the stairs.

And then, there was Chubb.

Chubb stared at Rachel. Rachel stared at Chubb. Gerry stared at Macko, who valiantly continued to stare at Rachel's cleavage. This tableau proceeded for what seemed an eternity, before Chubb finally broke this silence.

"Hello," he said flatly.

All parties present seemed rather uncertain how to move forward after this, so after another protracted caesura, Chubb tried again.

"I'm Gideon." No response. Then, with an effort, "Pleased to meet you."

This was social interaction with a female on an

almost unprecedented scale from Chubb, but he had now hit his stride.

"And you are?"

Rachel continued to stare silently at Chubb. Gerry, who had transferred his gaze from Macko to her, thought it eerily reminiscent of a scientist intent on some new species of bacillus beneath a microscope. Suddenly, out of nowhere, her face broke into a smile, and she extended her hand.

"Hi there Gideon. I'm Rachel."

Chubb was deep into uncharted territory by now, and it showed.

"Nice. Nice. I have to. Things to. Go now. Bye."

The inner Chubb, a churning mass of conflicting and confusing emotions, impressed upon the outer shell the urgency of exiting the scene, and suddenly he was gone, thump-thump-thump up the stairs, leaving behind only the inimitable Chubb perfume.

"Jesus, never seen Chubb talk to a lass before," observed Macko.

Rachel raised an eyebrow sardonically. "So he's just into aliens?"

"Pretty much."

"Doesn't like footie?"

"Nah." Then, hopefully, "Do you?"

"Oh, God, yeah."

Had angels sung hosannas in the highest at that moment, their impact on Macko would have been markedly less than that of Rachel's appreciation of the beautiful game.

"Would you be interested in coming in on a Sky Sports subscription?"

"You've got the sports channels? Tops!"

Macko himself was of a mind to sing hosannas to the Lord at this enthusiastic response. The edge was taken off his epiphany by a flash of jealousy when

Rachel plonked herself down on the sofa next to Gerry, but: *what the hell – she can sit next to you, Gerry. Just as long as she doesn't shag you. Then I'd have to kill you.*

"Who do you support then?" she asked, disturbing Macko's nascent murderous thoughts.

"Mighty red-shirted heroes," replied Macko proudly.

"How 'bout you, Gerry?"

"Oh. Liverpool. The red-shirted lot that ain't done quite so well recently."

Macko sniggered. "You're shit." Gerry did not demur.

"What about you, then?"

"Leeds."

She had to go and spoil it, thought Macko. *The most hated word in the English Language. Still, for that arse, I'll get over it.*

"Bloody hell," he said, shaking his head. "Well, in the spirit of friendly rivalry, I hope your lot go down this year.

"The feeling's mutual," she said sweetly.

V

The Clio was gone.

That in itself came as a shock to Laura: the chubby orange car had squatted on the curb outside the two-up, two-down terraced house for months, almost invariably flanked by an aging red Vauxhall Opal and a positively venerable, metallic green Ford Cortina; it had looked, Laura had thought when she first encountered the triumvirate, like a vehicular set of traffic lights.

There was the Vauxhall; there was the Ford; between them, fifteen feet of empty curb.

She opened the gate and walked, a trifle hesitantly,

up the path to the door. The garden was a mess, all long grass and weeds, but that was nothing new; Lisa had never been much of a gardener – never cared for gardening, she'd said, waste of a Saturday afternoon, she'd said – even when she'd been physically up to it.

She knocked on the door. Nothing.

Waited for twenty, thirty seconds, then again. Nothing.

She peered through the lounge window, straining to see through the gaps in the curtains. Difficult to see with all that shadow, but things were missing, furniture, ornaments -

The harsh monotone of her mobile phone rang out in her handbag, causing her to jump.

She answered. "Hello?"

"Is that Laura?"

Lisa. *Lisa!* But: wrong.

"Lisa! Babes, where are you?"

"I'm in Bristol. At Richard's."

"What the hell are you doing there? The guy's a dick, you said so yourself!"

For a moment, it seemed to Laura as though Lisa was momentarily nonplussed.

"Oh, look, it's just that – things are cool between us now. We're good. I'm just staying for a few days before I head off."

"Where?"

"Thailand, I think."

Laura reeled. "Thailand! Where did this come from?"

"I just need a break, you know. After the operation and all, I – well, I just want to do something different. Travel."

"But when are you coming back?"

"I'm not."

Laura didn't answer. She couldn't.

"Look, I've given notice to the agency; they're letting the house out again. I've brought some stuff down to Richard's; I've sold the TV, some books; I'll be selling the Clio next week, just to give me a little extra cash on top of my savings."

Silence.

"Laura, I'll miss you."

Laura found her voice. Or found a voice, a small, unhappy, bewildered voice. "Babes, you're just out of surgery, you need to rest up -"

Beep-beep-beep.

"Oh, that's the pips, you don't get much time ringing a mobile, do you?"

"Babes, don't do this -"

Beep-beep-beep. Click.

Twenty minutes later, Laura's Mini had hit the M1, bound for Bristol. *Wrong*, said Laura to *herself, all wrong, wrong, wrong.*

VI

In a callbox on the edge of Scrimpton, Rachel had stared at the payphone receiver for over a minute before replacing it on its rest. This Laura had been Lisa's friend; fortunately, it seemed, one of a comparatively small number; all, the better, since it meant less people to call, less people to lie to. Less people to become suspicious. Her reaction at the news that Lisa had travelled to stay with her relative – her *only* relative – would suggest that Lisa and Richard were not on the best of terms. That meant that her cover story – agreed over a drink with Pressdee – might not be as watertight as she'd supposed.

Would Laura continue to try to track her down? Probably. She might go to Bristol, and – when she drew a blank there – might go to the police. Would they then investigate? Possibly. Which meant that she needed to be more rigorous in covering her tracks

She had sold the Clio that morning, for six hundred pounds, cash, so that was out of the way; many other items – books, trinkets, small items of furniture, and most of Lisa's wardrobe – she had previously taken to a local amenities tip, thinking that it would probably be more trouble than it was worth to attempt to sell them on. She had also emptied Lisa's current and savings account – bringing her a further nine hundred and forty pounds – before carefully cutting Lisa's cards, cheque book and saving book into pieces and setting light to them. That would keep her going for a while, although she would clearly need to get a job at some stage. But what?

Anyway, that could wait. Back to covering her tracks. She needed to make an appointment with a hairdresser.

VII

"You know", said Macko, conversationally, "Life is good."

Gerry nodded sagely, although from his vantage point sprawled on one of the sofas he felt that he could have done without the sight of Macko idly scratching his testicles on the other. It did not, he felt, add significantly to the quality of his existence.

"Got to say I'd rather have Rachel lying there than you fella."

"Well, that's understandable. I mean, and much as I love you Taffy boy, I don't get a fucking rise out of your bod either. But think of it: the weather's picked up, we've just had a bloody good night in a bloody good pub, drunk bloody good beer, spent half the night staring at that new lass behind the bar, had a bloody good curry, and upstairs is a bird with tits and an arse to die for. Oh, and United dicked Wimbledon on Saturday. How did your lot do again?"

Gerry grunted. Macko looked at his watch.

"Porn comes on a few minutes. Although thinking about it," and he swung himself off the couch with the level of grace and elegance that could be expected after six pints, "now that we've got the lovely Rachel living upstairs, I don't feel the need for artificial stimulation. No, I'll just think of her while I knock one out."

"That's nice."

"Indeed. I look forward to it." He moved somewhat heavily to the door. "She is fit, though."

He ascended the stairs, happily preoccupied with carnal thoughts of Rachel Moran.

Gerry settled himself on the couch, reluctant to stir himself for the arduous journey up two flights of stairs to his bedroom. *Yes*, he thought to himself as he drifted off to sleep, *Macko's right. She is fit. Dead fit.*

CHAPTER FIVE

I

Gerry had woken, cold and cramped, at three and thereafter sought solace in his warm bed. It was approaching eight thirty when he prised himself free from its comforting embrace and stumbled blearily down the stairs, dimly conscious of the fact that he needed to be at the college in half an hour or so.

Mechanically he put the morning into motion, filling and turning on the kettle, putting two slices of bread in the toaster, taking the milk from the fridge. As he performed these necessarily rituals he caught sight of movement out of the corner his eye, a flash of colour in the lounge.

It was Rachel. Rachel in a short T-shirt and pyjama bottoms, eating toast and watching a magazine programme on the sports channel.

Rachel with short, red hair.

Well, shorter. The straight locks which had cascaded beyond her shoulders were history, now ending just above the nape of her neck. And were now a rich plum red.

She still looks fantastic, Gerry thought to himself. As if in response to that thought, Rachel looked up at him at smiled.

At which point Gerry became conscious of the fact that he in turn was only wearing a pair of boxer shorts.

"Hi, Gerry."

"Oh, hi, err, look, I forgot there was a girl in the house, look, I'll just nip up and get some clothes."

Gerry was gabbling, backing out of the room. *Please God*, he thought, *she didn't see my semi.*

"No, don't be silly, it's OK."

"No, no, really, just a sec." Gerry fled in search of a

73

pair of jeans. Jeans having been located and pulled on, he returned, abashed, a few moments later.

"Sorry about that." She smiled that smile at him again.

"Like I said, it's cool."

"Like your hair."

"Yeah, I had it done it town yesterday. Place on the Headrow. Just wanted a change of image, you know?"

Gerry nodded dumbly.

"You doing much today?"

"Oh, yeah, off up to the college. I'm a researcher there."

"Yes, you said yesterday."

"Did I? Oh shit, yeah, I did." Gerry blushed. "Look, I'm gonna have to get a move on: eat toast, brush teeth, drive to college, that kind of thing."

"Put shirt on."

"Yes, put shirt on, missed that one. And socks. And shoes, come to think of it."

"Shoes can be important."

From the kitchen came the faint *click* from the kettle as the water reached boiling point.

"I'm just gonna grab some tea and toast."

"Don't forget that shirt."

"No, that's on my to-do list, just a bit further down. Do you want a brew – tea, coffee?"

"Coffee please."

"Milk, sugar?"

"Just coffee, thanks."

Gerry smiled. "No, do you want milk or sugar in your coffee?"

"Oh, sorry: yes, please."

"One sugar?"

"Please." And there was that smile again. *Thank God I've got my jeans on.*

He accelerated, making tea and coffee, buttering

74

toast. He passed her the coffee then, munching his toast on the go, bolted up the stairs in search of that oft-mentioned shirt.

Minutes later he was out the door. Rachel watched him go, and sipped her coffee. *My first cup of coffee*, she thought proudly to herself. Rich, strong smelling, the bitterness of the taste partly offset by the sugar. *I like the caffeine hit.*

She reflected on her housemates. An interesting crew. He seems sweet, that Gerry; Gideon, though: she would have to be careful around him. He could be dangerous. And Macko, well a lack of finesse compared with – well, compared with most of those she had viewed en route on the training videos, but he likes his football, even if he does support bloody Man U. And he has quite a cute bum.

A cute bum. A few days, and she was already going native.

But that was good, wasn't it? That was what she had wanted all along.

II

While Gerry was driving to college and Rachel was sipping her coffee, Graham Mayhew was standing in the doorway to his office in Air Staff 2, wondering what on earth was going on.

A tall, thin man (late twenties, early thirties, thought Mayhew) with swept-back blonde hair was sitting at Mayhew's desk, peering closely at the monitor screen and tapping frenetically at the keyboard. A second man, partially obscured by the first, was leafing through the filing cabinet in the corner: as Mayhew watched, he extracted a file, stood up – revealing him to be tall like his associate, but thickset, older – and placed it on his desk. As he did so, he caught sight of Mayhew, and his face darkened.

"Yes?" Said with no little irritation.

"Well," said Mayhew carefully, "I do work here, you know."

"Not today you don't, Mr Mayhew. We're busy."

"Look, I'm afraid I'm going to need some identification…"

The younger man reached into his jacket pocket and casually tossed an ID card to Mayhew, who noted with an air of resignation that Peter Tremaine was one of Blackwater's lot.

"I'm still going to need to confirm this with the SEO…"

Tremaine gestured silently towards the phone on the desk and continued typing.

Mayhew walked round to the desk, ostensibly to call his superior, in reality to find out what Tremaine was working on. *An Access database – hang on, that's the duty log!* As Mayhew watched, Tremaine ejected a CD from the computer and tucked it into a pocket.

"Two copies should do it, Roy." The thickset man, who had returned to the filing cabinet, gave a grunt which Mayhew took as a sign of assent. Without further ado, Tremaine began manually erasing first the details of the records, then the records themselves. Mayhew was horrified.

"You can't do that!"

Tremaine smiled, and the thickset man looked up once more.

"Yes we can, Mr Mayhew. Now I'm sure you'd like to see some written authorisation for all of this, but you know us and paper trails. Very inconvenient, very messy. Bureaucracy just slows everything down."

"As, indeed, does history. History is a pain in the arse." That was Tremaine: where his colleague's voice carried the faintest West Country burr, Tremaine's was clipped Home Counties; he had temporarily ceased his deletions, and now stared wearily at Mayhew. "You have no idea what a pain in the arse history can be: like these files, Mr Mayhew. I must say, looking through them, you've been very diligent over the years. Dull, mundane logs of every supposed sighting. The imaginings of the Great British Public have kept you busy these past few years, obviously: there are thousands of these entries here. However, some of them – just a few, not many – are a little awkward for us. So they, well, for want a better expression, they need not to exist anymore. The events they purport to record need not to have happened. And the reason that this is a pain, Mr Mayhew, is that once I've deleted them I then have to change all the record numbers on the other files, so that some bright spark with time on his hands doesn't go through the database and say, 'Hang on, there's record four oblique two three six, there's four oblique two three nine, where's seven and eight gone?' So this is what I have to do for the rest of the day: tidy up bloody history."

Mayhew couldn't stop himself. "And what do I do?"

"Relax, Mr Mayhew. Go for a walk. Visit a museum – there is an excellent exhibition of Pre-Raphaelite art on at the National Gallery, I thoroughly recommend it. Catch a film at the Leicester Square Odeon-"

("*Saving Private Ryan* is definitely worth catching," chimed in the thickset man, who had re-engaged with the filing cabinet.)

"Or the theatre, Mr Mayhew. *The Blue Room* is on at the Donmar Warehouse, although you may struggle to get a ticket at short notice. Or a musical, perhaps? Or maybe" and here he leaned forward, almost conspiratorially, "if you're so inclined – and I'm not suggesting for a moment that you are, just that you may be – there are some rather more earthy attractions to be enjoyed in certain other establishments."

Mayhew said nothing, but stared coldly, fixedly, at Tremaine. Tremaine waited for a moment, then resumed his patronisation.

"Today, Mr Mayhew, the world is your oyster. I have merely proposed a few ways for you to pass your time. Go wherever you please: anywhere. Gallery; museum; cinema; theatre; brothel; anywhere. Except, that is, this office. That's strictly off limits for the time being."

Jesus, thought Mayhew, *I think I even prefer Blackwater to this pair. But – they're not worth it. My pension's just not worth it.* He sighed.

"And if any calls come in which need logging?"

"Leave that to us, Mr Mayhew. We'll log them – or not, as the case may be, depending on whether they're pertinent to our investigation. If they're not, we'll log them. But if they are, well..." Tremaine shrugged nonchalantly.

The thickset man stood up, half a dozen files under his arm. "Bloody hell," he said peevishly, "why do you chaps have to keep hard copies of everything? Take me half an hour to shred this little lot."

Mayhew turned to go.

"Oh, Mr Mayhew -?" Tremaine again. He had laid his hand softly on Mayhew's arm: almost a caress. Almost.

"If, over the next few weeks — few months, even — you get any calls, any reports coming through regarding, well, people who have recently been hospitalised behaving oddly - really no reason that you should, not really your bailiwick at all, just that if you do, don't log them. Just let me, or Mr Granville here, or of course Mr Blackwater, know."

Granville coughed.

He paused for a moment. "On reflection, there's no need to bother Mr Blackwater. Just myself or Mr Granville. Roy will give you the number to contact."

Roy was already doing so, passing Mayhew a small piece of card on which he had scribbled "Roy/Peter" and a mobile phone number.

Mayhew smiled bleakly. "And you'll deal with them?"

"That's right." Effortless condescension.

Peter Tremaine returned to his work, tap, tap, tapping the records out of existence; Roy Granville continued to shred files; and Mayhew, a bitter taste in his mouth, suddenly felt in need of a drink.

III

Gerry had become inordinately proud of his database.

His database. Not the college's database, not the Department of Sociology's database, not even the database of Dr Kent, its progenitor: *his* database.

When he had first been introduced to it two years previously, he had viewed it with profound suspicion and deep misgivings: it was, as Dr Kent had patiently explained to him shortly after he had taken the research post, an attempt to codify the outcomes of the various focus groups conducted across the department. To that end, Gerry would be obliged to sit in on some of the groups and watch video recordings of the remainder, and then to assign numeric values to the physical and verbal responses of the various participants who had turned up for the groups in return for a tenner apiece and a can of lager. Dr Kent had then talked Gerry through the database shell and data input procedure, thrust a file into his hand containing draft delineations of the various possible responses, pointed him in the direction of a large cupboard containing hundreds of video cassettes, wished him luck and scuttled off to a staff meeting to which Gerry had not been invited.

Gerry had stared at the file, open-mouthed, before phlegmatically choosing a tape at random and placing it into the player.

He had spent the next hour and half watching ten individuals – carefully selected from the DE social demographic – earnestly discussing their perceptions as to the impact of violence in children's television on society at large, occasionally pausing the tape to classify a particular response, occasionally adding new categories to the coding sheet, as Dr Kent had failed to include a code which could reasonably be said to cover responses such as "[Deliberately Emits Loud Fart to Derogate Argument Outlined by Fellow Participant]", occasionally rewinding the tape to focus on the substantive cleavage on show from a blowsy but attractive blonde lady of forty or thereabouts.

By the end of the day, having viewed and coded three focus groups, he had decided that this could be rather fun.

Over the next two years, he had assumed full ownership of the database and the attendant coding scheme, tending them, lavishing attention on them, constantly updating and refining the categories and sub-categories so that his colleagues – should they ever wish – could understand the key outcomes from a given group and could cut those findings in numerous ways: by age, by ethnicity, by sex, by attitude towards Sunday trading laws.

In that time he had worked his way through the entire historical back catalogue of department recordings; in fact, some of the videotapes had proved so entertaining that he had occasionally smuggled them out of the department for repeat viewings with Macko at Birch Lane, although he had felt obliged to reject some of Macko's more inspired codification suggestions regarding female participant breast measurements and "level of fecking bullshit spouted".

With the older material now coded, his work on the database was now largely limited to classifying focus groups as and when fresh recordings came in. Today, he had intended to begin work on a recording that a colleague had left on his desk at the end of the previous week: the scrawled label promised, "Magazine Nudity – AB fem 25-40" which suggested that an interesting debate was in prospect.

But today the database wasn't having any of it. Gerry was rudely denied access.

So he had called IT to report the fault. And, as always (for this was far from the first time that his baby had played up), he had received a lazy, drawling lecture from Bob Gibbs or Nathan Harrison or whichever of the geeks was at the end of the line, telling him to follow procedure and log his request via email in the system. Again — as always — Gerry had replied patiently that given that the designated response time to a logged request was four hours, and that the actual response time averaged somewhere between seven and ten days, procedure didn't really work and that telling IT about the problem might facilitate a speedier solution to the current difficulty.

This alternative procedure didn't work either. Gerry knew that, but at least it gave him the opportunity to let off steam. The first phone call would be followed by another, then another, then another, phone calls that were sequentially more abusive, colourful and threatening. Finally came the pleading — *look, guys, give me a break, I'm having a shitty day here* — but the pleading, however couched, rarely evoked a sympathetic response. IT danced to the beat of their own drum; remote, sarcastic other-worldly beings,

81

semi-detached from humanity and reality.

Recognising the futility of his task, Gerry resigned himself to a morning of reading the national newspapers, drinking coffee and browsing sports sites on the Internet, tasks that would occasionally be punctuated with calls to IT, to show willing. He was therefore rather surprised — and mildly annoyed — to have these plans interrupted by the appearance of the myopic Chubb.

"Database not loading properly?"

Gerry grunted. "S'buggered."

Chubb sidled into the room, peered at the screen for a moment and then began shutting the machine down. (*Fuck me*, thought Gerry, *he's going for a reboot. I would never in my wildest dreams have tried that. Well, 10 out of 10 for predictability, you smelly sod.*)

The machine, rebooted, still failed to load the database, so Chubb busied himself in the programme files, muttering away to himself (or perhaps the computer) in what Gerry imagined was some kind of impenetrable IT language. It could have been Swahili for all he knew. But whether it was IT, or Swahili, the computer appeared to respond, for a few moments later his precious matrix filled the screen: Chubb had got him in.

"What was the problem?"

Chubb carefully explained the issue in the argot of his tribe, so that at the end of the explanation Gerry was none the wiser. Nonetheless, so as not to appear foolish he had punctuated Chubb's flat monotone with what he hoped were timely and pertinent interjections, and when it appeared that the explanation had ended, had chimed in with, "Bloody stupid of me! Thanks. err, mate." Was Chubb fooled? Impossible to tell from that impassive, expressionless face. But then again, were any of them ever fooled?

(No.)

Gerry had assumed that these words signified the end of their meeting, but there was more.

"Heard about that business up in Ilkley?"

Gerry said no, no he hadn't. But, he thought grimly, he was about to, whether he wanted to or not.

"They sealed part of the moor off for three days the other week. Army helicopters, men in NBC suits — the Internet's full of it."

Gerry nodded. He noticed a smile beginning to creep around Chubb's face. It disturbed him.

"Two people posted that they saw people carrying items away from the site to the helicopters. And it wasn't just in Ilkley."

Gerry wondered whether that sentence had ever been delivered before.

"Liverpool, Manchester, Glasgow: all over. And d'ya know what they reckon?"

(Gerry didn't know. He didn't care, either.)

"Aliens. They reckon they've found aliens."

IV

The Glenlivet (or what was left of it) lived in the bottom of the French dresser in the sitting room, together with a bottle of some bloody French liqueur that Angela had insisted on buying a few years back, and a couple of crystal tumblers.

Mayhew poured himself a whisky and stared out of the window. It was dark; rain had started falling an hour or so earlier, and the pane of glass was streaked with water, obscuring any view of the archetypal suburban lawn that the lamps mounted on brackets above the window would otherwise permit. But Mayhew was staring, not looking; his mind's eye was fixed on his office in Air Staff 2, several hours earlier.

Peremptorily dismissed, he had proceeded mechanically to the Underground, taking the District Line back to Wimbledon, before deciding that he may as well take a walk on the Common. It was a well-trodden route, albeit not on a working day: he had used to keep a record of the birdlife he had observed, either alone or (for a period in recent years) with Gerry.

Not a great day for birdlife, today: a few mallard flying over; some pigeons; a sparrow or two. Nothing to match the time when he had disturbed a snipe, or when – during one particularly harsh winter – he had seen three waxwings greedily tearing berries from a rowan. No, the most colourful find of the day had been the tattered pages of a once-glossy pornographic magazine peeking coyly from beneath some bushes on the edge of the heath.

On a whim, he had stooped to examine what was left of the magazine. Well, now! Leafing through the pages, he recalled the visceral thrill, over forty years past, when he would surreptitiously slip his brother's well-thumbed copies of *Titbits* from their hiding place amongst LPs of Billie Holliday and Ella Fitzgerald, and engage in moments – almost always too brief to be classified as sessions – of frenetic, glorious and shame-filled masturbation.

As he returned to his chair, glass in hand, he wondered idly what had become of *Titbits*. Had it survived amongst the myriad publications that now inhabited that sector of the market euphemistically and vaguely described as "adult" by newsagents or otherwise – by a fellow student at Warwick and doubtless by others before and since – as "gentleman's relaxation material". And if it had survived, it had surely changed beyond all recognition from the *Titbits* of years gone by, when scantily-clad ladies (Heaven and the bloody censor forfend that there should be nudity!) were scattered amongst short stories and articles on cars. He remembered, in the joyous throes of self-abuse, straining his eyes to glimpse the nipples beneath the lingerie: these days, to judge from this magazine – and from similar magazines that Blackwater had accidentally-on-purpose left on his desk from time to time, you had to strain to find any lingerie. Would he, as a gangling adolescent, have preferred the modern, liberated cascades of full-frontals to the coy temptations of fifties *Titbits*? Probably. Nowadays: well, they produced no stirrings below the belt, only a cold incomprehension; the memories of *Titbits* prompted a faint, weary smile, nothing more.

The whisky burned his throat, at once bitter and invigorating. The forbidden schoolboy pleasure evoked by his recollection of *Titbits* had prompted a chain reaction of memories, and with them countless questions. He remembered recounting the tale of his *Titbits* discovery to a friend at Warwick University in the course of an evening invigorated and stimulated by the consumption of far too much beer – Roger Bell, no, Roger Beale, that was it. They had been quite close once, shared digs in a shabby little flat during their second year at university. Roger had studied History, when he bothered to study anything at all, and had been adamant that capitalist society would collapse by the end of the sixties, by which time he (Roger) would be on the National Executive of the Marxist Party, or whatever collective body it was that nominally controlled the warring factions of the Trots and pseudo-Trots. A pillock, Roger, but a fun pillock to be around. Then, after Roger took a year out – inadvertently, after failing his examinations – they had drifted apart, meetings limited to maybe three or four lunchtime pints on occasion in the college bar. Mayhew had seen him just once after university, eight or nine years on, a chance meeting on the underground platform at Victoria. The unruly mop of black hair reduced to a crew cut, the black polo neck replaced by a rather crumpled off-the-peg suit, the duffle bag now a briefcase. A short conversation had ensued: Roger was now a junior manager at the Department of Health, near Elephant and Castle. They had simultaneously apologised for their lack of contact, exchanged numbers, promised to keep in touch. They never had: the numbers, written on old ticket stubs, had been thrust carelessly into those parts of wallets that serve as out-trays, before being casually, inevitably binned with the rest of the accumulated detritus at some biannual clear-out. At least, that had happened on Mayhew's part: that always happened on Mayhew's part. He assumed Roger had done the same. Or maybe he just hadn't felt the urge to reignite their friendship. Maybe they had both changed beyond recognition, Mayhew already weakening under the twin yokes of the MoD and Angela, Roger's comical, revolutionary ardour sunk forever beneath a brown three-piece suit.

That led him to wonder about Angela. There had been some attraction once, even the occasional meeting of minds. *We both saw something, surely?* But perhaps they had both seen what they wanted to see: perhaps he had glimpsed a woman who would love him for all his faults, who would snuggle next to him on the sofa on a cold winter's evening and tenderly squeeze his hand. Perhaps Angela had convinced herself that she had seen a man with the confidence and ambition to pull himself to the very pinnacle of the civil service, who could in turn show her off at glamorous cocktail receptions. Perhaps: but if they had, then both had been mistaken. Any meeting of minds between them had been brief and transient, while the physical side of the relationship had begun to peter out well before Emma arrived. Hell, when was the last time they had had sex? This year? Last year? Mayhew couldn't remember: not that he really wanted to.

Wondered about Emma: a plumper, shriller version of her mother. He had doted on her as a little girl, an affection which – as Emma advanced into her teenage years – was reciprocated only sporadically. By the time she hit twenty, it was clear that – in concert with Angela – she regarded Mayhew simply as a rather embarrassing, dilapidated feature of the family residence that she was on occasion obliged to explain away to her various friends.

And boyfriends. Which led to him wondering about Gerry, the latest (and to him, far the most personable) of Emma's paramours. Now he was gone, like the others before him: he – unlike his predecessors – had fired the gun himself. Surely he should have felt anger: *you bastard, Gerry, ditching my little girl – and over the bloody telephone?* Instead, he had stood helplessly by, a bystander to his daughter's plaintive weeping; across the room, Angela too had said nothing, merely flashing her husband a look which both implicitly recognised and condemned her husband's ambivalence.

Do you know, he thought suddenly, *I never told Gerry about the waxwings. He'd have been impressed. And a bit jealous.*

And now there were these bloody sightings. And this business with Tremaine and Granville. Many years ago these would have set his nerves on edge, now only a weary dullness prevailed. *Leave it to Blackwater*, he thought. *It's his baby now.*

V

Blackwater's mobile rang just after eleven. Otherwise engaged, he thought briefly about ignoring it, but the name on the screen, or rather its connotations, quickened his pulse. Griff. Manchester. *Had the little bugger cracked it?*

'Better be good, Griff."

A broad grin spread slowly across his features as the operative updated him.

"You beauty... you're watching the house now, yeah?. If the target leaves the house. stick to it like shit to a blanket... That's right... Can you get Maurice to sort the logistics on this one, got a few things to finish off here... No, I'll ring Hartshorn later, but we'll need all the gear from the Upper Lupton labs. And can you tell him to get a car to come out for me? I've had a couple... No, no, not at my gaff, at Linda's... Linda's, not Lindsey's, haven't seen Lindsey in over a year... Look, you've done me proud, matey boy, but just get on to Maurice. Even Maurice can sort out the manpower and a couple of Chinooks... Sweet. Later, matey."

Blackwater lay back in the armchair. Griff had cracked it.

During the conversation he had almost forgotten the activity in his lap. He beamed a relaxed, condescending smile as the tousled blonde head rose from his groin.

"No, you carry on down there love. Car won't be here for fifteen minutes and we should be done and dusted long before then."

VI

Eric Grimes was running, or at least, his body was.

But while Eric's body had been invigorated by the possession that had occurred a couple of weeks previously, no amount of alien energy could disguise the fact that the body was fat, fifty-five and had short, chubby legs that had done no running for many a year.

Salt tears stung his eyes, of fury, frustration and despair.

The new incumbent of Eric's body had, so to speak, landed on its feet. It had discovered to its joy that Eric was a dyed-in-the-wool red, a season ticket holder of many years' standing. Thus, following Eric's wholly unexpected recovery from a coma, he merely continued broadly along the same happy path as before, with the added bonus of extended sick leave from his work in a nearby warehouse.

He had been standing in the front doorway, drawing pleasurably on a Silk Cut – his first of the day, hell, the hit was good – when he first noticed the car: a Jaguar, parked around sixty yards up the road; wholly out of place amongst the jaded Escorts, Fiestas and Nissan Bluebirds that otherwise crowded the curb of this redbrick street in Ordsall.

His eyes narrowed, focusing on the car: as he stared, there was a sudden blur of movement, as of someone ducking out of sight below the rear window.

He took another sharp drag on the cigarette, attempting to remain calm. He shifted his gaze first skywards, then down the road to where a couple of kids were having a kickabout with a football on the way to school, attempting to demonstrate to the world at large that here was just an insignificant middle-aged man surveying the world on a bright October morning, having a quiet fag.

Saw the man who didn't belong, a thin-faced, dark suited man ostensibly bending to tie a shoe lace on the fringes of the impromptu game, as out of place as the Jaguar.

Saw the glint of light reflecting from the glittering panel on the device that poked from the holdall at his feet.

Got to go now.

He ground the remains of the cigarette beneath his shoe, glanced at his wristwatch, adopted what he hoped was a passable expression of shock that *Christ, was that the time already*, and began to walk purposefully down the street, towards the football, towards the man.

The man looked up at his sudden approach, startled. Hesitating.

Punched the man, sent him spinning into the wall.

Run, as the street behind you erupts, as the game breaks up and the kids scream in confusion and fear; you hear shouts – barked, expletive-ridden instructions – and you know that the Jaguar is already in pursuit.

Sharp left down the ginnel, into the main street, left again, past a gaggle of laughing schoolchildren, past the corner shop, then sharp right down a second alleyway.

Knew they were gaining on him, on foot, in the car. Knew that it couldn't keep this up. Had to transfer. To what?

Saw the cat, staring at him from the garden wall. The cat was the last thing that Eric Grimes' eyes saw before his body fell lifeless, soulless to the pavement. And the falling Eric was the last thing that the cat saw before its mind was abruptly expunged from existence by the intruder.

Too late.

The car was braking, back doors opening, even as Eric was falling, mere yards away; the small, wiry man raising the strange device, an intricate mesh of crystalline semiconductors, metallic plating and elements hitherto unknown to this suburb of Manchester: raising it and activating it.

Still dazed from the emergency transfer, it had no chance. Tried to resist but was ineffably, inevitably drawn out. Sensed the cat falling from the wall, sensed the constriction. Sensed the field of energy holding it

90

locked within the tube. Realised, with an awful finality, that there would be no more football.

Breathing heavily, Griffiths clutched the device to his chest. Blackwater got out of the passenger seat and ambled over. He ignored his colleague, but bent down to the device, eyes glittering; face hard; smile smug, cruel.

He patted the containment tube, which now flickered with a dim, pulsating light amidst a cloud of dense, smoky gas.

"Gotcha, matey-boy."

CHAPTER SIX

I

November was cold, grey and damp.

II

Gerry and Macko continued to ply their respective trades at Scrimpton college (the former plying rather more assiduously than the latter); they came home; they lusted after Rachel (the latter far more overtly than the former); they adjourned to local public houses (occasionally in the company of Rachel, occasionally in the company of other like-minded individuals, but more often than not just the two of them). Sometimes they would move on to the fleshpots of Leeds; sometimes they would return home laden with the finest provender of the Punjab Tandoori or the Lucky Dragon, and on some of those occasions they would actually remain awake long enough to eat said provender.

Sometimes they would wake in their beds; sometimes on the sofa; always alone. The remainder of the alphabet remained safe from Macko's clutches in November, while the ghost of Emma still haunted Gerry. He had never been much good at chatting up girls, he thought to himself sadly after another evening staring soulfully across the dancefloor. Now he couldn't even bring himself to the chat in the first place.

III

Rachel had been in the South Stand at Elland Road to watch Jimmy-Floyd Hasselbaink and Jonathan Woodgate seal a 2-1 win over Sheffield Wednesday;

had raised the rooftops of the Taps with her screams of delight as the vidiprinter confirmed a 3-l victory at Anfield; had returned to Elland Road for a clinical (and thoroughly enjoyable) demolition of a hapless Derby County; and had stalked out of the Kings Arms after watching Bastard Nicky Butt hit a screamer to give bloody Man U a 3-2 win over Leeds on the big screen. (She had steered well clear of Macko after the game; for his part Macko, perhaps sensing that it was not wise to gloat on the streets and in the hostelries of West Yorkshire, had simply retired to the lounge with two fourpacks of lager and a videorecording of the game, subsequently replaying the game twice before passing into contented unconsciousness.)

And in between watching football matches, and avoiding Macko's taunts, she had become a lapdancer.

She had informed Gerry and Macko of her career move over breakfast.

"Got a job yesterday," she began brightly. "'Fantastic!" and a broad, beaming smile from Gerry; a thumbs up and mumbles of encouragement from Macko, who was otherwise engaged with a bacon sandwich.

"Yeah, I start on Monday. At Exotica."

Afterwards, Gerry was pretty sure his jaw had touched the floor at this point. Macko simply coughed violently and cast aside the remnants of his sandwich; breakfast was no longer a priority.

"You're fucking kidding!" he exclaimed. Rachel eyed him a trifle nervously.

"It's good money and they're short shifts," she replied. "'And they seem a nice bunch of girls there."

Gerry, attempting to maintain a passable facade of composure, gave what he hoped would appear to be a nonchalant shrug. "Well, if you don't mind, then. . . (*Say something positive! Say something positive!*) ". . .

bloody good luck to you, Rach!".

Slightly peeved at being suddenly outmanoeuvred in the Rachel stakes, Macko struggled to recover lost ground. "'I'm not knocking it, like, but, well... fuck me, getting your kit off in front of a lot of hairy-arsed blokes..." His voice tailed off as he contemplated the prospect, and then another thought struck him. "Have you done much of this before then, Rach?'"

She shook her head. "Nah. Think I'll need some practice before my first shift" - Macko and Gerry looked at one another in exultation, both internally thanking the Almighty for what they were about to receive – "so Liz and Poppy down at the club have offered to give me a quick lesson Monday lunchtime". Two identical dreams involving a naked Rachel dancing around the lounge were brutally exploded.

"Anyway, I'm off for a shower."

"Do we get discounts?'" asked Macko, only partly in jest. Rachel shook her head, blew him a kiss and headed for the stairs - where she bumped into Chubb, who then made every effort to appear as though he were descending purposefully to the kitchen rather than salaciously eavesdropping on their conversation. She flashed him a gentle smile and with a "Hey there, Gideon", the North's latest recruit to the noble art of lapdancing disappeared into the bathroom.

Chubb reddened and scuttled into the kitchen. Then, realising that he had absolutely no reason to be there, panicked. He stared, horrified, at Macko, who was watching him with a broad grin.

"Morning Chubbles! Out on the town last night were you?"

"No, no. Just in my room."

"Could've sworn I heard the moans of passion coming from your love nest. Haven't got a bit of skirt upstairs waiting for sloppy seconds, have you?"

94

Chubb lowered his head and hunched his shoulders. "No, just me. Just me."

Repeating the phrase, like a mantra, he turned and ascended to his lonely eyrie, closed the door, took a deep breath, then allowed himself to slip into a delicious, sweaty reverie involving Rachel, not dissimilar to that which had so recently but so briefly headlined the imaginings of both Gerry and Macko, but which was here allowed to run its inevitable course.

In the kitchen, and fortunately oblivious to the scene being played out in Chubb's mind (and to its real world consequences), Gerry looked at Macko reproachfully. "He can't help it."

"Neither can I", rejoined Macko hotly. "You know how it is when you're passing some kids playing footie in the park, and you get this urge to run up to them and kick that bloody ball between the posts? Well, this is the park and Chubb's the fucking ball."

IV

At Upper Lupton and - sod Hartshorn - at the Horse and Groom in Ascot - the smile on the face of Adam Blackwater had grown broader by the day. The Liverpool case – which had gone cold for a few weeks - had been tidied up in the first days of the month, thanks to some sharp work from Griff (again, good lad Griff) and (to Blackwater, somewhat surprisingly) Dimmond; and while Griff had been administering the coup de grace in a Toxteth bedsit, the remaining cylinder had finally been unearthed on moorland some twenty miles northwest of Glasgow. A further clutch of operatives had been dispatched north of the border, gently but persistently harassing the police and hospitals, some cruising the streets surrounding Celtic Park on match days.

On the evening of the penultimate Saturday in November, jubilant Celtic fans had been celebrating the 5-1 demolition of Rangers in bars around the ground and throughout the city. One such fan, rotund, balding and- after several hours hard at it in the drinking dens of Gallowsgate - distinctly inebriated, decided that enough was enough and that he'd better bid farewell to his two new chums. He had met them in the Saracen's Head an hour or so after the game: one had stumbled into him in the boiling, febrile melee at the bar, knocking his pint to the floor. Profusely apologetic, the guy had insisted not merely on buying him a replacement, but the next round as well. The guy – scrawny, grizzled, maybe mid-forties – had explained over the course of numerous beers and chasers spread across several pubs that he'd just come off a long stretch on one of the North Sea rigs, and that this was the first game he'd seen in an age: but what a game to come back to! He introduced the rotund, balding fan to his mate Bob – "a fecking Sassenach, but likes his footie and his booze, so he's OK by me" – and Bob had beamed, seized him in an iron bearhug, and spent the rest of the evening drinking Deuchars, smoking rollups and telling dirty jokes.

The balding, rotund fan now went under the name of Geoff, and had done for the past six weeks or so, ever since he'd risen from his hospital bed with an alien entity inside of him. Prior to that he had been Johnny, but Johnny had had a few too many mates. Johnny had been a bloody Rangers fan as well, although he'd apparently not gone to many games, or it could have caused a few problems around the ground.

He was three sheets to the wind, and needed to get home. English Bob and the scrawny guy – he had told Geoff his name, but Geoff had forgotten it immediately and didn't want to appear rude by asking it again – said that they, too, should be getting back: the scrawny guy said that they had a car down the road somewhere, he was sure he was up to driving, and did Geoff want a lift? Geoff said no, he needed a walk to clear his head, so there was a flurry of backslaps and farewells and his new chums veered off into the night.

Jesus, but they could knock it back, thought Geoff to himself.

He'd barely gone a hundred yards when the cold air took effect and he needed a pee. So he unzipped in the shadows and gave vent to his needs.

As he urinated, a car pulled alongside amidst raucous cries of "Hey, Geoff's taking a piss!" Turning, still urinating, he saw the scrawny guy's head emerge from the driver's window. Nice motor, he thought dimly. He could see Bob fumbling around in the back seat.

"Pissing on yer shoes, Geoff!"

"Thanks to you, yer bastard. Now drive safe, you hear me?"

The back door opened and Bob fell out onto the pavement, clutching something to his chest.

"Y'alright man?"

Bob nodded, looked up – and the body of Geoff, nee Johnny, slumped to the floor as the entity was consigned to its tubular prison.

V

So, we finally found a use for our Sweaty agent, thought Blackwater as he drained his pint. That just left Leeds. Hopefully they'll get it out the way soon, he told a disinterested blonde at the next table. There's a few decent lads on the case up there. They should manage to round the fucker up. Better had. I don't want to have to go up to that Northern shithole. Bad enough having

97

to spend a few hours in Manc the other week. You want another drink, love? Sure? Small one?

Even Blackwater eventually realised that his attempts at catching this particular fish were going nowhere, and so he sauntered across to the bar in search of a new pint and new prey. En route, his mobile rang. A short conversation ensued, predominantly one-sided, with Blackwater doing the bulk of the listening. When it ended Blackwater's mood had taken a marked turn for the worse.

Useless bunch of fucking twats up there, he thought bitterly. *Can't manage a piss-up in a brewery. Never thought they were much cop.*

Much to his annoyance, Blackwater was going to Leeds.

VI

And through the unimaginable vastness of the cold, grey-green void, all too occasionally irradiated by the faint pinpricks of distant stars, an object was travelling well beyond lightspeed, gradually but inexorably closing upon its destination.

Trillions of miles remained. But they would pass, soon enough.

CHAPTER SEVEN

I

Life is good, thought Rachel. *My job is great and Leeds won 2-0 last night and we're just a point behind the Scum! One point off the top!*

I'm never going back, she decided happily.

As for the job: well, she turned up, changed into the skimpiest of neon bikinis, chatted to the punters, danced, stripped; chatted, danced, stripped; went home with a pocketful of ten pound notes.

Rachel had rapidly become one of the more popular girls of Exotica. This was partly due to the fact that she was one of the prettiest of the dancers, but also because many of those who frequented the smoky, poorly-lit club - from overweight, perspiring bankers to heavily tattooed, shaven-headed shop floor workers - loved their football. And, this being Leeds, loved Leeds FC. Loved Hasselbaink and Bowyer, Molenaar and Kewell. So there was a natural bond between them from the outset. She and the punters had commiserated with one another over the agonising defeat at Old Trafford, had joyously talked through each of the four goals that had sent West Ham back to London with their tails between their legs. And then she had led them off to a side booth, collected her tenner, turned on the music, whipped off her bikini and all parties went home happy.

Many of the punters were regulars, and very rapidly she struck up a rapport with several of them: Dave, a plump accountant in his fifties who had been a season ticket holder at Elland Road since his teens; Danny, a close-cropped, thickset plumber from Chapeltown and a former member of the notorious Service Crew (with the tattoos and scars to prove it); Mike, a divorced lecturer who seamlessly laced their footballing chats with updates on the latest adventures of his small children; Alf, a lovely gentleman of advancing years who was always solicitous as to her welfare and knowledgeable about the beautiful game to boot (he was also, she soon discovered from a fellow dancer, a city councillor of long standing who infallibly put Exotica on his entertainment expenses, but since most of those expenses wound up tucked into her knickers, then it wasn't for her to grumble).

Dave and Mike had been in earlier in the evening, and had had their chat and their dances (in Dave's case, three with her alone; much appreciated, Dave!). Danny was sat at the bar, supping his pint, staring through the smoky fug at a TV screen on which the highlights of last night's game were unfolding; she would give him a few more minutes then sidle up to him. Alf never came in on Tuesdays, because he was off visiting his mistress in Huddersfield.

It was still fairly quiet, but then, it wasn't quite ten o'clock; many of the punters didn't come in until the bulk of their night's drinking was done. Besides Danny, there were half a dozen or so assorted customers arrayed at the bar; maybe as many more lounging around on sofas that had seen better days (as indeed had one or two of the dancers that attended them); Trisha and Roz were entertaining another couple of gentlemen in the booths; and that was it.

So she chatted for a few minutes to Danny, led him off to a booth, danced, pecked him on the cheek ("Ta, love!'") and climbed back into her bikini. When she emerged from the booth, Danny had gone back to the bar; he would probably have another pint or two, and another dance, though not with her; unfaithful bastard, she though wryly.

The number of punters had grown by one. The

newcomer was at the bar. On the short side, slim of build; jet-black, collar-length hair; nice suit. Very nice suit. She had only been in this body a couple of months, but in the last few weeks she had seen a lot of men in a lot of suits and that was a nice one - designer, made-to-measure. *Hel-lo!*

The suit's owner bought his drink - pint of lager - and turned to survey the club at his leisure. She caught sight of his face: rather thin, pinched, with dark eyes full, it seemed to her, of a brooding boredom and of profound irritation; a face that would rather be somewhere else but was making the best of a bad job.

She sidled across to him; flashed him a smile.

"Hiya." The man looked at her; looked her up and down; gaze lingered momentarily on her breasts before returning to her face. He's thinking: *she 'll do*. And, Rachel said to herself, *that'll do for me*.

"Leeds is a shit hole." He sipped his pint, and grimaced. "And the lager tastes like piss."

She smiled, in spite of herself. "Na, that's just in here. Better next door."

"Good job I've not come in here for the bleedin' beer then, isn't it?"

Faintest hint of a slur, there: had a few earlier, have we? All the better.

"I'm Rachel."

"Well, Rachel my gorgeous big-titted lovely, I'm Adam Blackwater. Pleased to meet you. But Leeds is still is a shit hole."

II

Blackwater was hating Leeds with all the vengeance of his preconceptions: hating it for everything it was not, and for being everything he'd expected it to be. It wasn't London or Upper Lupton, and it wasn't warm, and it wasn't the Horse and Groom; it was so bloody Northern, he had mused bitterly as he had shifted beer after beer in a wine bar on the Headrow; some of the birds are fit, but they're Northern too.

Worse still, his team had made no progress at all; unable to deploy his preferred option of declaring martial law in West Yorkshire and descending on every public and private hospital in the area with a handful of agents backed up by special forces troops, Blackwater had on this occasion been obliged to pursue a more moderate approach, his operatives assigned the task of obtaining confidential patient records from the various establishments so as to ascertain, as Blackwater put it, "which of the fuckers is most likely to be a walking corpse".

Unfortunately the operatives initially detailed with the task in Yorkshire were two of Blackwater's most recent recruits, who lionised their superior and sought to emulate him in all things. They were raw, keen, voluble individuals to whom moderation and subtlety did not come easily. Worse, they both hailed from parts well to the south of the Watford Gap and shared (or had rapidly assimilated) Blackwater's prejudices about the frozen wastelands above it. In their first attempts at contacting the relevant personnel by telephone they found that they were treated no differently by the healthcare authorities than the general public: that is to say, they were faced with a wall of cheerful, patronising indifference to their plight. As they were passed through what to their exasperated minds appeared to be every internal administrative extension at the hospital - some twice - their limited patience ebbed rapidly; having been passed back to the switchboard - via a brief and unrewarding conversation with an external helpdesk in Newcastle - the inevitable torrent of abuse was unleashed and, it should be said in all fairness, returned with interest by a lady of a certain age who had heard it all before. Suitably riled, the two operatives had opted to visit the hospital in person.

The net result was that Mike Griffiths, Blackwater's deputy, had been called across from Liverpool where he'd been supervising the post-operation debriefing to facilitate the release of his men from the care of the West Yorkshire constabulary. Faced with unflinching and unco-operative bureaucracy, the agents had wearied of debate and opted to attempt to remove the records by force; those members of the public waiting in A&E to be treated were therefore regaled by a lively and vigorous display of pugilism from the agents, a shift manager, three hospital security staff and - in the latter stages of the fracas - a heavily-tattooed bricklayer from Gipton who had reluctantly visited the establishment to seek attention to injuries incurred during a brief but violent contretemps earlier in the day, and who saw no reason to miss out on an opportunity for further entertainment. Two broken ribs, a broken jaw and a welter of bruises later, and both the agents and the bricklayer had been detained; surveying the wreckage of the Leeds operation, Griffiths - shaken after successive terse conversations with the police and the hospital - had decided to bite the bullet and call in Blackwater.

So Blackwater had come up on the train, bollocked Griffiths when he met him at the station, bollocked his wounded agents who had been waiting nervously in Griffiths' car, and attempted to make some headway whilst not actually having anyone locked up or shot. In the first instance, this involved being pleasant and apologetic to lots of individuals behind desks, an approach he undertook with great misgivings and only a modicum of success: the apologies were begrudgingly accepted, but unless he could provide more specific information as to the reason for his request then the answer was: no. Restraining himself with an effort, Blackwater had thanked the hospital staff for their help, apologised once more for the senseless way in which his employees had acted, before Griffiths drove him to the secluded estate in the affluent village of Menston, a dozen or so miles north of the city centre, where MIl3 had temporarily established an outpost. Once back at base, he spent the next hour swearing loudly and randomly at his colleagues before settling down in front of a computer with a list of the leading administrative staff at each of the nearby hospitals: and if we've got one speck of dirt on any of you, thought Blackwater, then you're going to give me exactly what I want or else come Sunday morning it's in the *News of the World*. And then, when you've shat yourself, begged me not to ruin your reputation and given me what I want, it's still going in the *News of the World*.

Disappointingly, no dirt had been forthcoming by six o'clock, by which time Blackwater had had enough for the day: so he got a taxi to the city centre, checked into his hotel, showered, dug out a change of clothes and strode out to see what Leeds had to offer; or, to be precise, to ensure – resolutely and defiantly, in the face of any evidence to the contrary - that it reinforced his existing prejudices.

Thus, beer was worse than in the south; the carbonara he ate at an Italian restaurant was a bleeding shadow of that served up at the Dolce Vita round the comer from the MoD offices; the bars and clubs were cheap and tatty compared with his usual haunts. And the girls were, well, Northern.

In the course of his cultural considerations, Blackwater had indeed had a few jars, his comparative criticisms notwithstanding. Quite a few, really. Rather a lot, in fact. And having failed to impress any of the aforementioned Northern birds in the wine bar, Blackwater had peevishly rung Griff and demanded to be told if he'd found any chuff-joints during his otherwise wasted time in Leeds and whether he could direct him to the nearest one.

So Griff had obliged.

III

"Someone's having a bad day…"

"Yes, it's bad because I'm having to spend it in Leeds."

"What's so bad about Leeds?"

Blackwater glowered at her, but said nothing. *Not the nicest of men, are you? Still, you've got money, Adam Designer Suit Blackwater. Which is all that matters...*

"Getting a Harvey Nicks here soon…"

He snorted, contemptuously. "Fuck me. What'll that be selling round here? Top of the range flat caps? Tetley's Bitter and caviar?"

To hell with the small talk. "Would you like a dance?"

Blackwater shrugged. "Yeah, go on - hang on a mo." He downed his pint, ordered another, and - after the impersonal ceremony whereby he had handed over a ten pound note to Rachel, she in turn had passed it on to the bartender, and the bartender had given Rachel a paper token so she could claim for the dance at the end of the evening - she led him by the hand off to a small booth off the main bar, with plush, red upholstered seating around the walls. R'n'B pumped out from a speaker above them. Blackwater sank into the seat and leaned back, expectant.

"We'll just wait for this track to end."

Blackwater nodded. He knew the form.

The song ended; the next kicked in, and with it Rachel began to dance.

Slowly, sensuously, gyrating in time with the music, turning away from him, her buttocks barely brushing his thigh...

"You know what I do for a living, Rachel?"

...turning to face him, cupping her breasts in both hands, staring deep into his eyes, whispering...

"What do you do, lover boy?"

"I hunt aliens. I've been sent to this northern shit hole to dig out a pain in the arse alien that's buggered off with some poor sod's body and is now running around inside it like a fucking Yorkshire zombie."

...losing the beat, losing the beat, lost the beat. Keep calm. Keep dancing.

"What do you say to that, Rach?"

Picking up the beat again, hands sliding either side of him, flat against the wall, staring straight ahead, pushing her breasts towards his face...

"I think you're talking bollocks. But tell me more."

"Do you like bollocks then, Rach?"

..and pushing herself backwards, arms curving back, hands tugging at the fastening of her bra behind her neck...

"Oh yes."

Bra falls away; hands slide down over and around her breasts, framing them for him alone...

"Well, Rachel, there's this security service called MIl3, and they're like the usual spooks, except that they deal with aliens. And, believe you me, there's loads of the little buggers out there. Most of 'em are no problem at all, much nicer than the Jocks, rather have them sat above England than the Sweaties I can tell you..."

Turning away from him, legs apart, bending down, fingers easing under her G-string...

106

"But this one shower - they're like clouds and – it's all political really – their government doesn't want them here. Upsets the clouds back home. So me and my boys have to catch them…"

The tiny triangle of cloth slips to the floor; bends lower, legs spreading further...

"And fuck me you've got a nice muff. So, yeah, we got sent all round the bloody country. Manchester, Liverpool, Jockoland. Got all the little buggers, all tucked up in ET chokey. Except One. One bastard bleeding cloud-shaped alien that's run off with a stiff from Leeds so that it can go and watch football. Did I tell you they liked football?"

Turning, so nearly straddling him, gyrating millimetres above his stiffening crotch...

"So, yeah, I hunt football-loving aliens. I pack 'em up in little tubes ready to send back to space. And I fucking love it."

His groin rose a fraction, meeting her; he leaned forward, whispering harshly. "Except when it means I have to come to fucking Leeds."

The music faded away; fighting every instinct in her being, she managed to bend down and kiss him on the cheek.

"Ta for that, Rach - you almost made me forget about this hole for a minute. Right, I'm going to finish my pint, go back to my hotel room, have a wank, have a kip, and find myself an alien."

And with that, he stalked off - resolutely if a trifle unsteadily - into a comer of the bar from where he stared moodily at the dancer on the central Stage.

IV

Somehow she finished the shift; somehow, kept smiling, kept dancing for a few more customers. Kept to the beat. And only then, long after Blackwater had finished his pint and slunk away, as she returned to the changing rooms at the rear of the club, did she let go; staggered, doubling over, hyperventilating. Only momentarily, though: gently she shooed away the ministrations of Trisha and Roz, assuring them it was just a touch of asthma and that she would be OK in a sec: she wanted to sob, to scream, to run; but sobbing and screaming would bring attention - might ultimately bring Blackwater or his agents. And as for running: there was no point in running; there was nowhere to run to.

Besides, she told herself as she pulled on her jacket and stepped into the chill December air - she wasn't here to run away; she had run away already, run to this place. The home of her dreams. Of Leeds United, of Johnny Giles and Terry Yorath, Billy Brenmer and Trevor Cherry, names that had passed into legend in the secret cults of the home world. She had begged to come; had exulted when chosen. She wasn't leaving, not because some chauvinistic oaf of an agent was looking out for an alien. Her face broke into a smile as she reached for the taxi door.

"Lisa? Lisa!"

She had been oblivious to the screech of brakes beyond her, but the voice rocked her world. Turned in shock and fear; saw that the woman was bearing down on her from fifty yards, now forty -

"Lisa!"

Rachel pulled open the taxi door, cried out her destination to the driver, pulled the door shut, tried to ignore the hammering on the window, the screaming,

108

the face contorted with hurt, bewilderment, pain as the taxi moved away; curtly dismissed the driver's concerns with a shake of her head as the fear flooded back and her beautiful world faced oblivion.

In the street outside the club, Laura was running hard for her car, and crying.

CHAPTER EIGHT

I

The house was falling down. That was Gerry's first thought, as he was dragged forcibly from his slumbers by a fearful, incessant hammering. His second, as he staggered out of bed in search of trousers, was that burglars were trying to gain entry, but then burglars – female burglars, by the sound of them - weren't normally given to yelling at the top of their voices while going about their clandestine activities.

Cautiously, feeling his way in the dark, he descended the stair; muffled thuds and curses behind him indicated that Macko had been roused; whimperings off the first floor told him that Chubb, too, was awake, although he didn't hold out much hope from that quarter if a defence of the property was required. As he reached the foot of the stairs, a flicker of movement caught his eye. Rachel was edging towards the kitchen wall, trembling, while the battering and yelling continued at the back door.

"What the fuck's going on?" whispered Gerry. Rachel ignored him, she was staring at the door through the gloom, eyes wide open.

"Lisa! Lisa! For fuck's sake let me in!" The landing light came on, pushing the kitchen darkness into shades of grey.

"Lisa! It's Laura! Laura!" Through the kitchen window to the side of the door, Gerry could see other lights coming on in the houses opposite. Then, framed in the window, a female face: pale, imploring, desperate.

"Lisa!"

Gerry stared at the face, dumbstruck. The face stared back, anything but. Desperation turned swiftly to anger.

"What the fuck have you done to Lisa, you bastard?"

"Fuck this. I'm calling Dibble." Gerry reached for the phone; Rachel's hand came down on his. "Don't. Please don't."

The kitchen was flooded with light, noise and motion. Macko had leapt down the stairs, three at a time, hit the light switch – revealing the disconcerting sight of Macko clad only in boxer shorts – picked up a frying pan from atop a mass of unwashed crockery and, holding it high above his head, flung open the back door, bellowing abuse the while. He crashed backwards, Laura's head driven into his midriff, the pan clattering into the wall. Laura and Macko landed in a flurry of limbs and curses; Laura recovered first and, ignoring the winded Macko, rose to face Gerry and Rachel. Gerry backed away; Rachel shrank behind him in terror.

What the fuck is happening, Gerry wondered. *Is she a druggie? Is she a nutter? Whoever she is, she's in our kitchen, she's just floored Macko, and she seems to be after Rachel.*

"Lisa, it's me! Don't you remember me?" Quieter, calmer now, for the moment at least. *Okay then: talk nicely to the druggie/nutter.*

"Love, you've got her mixed up with someone else. Her name's Rachel." Laura shook her head, but remained calm.

"Her name is Lisa Smith. Three months ago, she went into hospital for a routine operation on her heart. There were complications. They didn't think she'd make it; I didn't think she'd make it; I couldn't be there at the end. But she didn't die. She got up out of her hospital bed and disappeared. Didn't tell anyone where she'd gone or why, not her friends, ex-boyfriends, ex-colleagues, nobody. Well, she phoned up with some cock and bull story about visiting her arsehole cousin in Bristol – oh, he's still an arsehole, Lisa, you can take it from me – but for a while she seemed to have disappeared off the face of the earth. But now, by chance, I've found her. And I'd like some answers, please, Lisa, either from you or this pair of dickheads."

"Her name is Rachel, you psychopathic bitch." Laura turned; Macko was struggling to his feet. "Her name is Rachel Moran, she's a stripper at Exotica and she's a mate of mine. So leave off or God help me I'll fecking deck you."

Laura eyed him contemptuously. "Like hell you will," she said coolly and turned her attention once more to Gerry and Rachel. "Oh, you've got short red hair these days - rather suits you actually - but you're still Lisa. Still got that tattoo on your arm from that day out in Scarborough."

Aware that she was still moving towards them, Gerry edged back, still keeping himself between Rachel and the intruder.

"Come on Lisa, tell me why, babes? I need to know why you've done this. Did we upset you?"

"For God's sake, she's not Lisa, she's -"

"Lisa Smith is dead."

Gerry stopped and stared at Rachel. Laura froze; Macko, who had been snarling soundlessly at Laura behind her back, ceased his snarls.

"She was dying when I met her in the hospital. I'm sorry, Laura, really I am. But if it wasn't for me this body would be in the ground by now. Or cremated. I'm not sure which she would have wanted. Perhaps you know."

Laura shook her head. "What do you mean?"

Rachel smiled; a sad smile. "Can we sit down next door and talk about this? Please?" The fear was gone

112

from her face but, Gerry felt, there was undercurrent in her urgency of tone, of gesture. *Don't. Please don't.*

Macko shut the back door and they filed silently into the lounge. En route, Gerry glimpsed the round face of Chubb peeping nervously from behind his bedroom door. Gerry caught his eye, mouthed "Fuck knows" and shrugged his shoulders. The face disappeared, but the bedroom door remained ajar.

Rachel sat on one settee, Macko the other. Gerry stood in the middle of the room, Laura - confused, upset, hostile - in the doorway.

"Right then," began Rachel. "Did any of you hear about that weird business on Ilkley Moor a couple of months back?" Laura shook her head; but it struck a chord with Gerry.

"What, all those army blokes and helicopters? Training exercise, wasn't it? Although bloody Chubb kept harping on about. . ." His voice tailed off; Macko knew where this was heading.

"Aliens? Did bloody Chubb keep harping on about aliens?"

"Yeah, but that's. . ." Another sentence went unfinished; Macko stood up and, moving as close to Laura as he dared, shouted up the stairs to Chubb to get the fuck down here; Rachel continued regardless.

"The soldiers were looking for a landing craft that had made landfall in the early hours of the morning. I'm guessing they found it fairly quickly; not very big, the landers, but when they come down, they're travelling at one hell of a lick and it's pretty bloody obvious where they are."

"What's this got to do with you, Lisa?" Plaintive from Laura.

"Oh, Laura. . . I was in the lander. I needed form; I found Lisa. She was so near death, poor love; an hour, minutes even. She didn't need her body any more, so I

113

took it."

"Bollocks." Macko had regained his seat and found his voice. "This is big, hairy, sweaty fecking bollocks, Rach, and you know it. Now, I don't know if you're coming out with all this for Miss Loonybin 1998 here, or if one of the punters slipped you something a bit lively this evening, but whichever it is – it's bollocks all the same."

Miss Loonybin 1998 was staring at Rachel in disbelief.

"He's right, Lisa. Why are you saying this?"

Rachel's eyes flashed in sudden anger. "Because it's bloody true! Because Lisa is dead! Because, Laura, if Gerry had phoned the police just now, like he so very nearly did, that bastard Blackwater in the club tonight from MI13 would know where I was and would send in his goons after me!"

"Jesus Christ, Lisa!'" Laura was nearly screaming. "This is crap, crap, crap - "

"Woah there." Gerry had gone cold; a name, an organisation from a half-remembered conversation nearly two years ago. "Blackwater?"

"Yes, Adam Blackwater." Now Rachel was afraid again. Gerry leaned against the wall, his mind racing. *Christ, Graham hadn't been making it up.*

"Jesus, Macko, I think she's on the level." Macko opened his mouth to argue, but Laura beat him to it.

"Bullshit! I don't know what game you're playing, but -"

"Will you shut the fuck up for a minute?" Gerry glared at Laura; she glowered back, but held her tongue.

"Emma's dad was the bloke at the MoD who dealt with all the public enquiries about UFOs, funny lights in the sky, all that stuff. I got talking to him about it once, over a few beers one night in Wimbledon once

114

Emma and her mum had gone to bed. He said that most of it was a load of crap: well, maybe he didn't phrase it quite like that, but that was the gist of it. But he also said that sometimes these guys from MI13 would come down and take over the investigations. Said there was this one bloke, Blackwater, a right cocky guy." He thumped his forehead; this was making sense - frightening sense. "Look, these guys aren't supposed to exist, and if they do exist it's to chase aliens. If they're looking for Rachel, then..."

He temporarily abandoned his train of thought as he was drowned out in a flood of simultaneous observations: from Macko, "No, no, no, no"; from Laura, a peal of hysterical laughter than ended in a shrieked "Bullshit!"; from Rachel, a sudden "You know these people? You know Blackwater! Shit! Shit!"

Gerry sighed in exasperation. "Can I carry on please?"

"Not if you're going to come up with more of the same crap, no." Laura looked at him with an air of defiance.

"Well, love, I haven't heard anything better from you. All you've done so far is knock my butty on his arse and say 'Bullshit' a lot. And as for you" - turning to Rachel – "I didn't say I know these people, I know about them. I shouldn't, but Graham let it slip." He paused. "How did you say that you knew about them, by the way?"

"Blackwater came into the club. I danced for him. He was very drunk and very talkative."

Macko snorted contemptuously. "So your line is that you're a lapdancing alien?"

Rachel returned his gaze. "That's about it, yeah."

It was at this point that Chubb entered the room and began taking photographs.

II

The last dozen or so years of his life had been leading to this moment: all those hours imbibing *Twilight of the Gods* and *Arthur C Clarke's Mysterious World*, *Doctor Who* and *Blake's Seven*; all those hours plugged into the Internet, creating myriad Excel sheets of UFO sitings. This was Chubb's anointed hour. This was -

"First contact," explained Chubb, in response to Macko's bellowed demand as to what the feck he thought he was doing and a high-pitched "Jesus!" from Rachel, who was attempting to hide behind the settee. "Photographic evidence of first contact."

Laura rolled her eyes. Chubb warmed to his expository task, all the while clicking away on the dusty old Nikon that he'd hastily dug out from the bottom of his wardrobe.

"You see, most of the photographs of aliens are blurry, out-of-focus shots of saucers. Of close encounters of the first kind. Or maybe the second kind, where you can take pictures of how alien life forms have interacted with their surroundings – that's according to the Hynek Classification Scale, by the way, first introduced in 1972."

In the heat of the moment, the dense, opaque barrier that prevented this reticent, nervous, reclusive creature from sharing his world with those around him had been breached. Words flooded through the gap, embracing this rare opportunity to be heard.

"But what we have here is the third kind, or maybe even the fourth kind, I'm not sure if living in someone's body counts as an abduction. It would be a Ted Bloecher Type D, certainly. Anyway, what we can do here is get proper pictures. Aliens in the flesh. Well, maybe not their own flesh, but somebody's flesh."

They flooded through; but while both Macko and

116

Gerry were taken aback by this sudden outpouring, the finer points of the explanation were lost on them. Macko perceived only a fat lad in an oversize dressing gown, talking crap and taking pictures of a fit lass who clearly didn't want to be photographed. Gerry had been lost by the time that the Hynek Classification came up, but he had already spotted a flaw in Chubb's argument, and as Chubb paused for breath, pointed it out.

"Gideon, mate – in what way is this first contact? Not being funny, like, but have the past six weeks she's been living with us slipped your mind? It's not even first contact in this house let alone for Planet Earth."

"But we didn't know she was an alien until tonight."

"She is not an alien!" Laura punched the doorframe in frustration, and immediately regretted it. Her contribution to the debate was temporarily confined to a series of curses in the background as she nursed her reddening knuckles.

"I believe her. Can you come out from behind the sofa please – we mean you no harm..."

Gerry sometimes felt that living with Macko and Chubb was sometimes like inhabiting a particularly foul-mouthed, foul-smelling sitcom. Now it was turning into *Plan 9 from Outer Space*.

"Gideon, cut this out, she's terrified..."

The impromptu photosession was abruptly terminated as Macko snatched the camera from Chubb who, thus thwarted, reached into a capacious pocket and pulled out a small, leather-bound book and a biro.

"And can I have your autograph? More second kind evidence -"

"Oh, fuck that too." The book went the way of the camera. Chubb blinked furiously and squared up to Macko, but said nothing. Macko laughed.

"Just fucking try it."

Rachel emerged cautiously from her hiding place,

and cast a grateful look at Macko. Gerry gently interposed himself between his housemates then, placing a firm hand on Chubb's shoulder, directed him to the sofa recently vacated by Macko. Trembling slightly, Chubb sat, gaze now fixed on the floor. Gerry attempted to reassert some order into the proceedings.

"Can we all calm down, please? There's enough weird shit going down without you acting up like David Bailey and scaring the hell out of Rachel and you threating to start a fight and -"

He was on the point of directing a further request on etiquette at Laura, but at this point the conversation veered off wildly in a new and wholly unexpected direction.

Easily distracted from the matter in hand, Macko had begun poring through the pages of Chubb's book. The majority of the pages were blank, but his attention had been caught by a scrawl inside the front cover, helpfully identified by an annotation in small block capitals.

"Demis Roussos. You've got Demis Roussos's autograph."

Chubb nodded, dumbly. Macko gave him a look which conveyed the merest hint of admiration.

"My mam loves Demis Roussos. When did you get that?"

"In 1979. My mother got it after a concert."

"Who the hell is Demis Roussos?" During her journey to earth, the entity now going by the name of Rachel Moran had become versed in many aspects of British contemporary culture and society, her knowledge gleaned from the myriad snippets of broadcast data picked up by the powerful receivers dotted around the mother ship and amplified inside her travel tube. She knew all about the Blair landslide, Lady Diana's funeral, the Good Friday agreement, the

Blur-Oasis rivalry and France winning the World Cup. Demis Roussos had passed her by.

"Oh you, know…"

To help her out, Macko broke into song.

If Gerry thought his life had become a particularly appalling B Movie, Laura was now convinced hers was the by-product of some particularly dangerous hallucinatory drugs. Her best friend was claiming to be an alien; a geeky bloke clearly believed her and had tried to take pictures of her as she hid behind a sofa; and now this Macko, in a gruff baritone, helpfully backed up after a few bars by the light tenor of the taller guy and – most disturbing of all - by a hesitant, squeaky warble from the geeky bloke, were explaining Demis Roussos through the medium of song in a combination of voices that could not even loosely be described as three-part harmony. Rachel merely shook her head, uncomprehending.

Forever and Ever slowly faded to a standstill as, one by one, the performers realised they weren't getting their message across. Gerry also realised that, as far as the main business of the evening was concerned, they weren't making much progress either. He endeavoured to rectify this.

"OK, let's accept that you're an alien, inside a human body - and it's a big leap of faith I'm taking here - what the hell are you doing here?"

"Football."

This was not the reply any of them were expecting.

"We came to see football."

This time, Laura only got as far as "Bull". This was so way beyond "Bullshit" there didn't seem to be any reason to labour the point.

"Just over forty years ago, one of our mother ships crashed into the North Sea. There were six survivors. They used seabirds to get to land, then sought out more

119

suitable long term hosts."

Macko was staring at her in bewilderment. "Hang on a mo, I can only take so much bollocks in an evening. You're telling me you lot were jumping inside fecking seagulls?"

"That's right, yeah. Anyway, the survivors managed to rig up a distress beacon to alert the home world, but in the three months or so they were marooned in England they really enjoyed themselves – took the opportunity to see the sights, I suppose you'd say. And when they came back, they talked about this wonderful game that the humans played, this – this intense experience, the shared passions of the crowd as the patterns of movement were woven across the park. This football. And the word spread, back on the home world: about the games, about the rivalries, about the players – Bobby Charlton, Dennis Viollet, Peter Broadbent – about how this took life to a new level. This drama, this physicality: those who had seen it, experienced it, craved more. Those who now heard about it wanted to share in it. It became a cult.

"There was strong disapproval from the authorities, but they couldn't stop it. Sure, they could stop our people coming back, but they couldn't stop the stories. They couldn't stop Bobby Charlton. Then, just under twenty years later, an unlicensed ship came back. The authorities – yours and ours – tracked them down in the end, brought them back: but that just gave the rest of us new stories, new heroes, made us even more determined to try for ourselves. Every few years after that, another ship would make a break for it; none made it. Until ours. We made it."

She spoke defiantly, proudly. When she finished there was a brief silence, eventually broken by Macko, who had been nodding in mute appreciation at the mention of Charlton and Viollet, but who felt obliged to pick up on an earlier observation.

"Pardon me for asking, but did it not work out with the seagulls then? I mean, think of the fun – flying after trawlers, shitting on little lads on the beach…"

"Oh, stop taking the piss!" Suddenly angry. "We are bloody complex creatures, Macko! We need a half-decent brain to work with. We can only use seagulls as – as stopgaps. Jesus, when I first landed, I had to use a sodding pigeon as a host! It was so bloody cramped inside that bird's mind."

Gerry was eyeing her nervously. "What happened to the pigeon?"

"Its brain exploded."

Macko snorted. "And did you give a shit about that?"

"Honestly? Not really. If it came down to me or the pigeon, then I'm sorry, but it's me, every bloody time. What about you, Macko? Do you give a shit about the pigs you eat? Or the cows?"

"Did you give a shit about Lisa?" Gerry asked coldly.

Rachel didn't answer for a moment. "She would have been dead in an hour if I hadn't taken her as a host," she said finally.

"Hosts." Laura was scornful, but calm now, dangerously calm. "The pigeons and the seagulls were hosts, you said. Then those first aliens – they found 'suitable long term hosts'. Is that what Lisa's body is to you? A place to live?"

"No," replied Rachel, quickly. "She's much more than that. Without her I couldn't live as a human. I… love this body."

"But where is *she*?" demanded Laura. "Where did she go when you took her as a host?"

Rachel frowned. "It's hard to describe. I'm using Lisa's brain, her mind even, but I can't really know her experiences. I can't know what she knows; I don't know what she's been through. Those things happened to her, not me." She stopped and thought for a moment. "Look, this is difficult for me to put into words, but – it's like the memories of those experiences are tucked away somewhere, and every so often it feels as though this shadow falls across my mind; the shadow of this knowledge, these experiences, these feelings. But it's not the feeling: it's the shadow of the feeling. It tells me that she was fond of you, Laura, but that's all; I can't feel that feeling."

"Then can't you just jump out of her into someone else? Her body's fine now."

Rachel smiled sadly. "It doesn't work like that, Laura. Her body's fine because my energy's sustaining it. When I go, she goes."

Despite themselves, they were beginning to believe – apart, that is, from Chubb, who had been a devout believer from the outset and was now sitting in a mute personal nirvana. But Chubb aside, believing was one thing, approbation another. Macko's hackles were rising.

"So who's next then, Rach? Me? Jezza here?"

She shook her head. "Even if I wanted to – even if I was allowed to – I couldn't. You're fit, healthy: there's no way I could access your cerebral cortex."

"Cerebr -"

"Brain, Macko."

"Thanks."

"You're welcome. No, I couldn't. Wouldn't."

"Sorry, was that 'wouldn't' or 'couldn't'?" inquired Gerry.

"Both. You're a higher life form."

"Higher life form? What the hell does that mean?"

"Good point, Jez," chimed Macko. "Do you have a definition for 'higher life form', like? I mean, clearly

122

poor Lisa passed the test, but pigeons and seagulls would appear to be fucked. So where do cats and dogs fit in? Come on, let's be knowing."

"I can't remember the bloody definition, alright!" Rachel replied with some irritation. "Besides, in a lot of cases with new species it's about sensing the power of the mind in question."

("Hardwicke would've been toast if you'd met him first," opined Macko moodily.)

"She's dead, she's dead, she's dead…" Laura was crying freely. Belief had kicked its way past her scepticism, and with it her hopes lay shattered.

"Oh, shit…" Gerry turned to Macko. "What the fuck do we do?" Macko shrugged helplessly.

"Please don't tell them. They'll take me back. They'll hurt me."

Gerry breathed hard. *Think, think, think, Gerry: we can't call the police, we can't just go on as if nothing as happened, there's got to be something we can do, someone we can turn-*

"I need to speak to Emma's dad."

"No! He's one of them, you said, you can't -"

"Shut the fuck up!" Gerry glared at her in sudden, urgent anger; then, calmer. "We're not handing you in. Yet. Let's just say the jury's out on that one. But Graham: I trust him. He's a nice guy."

"You can't trust him!"

"I trust him because he doesn't trust them. Besides, not your decision. Our decision. In the meantime, the best friend of your 'host' is sobbing her heart out because you've bloody broken it, and so I'm going to get her out of your way for it a bit. Mack, can you keep an eye on her?"

Macko nodded, and did so. Gerry turned to Chubb.

"Gideon…" Gerry struggled inwardly to provide a role for Chubb in the present crisis. He failed. "Look, just go back to bed mate. We've got this covered."

Chubb was on the point of protesting, but then Macko provided added ballast to Gerry's request by gesturing forcefully at Chubb and the ceiling, before conveying through a series of simple and easily understandable mimes that if Chubb objected he could look forward to having his nose broken and his testicles crushed. Chubb shuffled out. The alien, he decided, could wait.

CHAPTER NINE

I

"Laura. Laura, love… Come on through here, sweetheart, I'll stick the kettle on for us…"

As Gerry gently shepherded an unresisting Laura through into the kitchen, Macko surveyed Rachel with an uneasy fascination.

"So, you're an alien then?" he began brightly.

"Yep."

"And you like football?"

"You know I like football, Macko. I sulked for four days after your lot turned us over."

"You said nice things about Bobby Charlton. Not like a Leeds fan to say that."

"Not all Leeds fans are one-eyed bastards, Macko. But then again, if he'd ever played in a game against Leeds and I was watching, then I'd be calling him all the names under the sun."

Macko nodded. They sat in silence for a moment, then: "Look, you're not going to try and take me over are you? 'Cause I just couldn't bear to have a Leeds fan inside of me."

"Like I said, Macko, I couldn't." Pause. "Unless you were dying."

"Right." More silence. "Can we just fucking clarify this, 'cause when you say 'dying', you don't mean a little bit under the fucking weather…"

"No, no…"

"We're not talking, 'little bit rough after a Saturday night on the pop'…"

"No, no, seriously, you're good."

Macko stared at the ceiling for a while, attempting to formulate a question. Before he got there, Rachel answered it for him.

"It would have to be terminal. No chance of recovery. The life essence would be leaving. I'd know."

"And – would you?"

"Well, you have got a nice bum."

Macko regarded her warily. "Do you mean 'nice' as in you'd like to wake up next to it or as in you'd like to wake up wearing it?"

"Well – either, really."

The evening had been punctuated by periods of silence, when – perhaps understandably given the extraordinarily precepts that those within this Birch Lane household had been obliged to digest – it had been difficult to articulate an immediate response to what had gone before. This was another such moment. Macko eventually came up with a tentative solution which neatly sidestepped the matter in hand.

"Shall I stick the telly on? Probably be replaying the game from earlier."

"Yeah, go on."

II

Laura sat motionless in her chair, staring into space, oblivious to Gerry's bustlings behind her. She barely registered the mug of coffee being placed in front of her, or Gerry gently manoeuvring himself into the chair opposite with a "Two sugars, wasn't it?"

Gerry sat and sipped his tea, and waited.

After a few minutes she came back to him from whichever sad, dark place she'd been contemplating, and looked at him with tired, cried-out eyes. When she spoke it was with a soft, cracked voice, all anger spent.

"It was the bloody football that did it," she whispered. "The rest of it could have been crap, but when she talked about the football like that, it was... it was like she was making it all into some beautiful, epic

126

poetry about gods and heroes instead of it being some hairy-arsed blokes hoofing a ball around. Lisa hated football. Couldn't see the point of it. Knew nothing about it."

"I'm sorry. We had no idea."

Laura laughed; a hollow, bitter laugh. A faint smile played across her face. "Why the hell would you? Why the hell would anyone?"

"Known her long?"

"Since we were kids. Her family moved to our estate when I was ten."

"Where are they now?"

"They were both killed in a car crash when we were in our first year at uni. Well, her dad was killed outright, her mum hung on for a couple of days. It was awful."

"Shit."

"Yeah, shit." She took a sip of coffee. "She was really quiet, you know? But lovely, funny, a good mate. My best mate."

"Your best mate?" Gerry had tried to couch it as delicately as he could; regretted it the moment he'd said it as he caught the anger that suddenly flickered across her face. But just as suddenly it died; there was nothing left to sustain it. She shook her head.

"Oh, why is it blokes think that just because you have a close girlfriend she must be that kind of 'girlfriend'? No, we weren't. But we were very close, she was like the sister I never had: she was the only one I could open up to when I was down, when my parents had been fighting, when the boys at school took the piss out of me for being a Goth and for being fat, when my first boyfriend dumped me…"

"I was a Goth. Well, kind of."

In spite of herself, she was intrigued. "Really? When was that?"

"Early nineties. Think I got rid of most of my gear a few years ago – except the CDs and the tapes, still play them a lot."

"Were you a student round here as well?"

"Yeah, in the college up the road. Work there now."

"Go to many gigs?"

"Used to go down the Cockpit a lot. See bands like Gethsemane, Die Laughing -"

"Oh my God! Die Laughing! I love them!" Her voice rose in delight; then realisation kicked back in and she sighed.

"I'm so sorry."

"Yeah, me too." She smiled at him. "Take it you like football, too, then?"

"Well, yeah. Although not as much as Macko or... or her." Laura looked down, fingering the pendant that hung from her neck. Gerry watched for a moment; watched the fiery red hair that cascaded over her shoulders to the black lace mesh below.

"Thing is," he continued, "I don't watch too many live matches when my team are playing. Can't."

"Why not?"

"It would bloody kill me. All the bloody tension, ninety minutes a week, thirty eight games a season. And it's worse 'cause it's Liverpool. Used to be great when I was growing up, we were winning everything. You'd watch a game, or listen to it, and Liverpool would win. Simple as. Or if they didn't, they'd win the next one, and the next one, and at the end of the season they'd wind up with the League Championship, or the European Cup, or sometimes both. But then seven, eight years ago Dalglish resigned, it all went tits up, and now we're lucky if we get to hang on to United's bloody coat tails. And now, even when we're winning, I expect us to bugger it up. So despite being a Liverpool fan, I sometimes avoid watching Liverpool

128

games. If that makes any sense."

"Not really. But then, like Lisa, I know bugger all about football." Laura paused, frowning. "Pardon me for asking, but how the hell are you a Liverpool fan? Not like you've got a bloody Scouse accent or anything."

Gerry grinned. "My oh my, you don't know much about footie, do you? When I was a kid, everyone was a Liverpool fan."

"So you followed the herd?"

"Not exactly. I followed my cousin."

She shot him a quizzical look and so, with a wry smile, Gerry elaborated. "Started getting interested in football – properly interested – when I was seven or eight. Before that it was just kicking a ball around with my mates. But then all the other kids were getting their replica shirts and their Panini albums and were supporting clubs: I was feeling a bit left out so I asked my cousin who I should support. I mean, he was twelve so he knew about stuff like that. Anyway, he supported Liverpool and told me to support Liverpool so I supported Liverpool even though I didn't know where Liverpool was. And I still support them. Well, in that fan-who's-too-shit-scared-to-watch-the-games-sense of supporting them."

"So which was your local club, then?"

"Newport County. They went bust a few years ago. Pity."

"Newport – I thought that accent was more Welsh than Scouse."

"Been up here so long it's turning into a Welsh-Yorkshire hybrid."

From the room beyond came a burst of noise, a television football commentary at high volume. Gerry stood up and rapped hard on the adjoining door. There was a muffled "Sorry" in unison from Macko and

Rachel, and the volume level dropped. Laura rolled her eyes. Gerry returned to his seat.

"What did Lisa like?" he asked quietly.

"Reading. Cinema. Classical music. Used to take the piss out of her for that." Laura suddenly looked hard at him. "Are either of you fucking her?"

"No."

She took a swig of coffee. "So," she said finally, "are you going to turn her in?"

"No – at least, not yet. Like I said, I want to speak to my ex-girlfriend's dad. He's on the fringes of all this stuff. Besides, I don't think she's going anywhere. All she's interested in is football."

"Bit like your friend Macko?"

"God, no. Macko likes lots of stuff besides football. Beer, porn…"

"OK, I get the picture."

Gerry stared at his watch. "Jesus, it's half two. Got to be in the college by nine, I'll be fucking knackered." He paused. "Fuck it," he said eventually. "I'm throwing a sickie in the morning. I think I've got just cause, although" he said almost as an afterthought, "I don't think I'll give them all the details when I ring in in the morning."

"I'm gonna go," she said quietly. "I think I need some time to myself after all this."

He nodded. "Sure."

"My car's parked out the back, round the corner."

"Look, I'll keep you posted, yeah. But, whoever she is now, she was shit scared of those guys who are after her."

"I won't say anything. Besides, who'd believe me?"

"They might."

Laura reached into her handbag and produced a pen and paper, and hastily scribbled her number down.

"Give me a call when you decide what to do."

"Will do."

She turned to go, then hesitated."

"It's Jez, isn't it?"

"Well, Jez or Gerry. Gerry Angel. Pleased to meet you."

"Thanks for the coffee, Gerry Angel." She squeezed his hand. "And mind how you go with – whatever's in Lisa."

And with that, she stepped out into the cold night air.

She held it together through the journey back to her Headingley flat, staring fixedly at the road ahead, resolutely singing to herself as she drove.

By the time she had worked her way through three Sisters of Mercy numbers she was home.

She shut the door, threw herself on the bed and wept.

III

Blackwater had been to pay him a visit.

It had been a while since he had had that privilege; two years, maybe. There he was, lounging against the wall, hands thrusts deep into pockets, an insolent smile playing on his face.

He had invited his visitor in, and Blackwater had disengaged himself from the wall and made himself comfortable in the flat's solitary armchair.

After some brief, unconvincing smalltalk about the furnishings (Blackwater had observed that the décor hadn't changed much, that another chair or two wouldn't go amiss, and was that a touch of dry rot in the corner) they got down to business: *What I'm after, matey boy, is the lowdown on your chum from that lander that came down over Ilkley a few weeks back.*

He had feigned ignorance, or at least, had begun to:

131

but barely had the first protestations of mock surprise left his lips than there was *No, no, no; cut the crap, sunshine. We know you know: and you know we know you know, so stop pissing about.*

He had smiled at this: Blackwater was almost refreshing when compared to some of his colleagues. You knew exactly where you stood with him.

So he had shrugged and said: *sure, I know about the lander in Ilkley; I know about all of them, in Liverpool, Manchester, Glasgow. I know that you've caught all the others; I felt you catch them. But between times, when they've taken hosts: the link is dulled, deadened; much of the energy is taken up sustaining the possession of the physical form. It's like encasing radioactive isotopes in a lead-lined room.*

Blackwater had said nothing for a moment, but had taken this on board.

I'm sorry, Mr Blackwater, but I can't help you. Wherever my... compatriot is now, I've no idea.

Come on matey-boy, you are bullshitting me!

Am I?

We know why your old mucker chose Leeds: exactly the same reason why you took that little aeroplane flight twenty one years ago. You both wanted to watch the team of cloggers down the road. So pardon me if I don't believe that you haven't met up to swap tales of Don Revie and how different life was in the old days before body-snatching was invented.

Not interested in the old days, Mr Blackwater. You know that. That's why I cut the deal with your office, all those years ago. That's why I put up with all that experimentation. That's why I missed a whole goddamn season after arriving in England. I remember every single incision, by the way. I remember it was very cold in those labs at night. I remember being so lonely but not being alone, because there were others down there with me. I remember the darkness crying out.

So: yes, my 'old mucker' is almost certainly living in Leeds; yes, my 'old mucker' will be trying to get to as many games as possible, perhaps home and away. But – so what? My old mucker is another Leeds fan. One among many. Now, when I'm at the game, I chant with the other Leeds fans; I punch the air with them when we score; I shout at the referee with them when he gives decisions against our boys. But I don't socialise with 'em after the game. I walk back here, make a cup of tea or take a beer out of the fridge and put Sky Sports on the telly. On my lonesome.

I'm the retiring type, Mr Blackwater. I've had to be.

I almost believe you, said Blackwater. *Almost. Oh, there's shit you're not telling me, and if and when I find out what that shit is, then your fucking season ticket will be revoked. So watch your ass, matey-boy. Because we will.*

Blackwater had got up to leave, before turning to Ellis with a puzzled expression.

Do you know what I can't understand? Out of all the places in the Universe – all the places in this planet – this shithole, this cold, wet, northern shithole – is where you decided to park up.

Because, Mr Blackwater, this shithole – this cold, wet, northern shithole – is where my boys play. Now I wouldn't expect you to understand that: but around this city – around this country – every single person who has queued up for a half-time pisspoor meat pie and a lukewarm cuppa would understand that. Because that's how it works.

Takes all sorts, said Blackwater. *But like I said, watch your ass.*

And that was that; Blackwater had sauntered off in search of a cab, leaving him alone once more.

Of course, he knew where the entity now known as

Rachel Moran was; as soon as he had sensed its presence on the incoming lander, he had set up the subsonic resonator beneath the armchair, which enabled the entity – once it had acquired its human host – to track him down; delicate adjustments to the resonance enabled the creation to provide a fairly rudimentary but mutually comprehensible messaging system, used by their kind when in host bodies since time immemorial, in this case telling the entity when and where they should meet. He had helped it create a new identity ("Hello, Rachel"); had advised it/Rachel on the best means of remaining undiscovered. Together, they had worked their way through the small ads in the *Yorkshire Evening Post* in search of suitable accommodation, and had decided that Birch Lane – not too close to Leeds, but with a thirty, forty minute bus journey from the Headrow, easily accessible – was perfect.

They had not seen one another again. After their meeting, he had dismantled the resonator; its parts now lay scattered in drawers and under the sink. He could not afford to get involved further; he had given Rachel a leg up, which was more than any of the others had received.

He was glad that the interview with Blackwater was over; he had been expecting one of them to show up, and was only surprised that it had taken MI13 that long to get round to it. But there were other things on his mind.

He knew what was coming; knew that a mother ship had entered the outer reaches of the solar system; knew who was aboard.

For the first time in more than twenty years, he was truly afraid.

CHAPTER TEN

I

Gerry and Macko surfaced late the following day. For Gerry, bed seemed a safe, familiar refuge from the unreal uncertainties that circumstances had thrown their way. He half-hoped, in the moments of waking, that he had dreamt up all up, that it had been some fucked up hallucination, but as he stumbled down the stairs at midday he had already accepted that a couple of cans of best bitter were not likely to have whipped up that much of a headfuck.

Macko emerged at five, although for him, this was not all that uncommon an experience. Deciding that sobriety was, for the present at least, a distinctly unpromising option, he had made a short visit to the corner shop, returning with a plastic bag groaning under the weight of Guinness and lager. He had shuffled silently into the lounge where Gerry was staring blankly at the TV, placed two cans at his feet and proceeded back up the stairs with the remainder of his purchases.

Gerry transferred his gaze to the cans; from the safety of his room, Macko slowly drank himself back into the comfort of oblivion.

If either Rachel or Chubb was up and about, they kept themselves to themselves.

After a while, the cans on the floor lost their appeal; besides, Gerry realised with a hint of trepidation, he had a phone call to make.

He took a deep breath, and dialled the number.

Please let it be Graham please let it be Graham please let it be Graham

"Hello?"

It was Angela. *Shit.*

"Is Graham there please?"

"Is that Gerry?"

"Yeah. Hi, Angela."

"Just one moment." Two hundred miles away, Gerry could sense lips being pursed at the memory of this uncouth Celtic youth who had callously abandoned Emma; this perennial student, this – this social scientist, of all things.

"Graham, it's – Gerry." *Christ, how much contempt can you get into two syllables?*

He dimly heard what sounded like an intrigued exclamation in the background, before Angela cut back in with a brusque, "Here he is Gerry. But first I'd just like to say that we felt that you behaved – abominably."

We felt? We? *That doesn't sound promising...*

"Hello, Gerry."

"Hey, Graham."

"This is a surprise."

"Yes, I imagined it might be."

"Keeping well?"

"Not bad, not bad..." Cut to the chase, cut to the chase. "Graham, I think I need your help. I can't say much, but – it's about Blackwater."

There was silence.

"It's about something he's looking for. And I know where it is."

II

Blackwater was not overly fond of jeeps, particularly jeeps that were travelling at an indecently rapid speed across unrelentingly bumpy terrain. *Christ*, he thought to himself as his driver dragged the vehicle sharply to the right in response to a crackled exhortation over the radio, *if ever there was a recipe for instant piles, this was it.*

Still, this little excursion over frozen farmland meant that, for the moment, he wasn't in Leeds.

Behind him, Griffiths was peering nervously and ineffectually out of the window in the vain hope that somewhere in the near blackness he might spy a landmark by which to gauge their progress or, failing that, any kind of light – moonlight, starlight, artificial light – to reassure him that their driver had taken the right turning at the last junction and hadn't inadvertently carted them off into some Godforsaken interdimensional void. Hell, the creatures that they had to deal with these days, he couldn't rule it out as an option.

Perhaps sensing the concerns of his passengers, the driver spoke up.

"'Bout five miles to go, sir."

"Glad some fucker knows where we are," grumbled Blackwater, wincing once more as a particularly hefty jolt made its presence felt all the way up his spine. Griffiths said nothing, unless the merest hint of a whimper could be said to comprise a response.

By the faint luminescence of the dashboard, Blackwater glanced at his watch. *Ten to one! Hell's tits, that's over an hour since the cylinder came down. Jesus, I get pissed off if I have to wait ten minutes for a train, and at least I've got the luxury of being able to wander up and down the platform, buy a 'paper , drink a coffee and scratch my arse. The fucker in the cylinder can't do any kind of wandering. It doesn't even have an arse to scratch. Yet.*

Griffiths' phone beeped plaintively. After a moment or two fumbling for it in his pocket, he retrieved and answered it. Blackwater waited expectantly as Griffiths listened intently; as his deputy ended the call with a slightly tremulous, "Thanks, sir", he barked: "Well?"

"There's an agent on site and another just arriving

137

with" - Griffiths swallowed – "a host."

A host. In spite of himself, Blackwater shivered, before black humour re-engaged itself. *Arse-scratching time coming right up*, he thought.

III

He had accepted death. Not at first, of course: there had been a stark rejection of what he was being told, even as his legs buckled underneath him and his heart pounded; later, there had been tears, bitter fury, hurling plates and glasses across the kitchen in unutterable despair; there had been more tears, lots of them, in the days and weeks that followed, but the rage had slowly subsided. As the condition worsened, as he grew weaker and more frail, he had recognised that he wasn't going to win this one; had decided that, since he was going to go, then at least he should go with a bit of dignity and decorum and leave the remainder of the crockery intact.

But now this.

He had been in a hospice on the outskirts of Cambridge when the man had come for him; a stocky, thickset man, his voice tinged by a faint West Country burr, telling him of this new treatment that could improve his condition, thrusting a sheaf of paperwork in his direction which – the man assured him – comprised a host of medical endorsements following clinical trials of the procedure. But he had to leave now, this instant: delay too long, and he might be too far gone for the treatment to have any effect.

Bewildered, scarcely daring to hope, Michael James had clambered painfully out of bed and into his towelling dressing gown, helped by his new friend, and had made his way to the man's black Audi. So had begun a long drive through the heartland of England: it

138

was nearly ten o'clock when they had hit the A10, and Michael had slept for much of the remainder of the journey; when he awoke, the Audi was coming to a halt in what appeared to be – as far as he could tell – a ploughed field.

"Not far to go now, sir. But we need to walk the last few yards. Just over the brow of the hill."

The man helped Michael out of the car. Michael took a few tentative steps, then nearly fell headlong as the ground seemed to give way in front of him: there was a steepish slope for maybe eighty, a hundred yards and then...

There were tents, thought Michael weakly. *Tents and bright lights. Tents and bright lights and soldiers.*

He turned to his companion in confusion and distress.

"Is it here? Is the hospital here?"

The man took Michael's arm and led him firmly but carefully down towards the slope towards one of the tents. It seemed to Michael that the air was warmer here than up on the rise, significantly so; there was a faint buzzing in his ear.

At the entrance to the nearest tent stood a young man, tall, slim, blonde-haired.

"How are you feeling, Mr James?"

Michael's pale, gaunt face looked up at him. "Are you the doctor – I'm sorry, I couldn't read everything that they gave me, I was too tired..." His voice tailed off.

The young man gave a wan smile. "We'll soon deal with your condition, Mr James. If you just come this way..."

Michael was led, unresisting, into the central tent, which was larger than the others. It was empty save for a deep hole in the earth at its centre; it seemed to be lit by a light coming from within that hole, a bluish light that pulsed and flickered.

The buzzing in his ear was growing stronger, more insistent.

Unable to help himself, he peered into the hole.

There was something down there, maybe thirty feet down, something – metallic? Whatever it was, it was the source of the strange light; it was so strong that he had to shield his rheumy eyes from the glare.

Behind him, Tremaine asked nonchalantly, "How is he?"

Granville shook his head. "He needs to be much weaker."

Tremaine gave a nod which signified both concurrence and assent. Granville reached into his jacket pocket.

There was a crack; James staggered, clutching his chest; a deep crimson stain spread rapidly across the front of his dressing gown as he tumbled sideways to the earth. From the depths, the light from the cylinder flared momentarily then, abruptly, faded into nothing.

Granville and Tremaine looked at one another but did not speak; Granville returned the Browning to its home.

At their feet, the body of Michael James opened its eyes.

"Good evening," said the ambassador.

IV

Chubb had gone, his plump figure shuffling off towards the bus-stop, holdall in hand. His holiday started here, and he was off to the parental abode for a week or so. He had been primed by Gerry not to utter a word to anyone – *you get that, anyone* - over the Christmas break, and he had nodded dutifully, inwardly savouring his part in this delicious conspiracy. His co-

conspirators were far less sanguine about the whole business, as they explained to Rachel over a belated breakfast. Macko put it simply.

"The thing is, Rach, we're shitting bricks here."

(Gerry noted from the three bacon-and-egg sandwiches that had been and gone from Macko's plate that his concerns had clearly not had an adverse on his appetite; he had previously observed in the toilet, much to his disgust, that – literally speaking – Macko's assertion didn't appear to be far from the truth. The dirty Irish bastard.)

Macko elaborated.

"What we're used to is, well, the everyday bollocks," he explained. "The nine-to-five shite, the having feck all money for the week before payday, the hot water not working and the landlord taking ages to sort it out; birds blowing you out in night clubs, pissed up twats trying to start on you on bus stops, the boss havin' a go 'cause he thinks you're an idle fecker. That kind of thing. This goes a bit beyond that. The boss havin' a go – he can call me what the feck he likes. I don't take it personally, I know he's a cock and that's that. But when I hear talk of tooled up spooks knockin' on the door lookin' for aliens, well – you could say I'm out of me comfort zone."

"I'm sorry," Rachel said quietly at length. "I didn't want to mess things up."

"Is there anyone else you know who might be able to help, Rachel?" inquired Gerry gently, as he piled his fork with a selection from his plate. "I mean, obviously Blackwater's rounded up everyone else from your planet, but any – well, friendly people besides us?"

She hesitated. *I have to trust these men; they have put their trust in me.*

"There is another of us."

The fork and its burden of egg, beans and bacon

halted in transit.

"Hang on – by another of us you mean – another alien, right?"

Rachel nodded. "Another Jackson."

Macko burst out laughing. "Jesus Christ – did I just hear that right? You're from the planet Jackson?"

Gerry couldn't stop himself: "Has it got five little moons called Michael, Tito, Jermaine…"

"We don't call ourselves Jacksons: it is the name by which we are known to them. Their little joke." Rachel's eyes were flashing with anger; she spoke with contempt. "We are so much more than a race of beings: we see ourselves as part of the fabric of the universe. But for the purpose of dealing with them, and of speaking about this to you, we must be classified: so we are Jacksons."

"OK, OK, so you're Jacksons against your will. I promise not to take the piss again." The anger faded from her face as Gerry continued. "But don't take it out on us: who the fuck came up with the name of Jackson?"

"MI13. Their little joke. To make us that much more inclusive; to enable them to talk about us in everyday conversation, I was told: 'Oh look, we've got a meeting with Mr Jackson today.' Doesn't raise so many eyebrows at the office canteen."

Both Gerry and Macko could see her point, and nodded as sagely as they were able under the circumstances.

"Anyway," Gerry continued, "you were saying, there's another one of you guys out there: can he help? Or can she help?" He paused for a moment. "I mean, I'm fairly new to all this but I'm assuming your mate is in human form, right."

"Right. And here in Leeds."

Macko exploded. "What is wrong with you aliens?"

he shouted, "Ninety two fecking football league clubs to choose from, and you pick the most goddawful bags of shite amongst the lot of 'em." A sudden thought struck him; he paled. "Jesus, Gerry, they're feckin' evil Nazi aliens. They must be. They all support Leeds. I'm not falling for any amount of 'we-mean-no-harm-to-your-planet' bollocks if they're all shouting the odds in the East Stand."

"Oh, fuck off, Macko." That was Gerry and Rachel, more or less in unison.

"Sorry," said Macko in a small voice.

"We're not all Leeds supporters, Macko," Rachel chided, "I told you that yesterday. Just the two of us that are left. They got everyone else."

"So who's your friend?" asked Gerry brightly. "Anyone we know?"

V

"I'm going down to Wales for Christmas to see Mam and Dad. On the way down I'm going to take a bit of a detour – I've arranged to meet up with Graham."

The George & Dragon was busy tonight; several of the local firms had knocked off for the year, and both the bar and the snug were crammed with regulars and irregulars. Gerry and Laura had managed to grab the last remaining table, near the door: relative piece and quiet, relative privacy.

"What did you tell him?"

"Couldn't tell him much – didn't want to say too much over the phone – but I didn't really have to. As soon as I mentioned Blackwater, that was it; he was keen for me to go down there."

"Gerry – you're sure about this?"

Gerry shrugged. "I'm not sure about anything, Laura. I'm bloody winging it, to be honest. But at least

Graham knows something about these guys; he might come up with a few ideas about how we deal with this..." – he struggled for a term to describe their present predicament, eventually setting on "shit" as covering all the bases.

"I don't know if there can be a good way out of this, Gerry. I mean, Lisa's dead, and now this thing is running round inside her body, and these spooks are chasing her."

"I know, I know." He hesitated.

"Look, there's something else. I know what we've been through is fucked up beyond belief, but this morning Rachel told me – well, she told me that..."

VI

"No fucking way."

Firstly Rachel had muttered the words under her breath; Macko, assuming he'd misheard, asked her to repeat them. Which she did, at the top of her voice.

Elvis Presley.

"Look, he came over from America back in '77. The cylinder crashlanded in the States and he was the nearest host. That's all I know."

And Gerry's mind went back to a smoky bar in August, where an old soak was telling them about a chance encounter.

"Macko, it's true! That old bloke in the pub: he saw Elvis after the game!"

Everything was coming together.

"Have you met him? Have you seen him?"

"Just once. He helped me get myself sorted out – showed me the ropes. But it's not safe for me to see him again. He said that MI13 keep a watch on him."

"So what's he calling himself these days?" Macko was intrigued. "I mean, I'm assuming that, like

144

yourself, he decided that a new name was in order. Because otherwise, people might get a bit suspicious: you know, if there was a Mr Elvis Presley livin' down the road who was a fecking dead ringer for Elvis Presley."

Now it was Rachel's turn to smile. "These days he's called Pressdee. Ellis Pressdee."

Macko let out an involuntary laugh. "Well, what a cunning disguise, calling yerself Ellis Pressdee. No one's gonna figure that one out. 'So, what's your name?' 'Ellis Pressdee.' 'God, that's funny, sounds a bit like Elvis Presley. And do you know what, you look just like him as well. Go on, give us a song.'"

"He didn't choose it, Macko. They did. MI13."

Gerry and Macko both looked baffled, so Rachel continued. "They let him stay, they let him watch the football, but they didn't want him, well, getting to know humans. Just one other safety measure – and another of their little jokes."

Little jokes. Rachel almost spat out the phrase. They could tell she wasn't that amused.

She stood up. "I hope this meeting you fixed it last night goes well, Gerry. Really I do. But I'm not counting on it." Her lip was trembling as she ran out.

It's not safe for me to see him. But nothing's safe any more, is it?

VII

"So, what you're telling me is that Elvis Presley is an alien from the planet Jackson who likes football?"

"Keep your voice down, for fuck's sake. And it's not the planet Jackson. It's just a cover name for the species. Rachel was most emphatic on that point. Right, my shout."

She laughed as she drained the glass of lager. "Oh,

Gerry, this is mad. Mad, mad, mad. We're trying to look after a football mad alien who's living inside the dead body of my best friend, and her best friend is living inside the dead body of Elvis Presley. Tell you what," she added, as Gerry rose and picked up their empty glasses. "I didn't like football before all this kicked off. Bloody hate it now."

Gerry shrugged helplessly and disappeared temporarily into the throng at the bar. *He's a nice guy*, she thought, fingering the elaborate crucifix that hung at her neck. *Holy crap, I hope this works out OK.*

As he waited at the bar, Gerry cast the occasional, furtive glance back at the plump, red-haired figure at the table. *Stop it*, he told himself. *Stop it! But still...*

He returned a few minutes later with the drinks.

"What are you doing for Christmas, then?"

"Watching crap telly under a duvet with a hangover."

Gerry nodded. "Fair enough."

"What's *she* doing?"

"Rachel? She's staying here with Macko for a few days. He'll look after her." *I hope.*

VIII

He had seen her within seconds of entering the club, sitting at a table near the bar with a middle-aged, heavily built guy. She had looked up as he walked past her, barely registering his presence, then returned to her pre-dance smalltalk.

He had ordered a beer, found a table and waited. Had endured a brief conversation and subsequent dance from Vicki, then one from another girl who might have been called Shirley or Shelley – her accent was so thick he couldn't be sure; Hell knows what else she'd been saying. After each dance he had returned to his table and sipped at his pint.

Not his scene at all. Had they sensed his disinterest? He had tried his damndest to feign enjoyment, but – despite the fact that his DNA was attuned to that of his host – had felt no stirrings, no arousal. Never had. But he couldn't just wait for Rachel; had to assume that he was being watched, had to throw them off the scent; had to make out that Ellis had started getting off on girls. Even that would make Blackwater suspicious; also, he guessed, a little bit proud of him.

A small screen above the bar was showing the highlights of that afternoon's Arsenal-Leeds game at Highbury. He had already seen the match live, and was not inclined to watch it again: Leeds had been soundly beaten. The ensemble of grumbles and curses that broke out from customers around the club at this juncture demonstrated that his was not an isolated opinion.

"That result was a bit of a pisser, wasn't it?"

He had looked up to see Rachel smiling down at him.

They had exchanged some faux-introductory banter about the game – *that Molenaar's a fat knacker, has he been training on a football pitch or in a pie factory; nice goal from Hasselbaink, mind* – before she led him into the seclusion of an alcove, switched on the cassette and began to dance.

"You're my third dance."

"That's nice."

"Not especially. Nothin' doin' down there."

She smirked as she gyrated. "Ellis, if you were any other client, I'd be pissed off." She unclipped the clasp of her bra. "I've seen Blackwater. At this club."

"I take it from the fact that you're dancing in front of me in a bikini – sorry, half a bikini – that his visit was for pleasure rather than business."

"If it had been for business, then I'm pretty sure I wouldn't have done any more dancing afterwards."

"So to him you're just another girl who gets her tits out. You should be grateful he's so superficial."

She shook her head as she pushed her breasts towards his face. "No, it's worse than that. There's this girl, Laura: she recognised my host as I left the club, followed me home, woke my housemates – she was threatening to tell the police, I had to tell them…"

He raised an eyebrow. "What did you tell them exactly?"

She sighed as she slipped her G-string to the floor. "You know. Oh, Ellis, it's a mess."

"And?"

"They believed me, I think." She paused. "One of them had heard of Blackwater."

This was unexpected. This was dangerous. As she leaned back on the floor in front of him and spread her legs, he tried to gather his thoughts.

She answered the first few questions without waiting for him to verbalise them. "Gerry – my housemate - used to go out with a girl whose father worked as some kind of public liaison for the MoD on UFOs. He got drunk one night and told Gerry a bit about his job, mentioned Blackwater."

"So you've got an agent who tells people top-secret information when he's drunk. Sounds just like Blackwater." He whistled. "Hell, you're in shit, kid."

"I don't think he is – like Blackwater, I mean. From the way Gerry described him, he sounds like a nice guy. At least, I hope he is. Gerry's driving down to see him in a few days."

Somehow he managed to stop himself grabbing her, shaking her, shouting into her face. He gripped the arms of his chair tightly, his nails digging deep into the foam beneath the ripped plastic covering. As she rose

148

and thrust her pelvis towards him, he hissed in fury, in frustration, "And you thought that was a good idea?"

Gettin' Jiggy Wit It faded out; she kissed him on the cheek. "It was the least worst idea, Ellis," she whispered. "But if you've got any better plans, I'm all ears."

"Not for the moment." He rose slowly from the chair. "I'm sure you're aware of the other complication. You surely felt it."

She turned, momentarily puzzled, as she stepped back into her G-String. Then realisation dawned, and her face clouded.

"Have you told your housemates about that? About what that means?"

"Jesus, Ellis, of course not!" Now Rachel was looking scared.

"I know who they've sent. Believe me, it's not just some minor official like we've had in the past. I know him. I know what he will do." He gave her a grim smile. "Tell you what, kid – I'm just gonna finish my pint and have another dance with Vicki. Then I'll get another drink in and you can strut your stuff for me again. And then I can give you some background material on our friend. After that – well, maybe Blackwater won't seem like such a bad guy after all."

He paused. "Oh, and at some point you can pay me back for tonight. Because all this dancing is making inroads into my savings. I don't get much of an allowance, you know, and I'd rather spend it on match programmes and half-time pies than lapdancing."

CHAPTER ELEVEN

I

Deep within the bowels of the Upper Lupton complex, Giles Hartshorn sat at his desk, the tip of an index finger fondly tracing a pattern across his cheek as he waited for the ambassador to be shown in, a wry smile playing across his silken visage.

Well, well, he thought, Dr Grant had told you at Eton that you would make an excellent career diplomat, but presumably the good doctor had never dreamed that you would reach the pinnacle of your career in a role that required you to smooth relations between species. Although, Hartshorn mused, Dr Grant had wholeheartedly espoused and championed the "Wogs begin at Calais" mentality, so to him Frenchmen, Italians, Indians and indeed Jacksons would be one and the same: Xenos; Un-British.

And yet, Hartshorn thought: in the great scheme of things: Paris; Rome; Mumbai; a planet in the constellation of Orion; what was the difference?

St John's, Oxford had followed Eton, and Hartshorn had effortlessly collected a clutch of academic prizes on his way to a double first, earning the admiration of both his peers and his tutors. But, oh, this admiration had extended well beyond his prowess at the Classics. Many times this beautiful youth had dined with his tutors, patiently accepting the attentions lavished upon him before slipping out silently in the early hours of the morning. Occasionally he was apprehended by the porters, in which case a note or two might be required to avoid a scene; but he was soon reimbursed by his dining companions. Fair-haired, fresh-faced Hartshorn, always eager, always willing to learn.

After stints in Cyprus and Malaya during National

Service, Hartshorn had returned – briefly – to the mother country, before he was posted as a Foreign Office attaché to a small central American state which had at that point achieved a level of democracy and stability quite unusual for the region, one which was quite at odds with British requirements at the time; by the time Hartshorn had worked his way up to First Secretary at the embassy, this unfortunate state of affairs had been rectified and military coups were happily occurring on pretty much an annual basis. One could argue that much of the credit for this could be given to Hartshorn himself, whose discreet negotiations with the various interested parties always hinted at, rather than promised, financial aid and military assistance; thus, during one particularly busy and vigorously contested uprising, all five of the warring factions were confident that within days they would be reinforced by British special forces: none were. Hartshorn himself of course would demur; would in fact be appalled at the merest suggestion that in some way he was indirectly responsible for the chaos and bloodshed. Which is why he became so successful; why is why he latterly rose to the position of Permanent Secretary; which is why, one warm autumn evening, he had received an unexpected visitor at his Greek villa.

Hartshorn had never heard of MI13, but didn't bat an eyelid.

Two weeks' later, he was ensconced at Upper Lupton.

That had been ten years ago. Over the intervening period, MI13 had evolved, slowly but surely, into Hartshorn's creature. He had brought in mavericks such as Blackwater to shake up and breathe new life into the old order, while quietly but assiduously promoting others – most notably Peter Tremaine – who could be relied upon to maintain the necessarily levels of

151

discrete interplanetary diplomacy.

Discrete but, when necessarily, implacably ruthless.

II

Blackwater and the Jackson ambassador waited silently in the anteroom outside Hartshorn's office.

Blackwater felt that their relationship had got off on an awkward footing: upon meeting the ambassador, outside the tent in that godforsaken part of Salisbury plain, he had inquired as to whether the ambassador was feeling a little stiff after his long journey, and spent the next minute cursing inwardly following the immediate realisation that "stiff" was equally applicable in this context as a noun as well as an adjective. Fortunately the ambassador had either failed to pick up on the connotation, or was too diplomatic to mention it: in any event, conversation had not exactly flowed in the journey back to Upper Lupton. Blackwater couldn't really think of any subject on which there might be common ground between them; besides, the ambassador didn't look like one for small talk. Blackwater also got the distinct impression that the ambassador was looking to deal with the organ grinder rather than the monkey, and his own sense of self-importance notwithstanding, recognised that as far as he and Hartshorn were concerned, then he most definitely fulfilled the small hairy primate part of the equation.

Mercifully for Blackwater, their wait was short: after less than a minute, Hartshorn emerged with a grave expression on his face.

"Ambassador Jackson."

"Mr Hartshorn."

"This way, please – and thank you Adam, that will be all."

Blackwater slunk away, grateful that this ordeal was over, but fully mindful of the fact that he was now heading back to That Shithole In The North.

Within Hartshorn's small but comfortably and elegantly furnished office, the two diplomats got down to business.

"I take it that there has been no change in the situation since our last communication?" said the ambassador at length.

"None," replied Hartshorn. "That is to say, the cloud entities which landed in Manchester, Liverpool and Glasgow and which subsequently acquired human host bodies were all identified and apprehended within a relatively short space of time after planetfall. They have been confined to cylinders in the isolation bays within this complex; they can be teleported back to your mother ship at your convenience. The fourth, however, which landed near Leeds – that still evades us."

The ambassador frowned.

"A pity. We need that particular cloud – far more than the others. There are areas of our own solar system which are hostile to most individuals of our species, and yet are also rich in nutrients which could, if correctly synthesised, provide a valuable long-term alternative source of sustenance. The cloud in question has unusually high levels of key trace elements in its genetic makeup which we believe can offset the corrosive effects of these atmospheres. When this cloud is reconstituted, we believe it will be capable of performing the role of – of scout for us."

The ambassador gazed levelly at Hartshorn. Did the ambassador recognise the expression "guinea pig" wondered Hartshorn? In any event, in these rarified circles, it would not have been appropriate for the ambassador to couch the explanation in such vulgar terms, nor for Hartshorn to respond to the obvious

153

implication of his statement. That was a matter for internal politics, and Hartshorn both understood and sympathised.

The ambassador continued. "Furthermore, given this cloud's interesting genetic structure, we were hoping that, in the medium term, fission might produce a number of genetically identical clouds which might also be capable of surviving in these particularly harsh environs."

Hartshorn was intrigued. "What of this cloud's – forgive my rather clumsy nomenclature – parent? Was it not suitable?"

"Good question, Mr Hartshorn. However, the cloud's own structure was unique – we have a number of methods of reproduction besides asexual fission. This cloud was created through the temporary merger of two other cloud entities. There is a kind of meiosis; shortly afterwards, a new cloud emerges from the union, a combination of the genetics of its – ahem – parents. This is perhaps the most popular form of reproductive activity: personally, I eschew it, but there you are."

Hartshorn understood, on so many levels. He, too, eschewed the most popular form of reproductive activity.

"So the cloud is unique, and we need it back. We have no wish to cause a scene, but if it comes down to leaving without the cloud or causing a scene, well…" The ambassador spread his hands in apology.

"How much longer do we have?"

"Mr Hartshorn, we have no wish to sour the excellent diplomatic relations which exist between ourselves and your particular arm of government. There is, as you have said to us in the past, no need for your various parliamentary bodies, national or international, to be troubled by the knowledge of our existence. Mr

Hartshorn, our own government doesn't know that you exist, and we would like to keep it that way. They suspect an awful lot, and these rather taxing long-haul sporting trips add fuel to their suspicions, but they don't actually know anything.

"It has become an unfortunate fashion within our society for governments to be elected by a majority of the populace – I believe you suffer from a similar affliction – and the populace can be so unreasonable, so emotional about things. Mr Hartshorn, if they knew about your species, or indeed about any of the other broadly intelligent life-forms that we both know have developed civilisations of a sort – well, there would be hysteria, plain and simple. It is far better to retain the comforting belief that the universe revolves around you alone. The realisation that one must share the spotlight with myriad others would mean the end to a thousand comforting belief-systems.

"We do not want that to happen. For our own part, we will not let it happen."

Hartshorn understood, but said nothing. The ambassador leaned back in his chair.

"We have an additional request. The cloud that has taken on the identity of Pressdee has become, frankly, something of an embarrassment. We think it would be better for all parties if he no longer resided among you."

"You wish the entity's exile to end?"

"You misunderstand me. Pressdee could not return; he would be a loose cannon. No – and here I must emphasise that while all our conversations are, as you term it, off the record – it is simply that we feel it would be far more agreeable for us all if he no longer existed."

The ambassador gazed fixedly at Hartshorn. If the latter was surprised, he did not show it. Coolly, he returned the other's gaze before delicately, thoughtfully stroking his chin with the tip of a forefinger.

"In principle," he responded cautiously, "I have no objection to that. In practice, what you require might be problematic. We know how to capture specific individuals; we had suspected, before you confirmed it, that cylinders could be calibrated to respond to a particular cloud; that, if a precise stimulus were applied, then it might be possible to coerce a cloud into such a cylinder. You were kind enough to suggest not only how that stimulation might occur, but also how the component molecules of the cylinder might then be excited in such a way as to prevent the cloud entity from leaving. So far, so good. But confining an entity is one thing; disposing of it, well…"

The ghost of a smile played across the ambassador's lips. "Under certain atmospheric conditions, our species will dissipate, disperse – effectively, die – within a short space of time unless a host body is available. But we are a persistent species, Mr Hartshorn, like your own; we go to great lengths to avoid our demise. That said, there are ways and means. I would suggest that once Pressdee has been confined, his cylinder is placed within a secure, airtight room, filled with a mixture of gases whose composition I will provide. The cylinder can then be remotely detonated and the issue resolved."

The ambassador stood up. "I have already stressed that this is a time-critical issue. Like I said, we need that cloud; we are prepared to be accommodating to a certain extent, to allow you to use your own methods to locate, isolate and capture it. However, our patience is not inexhaustible; if you fail to deliver it, then we must use our own methods.

"You have two weeks, Mr Hartshorn. Two weeks."

III

The heathland was alive in Summer, a haven on the
outskirts of the metropolis. From February onwards, the
skylarks would start up, doing their utmost to drown
out the low rumble of near-distant traffic; from late
April, they would be joined by a host of migrants:
yellowhammers, swallows, chiffchaffs, whitethroats,
the whitethroats apparently – so Gerry always thought
– attempting to emulate the skylarks in their mazy,
weaving display flight, but without the elevation or the
sheer intensity of song; but they always seemed to give
it their best shot nonetheless. By June, a cacophony of
birdsong was the constant soundtrack to a walk, where
– if you were lucky – you might also catch a lizard or
grass snake basking on the warm earth; you would
almost certainly see a host of butterflies – Brimstone in
early summer, then Gatekeeper, Meadow Brown,
Marbled White as the season wore on.

But in cold, bleak, austere December, the swallows
and whitethroats were respectively skimming over
sunkissed ponds and chattering querulously from
bushes in sub-Saharan Africa; the yellowhammers and
skylarks had fallen silent; there was the occasional
cawing of a solitary passing crow, the odd staccato burr
from the perennial stonechats, and that was that: Nature
had pretty much shut down for the time being.

Nor did either Gerry or Mayhew disturb this silence
overmuch, save for the crunching of feet on stony, icy
footpath: as they ploughed on determinedly across the
heath, heads down into the wind, conversation was
waiting to happen, but – hesitant as to a suitable
opening – failed to materialize for a good while.
Indeed, their meeting in the layby – Gerry had sat
drumming his fingers on the dashboard of the Focus
while waiting for Mayhew's old Ford Orion to show up

- had been a taciturn affair, conducted in facial expressions which expressed merely acknowledgement of their mutual arrival and the need to get some way off the road before words were exchanged.

Only when they had reached the slight ridge, maybe three quarters of a mile down the track, did Mayhew venture an opening.

"Do you know when things started getting awkward with Angela?"

To be honest, this hadn't been the intro that Gerry was expecting; possibly a question about Rachel, and how he came to know here; possibly an awkward question about the end of his relationship with Emma; possibly even a fairly all-encompassing tee-off along the lines of, "So, how are things?"; this was definitely out of left field.

No, said Gerry.

"It was the Vimto."

Gerry thought at this point that a line of inquiry involving alien life could well be rather less mysterious and tortured than the direction in which this appeared to be heading, but he went with the flow.

Oh yes, said Gerry.

"It was one evening, back in the late sixties – we'd been married for a couple of years then – and we went out for a meal on the town. It was an Italian – La Famiglia, I think, rather pricey but wonderful food, well worth it, still there I believe – and afterwards we got a cab back – you know we were living in a flat in Fulham in those days – well anyway we got back home, and Angela was actually looking rather lovely – she did have a wonderful figure in those days – still pretty good I would suppose – but one thing led to another, as it did from time to time back then, and pretty soon clothes were off and fun was being had."

Mayhew paused, and looked at Gerry. For what?

Gerry wondered. Approval? Approbation? A sly wink of appreciation?

Good show, he said rather limply.

Mayhew nodded. "Yes," he said. "Yes, I suppose so. Well, at the end of it all, when I'd done my bit, my first thought – my very first thought – was, 'I really fancy a nice glass of Vimto.' Not – 'Wow – that was fantastic' or 'Sex is superb!' but 'Vimto'."

He sighed, wistfully, and, with a perceptible note of regret, "And I told Angela. Perhaps, on reflection, not the best of moves. It all went a bit downhill after that. I mean, there was the occasional liaison after that – one of them produced Emma – but the fun went out of it after that. I think the Vimto left rather a bad taste."

Gerry nodded his head in mute demonstration of sympathy.

"Do you like Vimto?"

Gerry shrugged. "Never tried it."

"No? I used to drink it a lot in my teens. Developed quite a taste for it. But, there you go, there you go…" His voice tailed off, and he fiddled distractedly with a button on his overcoat. "That was my Vimto moment. Anyway," and here he lost interest in the button and stared straight at Gerry, "This business. It's, well, pretty bad, Gerry."

Knowing Mayhew's tendency for gentle understatement, Gerry recognized that "pretty bad" was rather too close to "apocalyptic" for his liking. But then, any scenario involving aliens, spooks and the living dead was never going to be tea-party territory.

"To be honest, Graham, it seems totally fucked to me."

"Oh no," said Graham earnestly. "It's far worse than that."

Gerry waited for Mayhew to elaborate, but his expectations were disappointed; instead, Mayhew was squinting against the weak December sunlight at a large, dark bird which was winging its way heavily through the sky.

"Just a crow. Thought for a minute it might be a buzzard. Never mind." He turned to Gerry. "Going to do any walking with your Dad over Christmas?"

"Probably go up the Skirrid on Boxing Day if this weather holds."

"Good," said Mayhew, and devoted his attention to the button once more. "I mentioned Blackwater, did I? Was I drunk?"

"A little. New Year's Eve, couple of years ago."

Mayhew shook his head sadly. "Well, bang goes the Official Secrets Act, then. Not, incidentally, that Blackwater ever gave a damn about it. The most indiscreet man I ever met. I often wondered how he kept his job."

"That's how it all came out. Because of Blackwater shooting his mouth off. Rachel was dancing for him and he told her who he was and what he was looking for."

"And, I take it, Rachel *is* what Blackwater is looking for?"

"Yes."

"Why did she tell you?"

"Housemate – no one else to turn to. Also – which kind of forced the issue – a friend of, well, a friend who she used to be, came a-callin'."

"Why didn't you hand her in?"

"Because I'm guessing she'd be killed. And all this girl wants to do is watch football."

Mayhew shot him an amused glance. "Really?"

"Really."

"It was still very noble of you."

"Noble doesn't enter into it. I just don't want to see anyone get hurt."

160

"Good – although unless you're very careful – very careful – it might not just be this Rachel who gets hurt."

They had reached a stile; Mayhew took the opportunity for a rest, and to catch his breath, while Gerry waited apprehensively.

"I'm just the middle man, Gerry. Joe Public rings me up with reports of strange lights in the sky, and I ring up some other people at the MoD, and then I usually get back to Joe Public to tell him that what he's seen is a military exercise or some freak of natural lighting or whatever. But occasionally, just occasionally, Blackwater or his colleagues will come down from their offices to tell me that under no circumstances do I reply to Joe Public; that they will be dealing with Joe Public." He sighed. "And you see, what can happen next, is that Joe Public disappears."

There was little enough heat from the December sun, but it was not the cold that made Gerry shiver.

"I suspect you already know much more than I do about this, but… I did a bit of digging, Gerry. I've had to be careful – this business meant that I was turned out of my own office for a few days, and these chaps don't leave much evidence behind them, and this stuff is way, way above my pay grade – but what I can tell you is that about three months or so ago, there was a lot of activity: lights in the sky, objects that we've said were meteors but which weren't. Objects which fell to earth. Objects that MI13 have recovered. That these objects had contained something that was no longer around when MI13 turned up. That triggered manhunts in a twenty mile radius around where these objects landed. One of these manhunts – in Leeds – is still very much ongoing."

Not without difficulty, Mayhew clambered over the stile.

"There's something else. Last night, about an hour before I left work, we started getting a lot of calls – one hell of a lot of calls – that pretty much corresponded to that bunch in early-September. Then I got a call from Blackwater wishing me Merry Christmas and telling me that any photographic or video evidence that came in was to be handed over immediately to MI13, and that we were to say that if anybody asked that there had been a heavy meteor shower.

"For what it's worth: I think your friend has company."

IV

There was a third vehicle in the layby now, a black Audi.

Granville leaned against the car and watched the pair through his binoculars for a while. He had already noted the registration number of the Focus; had already snapped the walkers as they paused at the stile with the compact SLR that he had now returned to his coat pocket. As the two continued on their way, he returned to the relative warmth of the Audi. That would do, he said to himself.

Besides, he had plenty to be going on with.

CHAPTER TWELVE

I

The Skirrid Fawr is not the tallest mountain in South Wales by any means — it is maybe two-thirds the height of the Sugar Loaf, a few miles west, and falls a thousand feet shy of the brooding Pen-y-fan, where Gerry had experienced blazing sunshine at the base and a wind-whipped snowstorm at the summit — but it was a fine walk for a Boxing Day, up through the woods of the lower slopes and then, when you thought you were nearing the final approach and clambering breathless towards your goal, the true peak of the mountain reared unexpectedly, wickedly into view, and you realised that you had merely attained the penultimate plateau and there were another fifteen, twenty minutes of arduous hiking through the rock and heather before you could feast your eyes upon the view.

Gerry and his dad surveyed that view in silence for several minutes. The weather had been kind to them — a few fleeting early morning squalls had given way to weak winter sunshine, light winds edging the dark clouds towards the Brecon Beacons, the black bulk of those hills flecked with auburn, gold and purple. Pen-y-fan would catch it again, Gerry thought wryly. Southeast lay the Severn, a grey sliver dappled with dazzling gold; he could see both bridges easily, and the Malvern hills beyond.

"Kite! Gerry, kite!"

His reverie was disturbed by his dad's excited shout — there, above them, was the red kite, soaring high above them, forked tail clearly visible. Gerry had seen his first kite here, more than twenty years before, when his father had carried him to the summit on his shoulders. Then the birds had been a rarity, the few remaining breeding pairs driven to the more remote and isolated mountain-tops. As the poisonings, the shootings and the wanton destruction of nests had ceased, so the birds had begun to flourish once more, both in Wales and beyond. Gerry had seen many more kites; and always admired them. They were worthy of awe.

When the kite had followed the rainclouds towards the Beacons and become a speck in the distance, the two settled down to the business of unpacking the turkey sandwiches, bacon-wrapped sausages and other wondrous flotsam and jetsam that Gerry's mam had carefully salvaged from the previous day's excesses and prepared for them. She had — as tradition demanded — driven across to Caerphilly to visit her cousin early that morning, leaving the vicissitudes of the Skirrid to her partner and her offspring. That had become their tradition, after all.

II

Gerry liked Christmas tradition. For ten years, he had joined his dad in the Kings Arms at midday on Christmas morning while his mam, keen to get them out of her hair, patiently, efficiently (and, to Gerry, somewhat magically) engaged in the preparation of turkey, vegetables, and trimmings, so that when the two made their way back home two or three pints later, the table was laid and the assorted ingredients were on the final furlong of their mystical transformation into the best Christmas dinner ever, a dinner where you didn't know what to attack first: the turkey, with a spot of cranberry and homemade stuffing? The potatoes, roasted in goosefat with garlic and a few sprigs of rosemary from the garden? The honey-glazed parsnips? The chestnuts? The sprouts? The carrots? Almost invariably, Gerry attempted to get some of everything onto his fork before dousing his tastebuds in a bewildering, joyous assortment of flavours.

The feast would be accompanied by an affable bottle of dry white wine – usually German, sometimes French – before the rich, brandy-soaked puddings appeared, themselves followed by an enticing selection of cheeses and (from the depth's of his dad's drinks cabinet) the inevitable bottle of port. Around three o'clock the meal would be reaching its natural conclusion, and all parties would repair to the lounge – Gerry and Dad with their port, the lady of the house with her sherry – to view Her Majesty's annual statement, before lapsing into a prolonged, convivial slumber, occasionally punctuated by farts which would have been described as loud, poignant and odoriferous had anyone been awake to mark their passing.

Some hours later, these three happy individuals would emerge from their post-prandial naps; Gerry and Dad would share the washing up duties, while the redoubtable Mrs Angel would bury herself in the wreck of the turkey and appear shortly afterwards with plates laden with drumsticks and sandwiches crammed with meat and stuffing. She herself would shortly retire to bed, while the two beneficiaries of this secondary feast would talk over the important issues of the day – usually incorporating such matters as rugby, football, politics, Gerry's job, his dad's job, the boobs on the barmaid at the Kings', the execrable prose of A A Gill – while polishing off a further two or three cans of bitter apiece.

Thus was Christmas in the Angel household.

III

The two did not arrive home until six – it had been a

leisurely amble down from the summit, and this had been followed by a short, picturesque drive out to a pub near Tintern where his dad knew the landlord and liked the beer; rather reluctantly, Gerry found himself entrusted with the car keys, reluctantly because he too would have preferred to sample more than a couple of pints.

Mrs Angel had been back for several hours, and was deeply engrossed in a wordsearch puzzle when they returned. Mr Angel, bucolic, red-cheeked and filled with the spirit of the season (as dispensed by Tintern's finest alehouse), leaned down and genially bestowed a kiss upon her lips.

"How was Yvonne?"

Mrs Angel smiled and embarked upon an effortless monologue only tangentially connected with the inquiry.

"Oh, it was lovely. Michelle popped in with the girls, and the girls are getting so big now, that Rhiannon is a darling, looks just like Yvonne did at that age, a lovely smile, such a pretty smile, but Michelle's going to have her hands full when she gets older – if Rhiannon's anything like Yvonne was, God help her – I remember one night when we were off down the 'Stute and Uncle George had told her not to stay out after ten, and if she did, well Uncle George came stomping down the 'Stute and dragged her out in front of all the boys and she was tamping mad and she said, 'Dad, how dare you do that to me?' and Uncle George said, 'I told you to be in by ten o'clock and you didn't come in. And I told you to come in by ten because I know what those boys from Blackwood are like and what they're after. Now you disobey me again and I'll tan your behind, I don't care whether you're eighteen years old or eighteen months. I want you up those stairs this minute.' And she gave him a filthy look but she didn't say another word and off to bed she went. And I remember one of the boys gave Uncle George a bit of chat and the next thing you know Uncle George had him up against the wall and said that if he ever saw him even looking at Yvonne again he'd do things to him that meant he wouldn't need to look at any girl afterwards. Mind you, Michelle was a little bugger too, Yvonne used to ring me up in tears, she said, 'Anne, my Michelle is a proper little madam, she doesn't listen to a word I say.' Hot around the drawers, as our dad would say. And Rachel spent all the time playing with this little dolly, Barbie I think it was, that Yvonne had got her for Christmas: you can see she absolutely adores Rhiannon, the way she looks at her sister. And Gerry, Roddy's been trying to get hold of you. Says it's really important."

This rude interruption of the present into the confusing and occasionally impenetrable memoirs of Mrs Angel took several seconds to permeate Gerry's consciousness, which had been battered and dazed by a series of anecdotes concerning relatives of whose existence he was only dimly aware (and about whom, following the exposition, he was still none the wiser); when it finally kicked in, it chilled him to the marrow.

Shit. Have they found her?

"What was it about?"

"He wouldn't say. He left two messages while I was out asking you to call him back, then called back twice after I got home."

Gerry was already slamming the parlour door, picking up the receiver of the handset in the hallway.

The bastards. Has Macko told Laura? Is he OK?

The phone was ringing.

Answer, Macko, please…

Still ringing. Three tones, four…

Shit shit shit…

Five, six…

"Hello?"

"Macko? Macko! What the hell's happening? Is Rachel OK?"

"Oh fuck yeah, she's cool. She's not back from the footie yet, she's gone over to Newcastle for the game."

"Mate, what's going on? Mam said you'd left lots of messages."

"Jez, I really needed to get hold of you mate. I shagged the fucking arse off it. Three times last night, once this morning. Best Christmas I've ever had, I can tell you."

Gerry reeled.

After a moment, he managed a pained whisper, through gritted teeth. "So you rang to tell me you've been having it away with Rachel."

"Jez boy, it was the doggie's bollocks. Every which fucking way, every which fucking room – not yours obviously, certainly not Gideon's, that would have been sick, but me bedroom, her bedroom, kitchen, lounge – I'm shagged out. Glad she wanted to go to the footie, me knackers are flat as pancakes."

"I'm so pleased for you."

"Oh, Jez, you can't imagine – look, you're not coming back for a few days, are you?"

"I'd planned on coming back tomorrow."

"Look, can you hold fire for a day or two – only you being around might cramp me style…"

Gerry paused. Tradition was all very well, but traditions – particularly when enjoyed in the company of members of a preceding, or subsequent, generation – retain their appeal precisely because they typical comprise events of limited duration. Extend them beyond these short, succinct periods, and the appeal palls for all parties.

Besides, he had promised Laura that he would look

after Lisa/Rachel. Not that Lisa/Rachel needed much looking after, he thought bitterly. Oh yes, Macko had been giving her a good looking after, by the sound of it.

And yet – even in the momentary resentment at Macko's extracurricular activities – he felt another, more pressing reason to return. He wanted to see Laura again.

"Jez?"

"Soz, buddy, enjoy it while you can. I'll be with you tomorrow about six."

"You utter twat."

"Love you too, Macko. Bysie-bye."

"'Koff." Click.

IV

This is how it all came about.

Two days earlier, just as Gerry was pulling away in the Focus, Rachel had been asking about Christmas dinners. They sounded, well, intriguing; the turkey, the trimmings, the crackers, the booze; the occasion. In a fit of bravado, Macko had agreed to sort one out.

To be fair, Macko had shown willing. He would have been the first to admit that cooking was not his forte; roast dinners were hearty rarities to be enjoyed in the comfort of other people's dining rooms: historically, at Ma and Pa McCall's in Belfast; in the more recent past, at the parental homes of the occasional paramour who was rash or naïve enough to effect a meeting between Macko and her family. These were strictly one off events; in each case, the relationship had ended soon afterwards, terminations which were always accelerated by these ill-starred lunches.

So when Rachel raised the prospect of a roast for Christmas lunch, it understandably gave Macko pause for thought once the initial bravado had worn off.

The social connotations of roast dinners notwithstanding, there were severe practical implications. For Macko, food came primarily in tins, or cellophane-wrapped trays, or whichever kebab van he happened to stumble against. You stuck it in a saucepan and warmed it up; you bunged it in the microwave; you asked for it with extra garlic and chilli sauce. You didn't spend hours chopping vegetables and basting turkeys for it. Until now.

The previous day – Christmas bloody Eve, for feck's sake – he had wandered the aisles of Morrison's in search of unfamiliar ingredients, checking them off one by one against a scrawled list: parsnips, check; potatoes, check; stuffing, check; cranberry sauce, check.

Only when he was on the bus and half way home did he realise that he had forgotten the turkey.

He apologised, shamefacedly, to the flock of elderly ladies that constituted the majority of his fellow passengers, after the inevitable, uncontrollable outpouring of expletives that emerged at this realisation; alighted from the bus at the next stop; and stalked grimly back to Morrison's, dispensing vast quantities of fucks and bastards in his wake.

But now it was done and eaten. Sure, the carrots had gone by the wayside after he couldn't remember where he'd put them after he'd peeled them, the little orange shites, and he'd forgotten to put the Aunt Bessie's Yorkshire puddings in, but what the hell, he thought, that dinner was the dog's bollocks. She might even lick mine after – *woah, Roddy don't go there*.

And Rachel was impressed, partly because it did look and smell fairly appetising, partly because it tasted almost as good as it looked, and partly because she recognised that, for Macko, this represented a truly

170

Herculean effort.

After the feast, they had retired to the lounge with a bottle of winter ale apiece and, as the Angels were sinking into blissful, turkeyfull oblivion in Leeds, Macko and Rachel had stretched out on their respective sofas and then marked their appreciation of the BBC's Christmas film by sleeping through it.

Macko awoke around six, still heavy with undigested turkey. Through bleary, sleep-soaked eyes he saw that Rachel was surfing through the Sky channels in search of some football. *That's my girl*, thought Macko. *You may be an alien, but you like your footie, and you have great tits.*

Seeing her flatmate stirring, Rachel smiled. "Thought you'd be waking up soon," she said. "There's another beer for you down there."

Macko beamed. "Tops!" He raised himself into a sitting position. "Much on the box?"

"Showing some of the highlights from the World Cup. England-Argentina game should be on in a minute."

"Cool." Macko took a swig from the bottle. *God, she is fit as fuck...*

"Dinner OK then?" he remarked casually.

"Macko, it was gorgeous. Thank you."

"I didn't think we'd need a full bird, like, so I just got those turkey breast fillets..."

"You know, that's only the third time you've told me that. But it was still lovely."

She smiled at him again, causing Macko to blush. Behind her, on the television screen, Richard Keys was extolling the virtues of Michael Owen. Under normal circumstances, Macko would have felt obliged to pass a comment on hairy-handed commentators and overrated Scouse strikers. Then again, with a beautiful, slightly tipsy human-possessed-by-an-alien smiling at him,

171

these were not normal circumstances.

"You know, there's a tradition in Yorkshire that if you like the dinner, you have to shag the chef."

"OK then."

"Particularly if you're really fit and hang on could you repeat that?"

"I said, 'OK then'."

"Right." Macko's heart had upped a gear. "You do know that I was joking? Only I'd hate to get you into the sack under false pretences."

Rachel shot him an amused, quizzical look. "So are you saying you don't want to shag me?"

"No, no, no, I mean – fuck, yeah, but…"

Macko's confused stammerings were cut short as Rachel kissed him on the lips.

As he followed her up the stairs, Macko was mentally scratching the letter "R" from his alphabet sex list.

V

And so it went pretty much as Macko had breathlessly described to Gerry; every which fucking way, every which fucking room. But amidst the activity, there had been interludes of relative calm: during one, as they had lain on their backs on the unkempt mess that passed for Macko's bed, Macko had asked Rachel – in a rare moment of intellectual curiosity – what life was like on her home planet, and how the hell had she got into this body-snatching business.

So Rachel told him. Told him of the glittering, crystalline cities that hung suspended above fiery lakes of burning adamant; of skies dappled with silica clouds that wept with colour at a twin sunrise; of great pinnacles of rock that burst vertically from bubbling seas and soared more than fifty thousand metres into the stratosphere; of the forests of light where the soul cried out with joy; of a thousand creatures from an ecosystem beyond imaginings.

Told him of the evolution of her species; how their bodies had atrophied as their consciousness had developed; how they had built a vast array of artificial infrastructures to act as temporary domiciles, both intra- and interplanetary; how they had first discovered that, in extremis, their consciousness could migrate to the bodies of other creatures; how, when unencumbered by physical forms, they would congregate in vast swarms, sharing thoughts, ideas, passions in a graceful, swirling dance of minds.

Unfortunately, Macko very quickly became distracted by some fluff he had espied in his belly button; Rachel's excited, animated descriptions were drowned out by his subsequent internal ruminations on the origins of belly button fluff and related thoughts on the lengths of pubic hair. Thus the extent of human knowledge of alien environments remained broadly as it had done prior to the beginning of their conversation.

VI

Rachel arrived home late, drunk on the high of a 3-0 victory and on the alcohol of five bottles of Newcastle Brown; she immediately pulled Macko into her bedroom for a further bout. *Maybe it's a good idea Gerry's coming home*, thought Macko two hours later as he drifted gratefully into sleep: *the heart is willing but the knob is weak*.

VII

It had been a fairly trouble-free journey back – spot of heavy traffic on the M42, but otherwise fine. Still, it was good to get home; as Gerry eased the Focus into a parking space adjacent to the house, his face broke into a smile.

Then, as he entered the house by the back door, his expression changed to one of shock. While household hygiene standards had inevitably slipped from the zenith achieved in that urgent, Erasure-fuelled cleanup prior to Rachel's arrival, the kitchen had nevertheless retained a modicum of cleanliness. However, in Gerry's absence, there had been a most definite and dramatic fall in standards, a decline precipitated by Macko's roast dinner, a fry up the following morning and several enthusiastic sex sessions on and around the kitchen table.

Gerry gave a sharp intake of breath, staring in disbelief at the resulting carnage and hoping to Christ that it wasn't a used condom that he could see emerging from the gravy boat.

His mobile rang. Gerry answered it mechanically, still unable to take his eyes from the gravy boat.

"Yes?"

"Is that Gerry?"

He froze. *I know that voice. From the TV, from the radio, from my Uncle Derwyn's record collection. I know that voice. That voice is dead.*

"Gerry Angel?"

"Yes, this is Gerry."

"Hi Gerry, this is Ellis. Are you going to be in this evening? I think we need to touch base on a few things."

CHAPTER THIRTEEN

I

He came, as he said he would. A gentle knock on the back door, and there he was: Ellis, formerly known as Elvis, otherwise known as The King, resplendent in replica Leeds shirt under a bomber jacket. He stepped rather gingerly into the kitchen which, after some frantic cleaning by Gerry, now appeared merely grubby and unsavoury rather than highly toxic.

Gerry apologised for only having instant coffee. Ellis said that he didn't mind. Gerry asked whether he'd care to come through into the lounge. Ellis said, thank you, and made himself comfortable on the sofa. By the time Gerry came through with the coffee, his guest was engrossed in Sky Sports. Ellis took the coffee with a murmur of thanks, eyes fixed on the football highlights.

Gerry stared at him. *This is Elvis the Pelvis*, he thought; *this is the man who sent tens of millions of teenage girls into lust-filled hysteria, the living embodiment of rock n' roll that outraged the establishment; this is the man who had – what was the answer in the pub quiz , was it fifteen number ones? I mean, for fuck's sake: he's in my house – well, the house I rent from that tight-arsed hairy bastard in Chapel Allerton – sitting on my sofa! Drinking my coffee! What the fuck do I say to the King?*

But just as these thoughts were sending his mind into a tailspin, they were pushed aside by a calm, sober, downbeat voice that gently insisted: *But it isn't Elvis. Elvis is dead, long gone. This is Ellis. And you know what Ellis likes...*

"Not a bad season for your boys, is it?"

"S'alright. Need a good run if we're going to get

175

into Europe again."

"Good win yesterday, though, wasn't it?"

"Three nil! Showed those bloody Geordies what for. Would have been nice to get up to see the game, but, well, the terms of my, er, parole generally preclude me from going to away fixtures."

Even in the midst of his nervous excitement, Gerry noted the occasional, odd inflection in the deep voice; the broad accent of the southern states (Mississippi was it? Tennessee?) flecked with Yorkshire intonations. *You're going native*, thought Gerry, *just like me*. And then, a realisation of sheer delight: this great voice, this historic voice, now shot through with those Yorkshire intonations, was depicting its owner's passion for the greatest game on earth. *Elvis is on my sofa! Talking about football!*

But it's not Elvis, it's Ellis, said the calm voice.

Sod off, said the excitement, *I'm going to run with this one, it's* Elvis, *talking about football, on* my *sofa*.

Their meeting was interrupted before it had barely begun. The back door was flung wide and Macko stood on the threshold, clutching a half-empty bottle of Grolsch in one hand and a half-eaten slice of pizza in the other, a thoughtful expression upon his face.

"If we both pulled down our kecks, pressed our bum cheeks together and I farted up your arse," he pondered through a mouthful of stuffed crust, "Would that be gay or just fecking funny?"

Silently, Gerry gestured to its housemate that they were in the presence of a third party. Macko's eyes widened in astonishment, his jaw sagged; the gay/fecking funny conundrum was immediately forgotten.

"It's yerself! Fuck a duck, Gerry, it's The King!"

Gerry rolled his eyes. "Ellis, this is Macko; Macko, meet Ellis."

Ellis nodded, shyly, and enquired if there was any more of that pizza going around, as he was kinda hungry. Macko stared dumbly at him for a moment, before shaking his head ruefully.

"Er, no, soz. I et it on the way home."

Was there anything else to eat, Ellis wondered.

"I could fix yous a bit of toast."

That would be good, said Ellis.

"I'll be… getting the toast and shit, then." Macko moved into the kitchen as in a dream. Gerry held up his hands in apology.

"Man U fan," he explained. Ellis gave a gentle nod of understanding, and sipped his coffee. "Right then, Gerry, down to business. But before we begin – I take it Rachel's at work this evening?"

Gerry shrugged. "As far as I know."

"Good, good. It was you and Mr Macko I wanted to meet, in any case. I think you appreciate we have a problem here around your new housemate."

"Blackwater and his buddies at MI13?"

"Blackwater is a nasty bit of work, that's for sure. I met him again recently – does a lot of the dirty work for a very dirty department. He's loud, crude – he's an asshole. But he's sharp, much sharper than he looks." He paused. "Rachel tells me you've been speaking to someone at the MoD."

"He's their UFO liaison guy – I mean, he collects all the public reports on UFOs."

Ellis nodded. "Air Staff 2. You trust him?"

"With my life. Lovely guy."

"Still a very dangerous thing to have done, Gerry."

"To be honest, Ellis, I didn't know what else to do."

"That's fair enough. Not everyday you get landed with something like this." He leaned forward. "So your friend knows Blackwater, yes?"

"Yeah. Doesn't like him one little bit."

"Then that is in his favour. When you spoke to him, did he mention a man called Giles Hartshorn?" Gerry shook his head. "He can't have come across him. It's not surprising – Hartshorn is the head of MI13. It's Hartshorn who suffers me to remain at liberty – in return for the occasional experiment upon my person." He broke off for a moment, staring at the floor, then recovered. "He's a far more polished guy than Blackwater – and far more dangerous. You see, Gerry, I don't exist, I'm not here talking to you now, I don't go to watch Leeds play at Elland Road, I don't make occasional trips in cars with blacked out windows to a complex in Upper Lupton that doesn't exist to have my blood tested and my brain scanned. So if someone were to have evidence that I did exist, that all these things went on, well..." He spread his hands in apology. "They wouldn't exist either. Hartshorn would see to that.

"So, Gerry, that's the problem we have. A number of people – you, your housemates, Laura, this friend of yours at the MoD – have what they believe is evidence that I exist. It's nonsense – must be nonsense, I don't exist, how can I? – but then, hey, Hartshorn hears about it, and the next thing you know, there's been this terrible fire, and all these young guys are killed, and it's all so sad – and meanwhile I go back to not existing."

Gerry held his head in his hands. "What the hell do we do?" he whispered.

Ellis shrugged. "I don't pretend to have answers, Gerry. At least, not yet. But, hell – I'm open to ideas."

The tableau was broken as Macko returned with a plate of buttered toast, and Ellis set to with relish. Oblivious to Gerry's distress, Macko's attention was wholly focused upon their visitor. He had his own pressing questions that needed answers.

"So did you really die having a shit, then, Elvis?"

178

To be fair, Ellis took that one in his stride.

"First things first, Macko: it's Ellis, not, Elvis", he chided gently as he worked his way through the toast. "And I don't know if you'd noticed, but I am very much alive, sitting on your sofa, and eating the mighty fine toast that you've made for me. But as for Elvis, well, he was in pretty poor shape when I came across him."

Having finally found his tongue, Macko was keen to give it free rein. "So, Ellis – as a Leeds fan back in the seventies, you were presumably looking for Billy Bremner and the other dirty shites: how come you wound up in the deep South? I mean it's not like you'd have had a fecking away fixture in that neck of the woods."

"Pure chance. I was aiming for the moors to the north of the city – pretty much where Rachel came down a few months back – but as I was entering the upper atmosphere the cylinder got caught up in a meteor shower, threw out the guidance systems completely. Damn lucky I didn't hit the ocean. Anyhow, I crashed in the Graceland estate, in need of a near-deceased, found Mr Presley on the floor of the john, vitals signs fading – and one thing led to another."

"You pinched Elvis Presley's body?"

"Believe you me, Macko, he had no further use for it." The last of the toast disappeared. "No doctor on Earth could have saved him. The poor guy had had a seizure and was lying face down in a pool of vomit when I found him. And the pills that guy had been poppin' – Jesus, his body was a pharmacy. Although, to be honest, I wasn't in much better shape myself: the lander had been damaged in the crash, my molecules were beginning to disperse. I just lay dormant until they took my body - "

179

"Elvis's body!"

"*My host* body to the Baptist Memorial Hospital. That's where I woke up. And that's where things, shall we say, diverge from the official history."

Gerry couldn't let this pass. "Who knew?" he demanded, a trifle icily.

"A few... of the guys. Maybe not so many as you'd suppose. Sure, they thought I was joking with them at first, but after I showed them the wreckage of the lander – and after I wouldn't shut up about this goddamn soccer team called Leeds United from someplace in England – they began to come round."

"Do you sing much these days?"

Ellis smiled. "Macko, I only sing when we're winning."

Macko shook his head in irritation. "No, no, no, I'm talking proper singing. I'm talking 'Bossa Nova', I'm talking 'Hound Dog', I'm talking Elvis numbers; I'm not talking 'You're going home in a Tottenham ambulance'".

"No, Macko." Was that a fleeting trace of regret, wondered Gerry. "Singing isn't just about a voice – it's about what you bring to it. You could have the voice of Elvis, or Caruso, or Pavarotti – but if you don't have the soul of Elvis, or Caruso, or Pavarotti, then what that voice sings won't have the depth, the meaning, the emotion that those guys could bring to a song. It won't be able to convey what they feel, what they have felt, what they've touched, what they've loved. I have Elvis's voice, sure, but beyond that – nothing. I'm not the guy who grew up in East Tupelo and grew up on gospel music, who scared the crap out of a nation on the Ed Sullivan Show and played to packed houses in Vegas. That's not me at all." He paused. "I just heard about that guy in a few BBC documentaries over the years."

180

Macko and Gerry were silent. Macko fingered his stubble thoughtfully.

"That was fecking profound, Ellis, but at the end of the day you're missing a trick here: I mean, a Beatles reunion would be nothing on an Elvis comeback."

Gerry shot him a pained look; Ellis coughed delicately.

"Don't you understand, Macko? I'm not Elvis; never have been. I just inhabit his body. But let's suppose I wanted to go down that road; that I wanted to be Elvis. There are certain complications, Macko, which I've already gone through with Gerry. What you might call *bureaucratic* issues which would make any potential comeback rather... difficult. But even without those issues, any comeback, well...

"Can you imagine what would happen if Elvis came back? All the questions: 'Where were you, Elvis? Why did you run away?' And it wouldn't end there. There'd be a thousand and one women out there, all claiming to have had a love child by Elvis at some point over the past twenty years. Can you imagine how Lisa Marie would feel? That her Daddy was still alive but had turned his back on her?

"I'm a strictly low-profile guy, Macko. That's the reason I'm still here. You want to be high-profile – to be Elvis's manager, the new Colonel Parker? Trust me; you don't want that. And I certainly don't."

For a moment it seemed that Macko was a beaten man. His shoulders drooped; he shrugged, reached into his breast pocket and withdrew a packet of cigarettes. Casting a hurt, sorrowful glance at Ellis, he carefully withdrew a cigarette, replaced the packet and loped into the kitchen in search of a lighter. Moments later the puffs of smoke and the gravelly, retching cough informed Gerry and Ellis that he had found one. There was a heavy silence in the lounge, punctuated only by occasional noises off: a further series of staccato coughs and a mournful, high-pitched fart. Ellis sighed and looked at Gerry.

"It wouldn't work, you know."

Gerry stared at him bitterly. "To be honest, Ellis, I'm not that bothered about the bloody ramifications of an Elvis Presley comeback. I'm more worried about some sodding spooks burning down the house or putting a sodding bullet in me."

Ellis nodded. "Yeah, we did get kinda sidetracked."

"Macko does that." Gerry paused, Mayhew's words cold and clear in his mind: *I think your friend has company.*

"Blackwater, Hartshorn: they're only part of the problem, aren't they, Ellis?"

Ellis raised an eyebrow. "I'm sorry?"

"Graham – the Air Staff guy – told me that there was some… activity the other night. Just like a few months ago."

Ellis's face sagged, darkened; he sighed deeply. "Although we – Rachel, myself – are living in human hosts, we can still sense the presence of others of our kind. We each have a unique aura; it's a bit like a body odour in humans, I guess, only in some cases you can pick it up, identify it, when it's a million miles away."

Gerry empathised. Chubb was like that.

"The other night I sensed an aura. One that I knew from way back. I can't sense it any more, which means that my old acquaintance has almost certainly taken on human form. And he – or she as the case may be – isn't here to watch football, Gerry. He or she is here to take Rachel back."

"What about you?"

Ellis stared at him bleakly. "We have history. When we – me, MI13, my home government – cut a deal so that I could stay, this guy wasn't best pleased, made

182

that clear to me. Called me an obscene deviation. But this guy was a relatively minor council member in those days. Times have clearly changed if they've sent him."

He stood up. "Put it this way, I don't think he's here to take me back."

"Fucking yes!"

And Macko was back, wild-eyed, exultant.

"Elvis impersonator! We can fucking do this!"

II

There was a brief but lively tricornered discussion, or to be more precise, three individuals simultaneously expressing their opinion on aspects of the matter in hand without taking heed of what their companions were saying.

Macko was firmly of the view that an Elvis impersonator was the way forward. There was a competition in town in two days time, he remembered reading about it in the *Evening Post*; if that was too soon, well, these things cropped up fairly fecking regular and they could do the next one along. Hell, they could do both if Ellis was up for it. They could buy a few Greatest Hits CDs, print out the lyrics for Ellis to relearn, dig out a white jumpsuit from that fancy dress shop in Guiseley and they were away.

Gerry was advocating a long holiday in Mexico. Or Brazil. Or the Democratic Republic of Congo. Anywhere, in fact, that put mileage between himself and the detached and violent arm of the British government comprised by MI13. Anywhere that didn't involve queuing for a visa for a lengthy period, or too many painful injections, or a language whose alphabet had little or no association with that with which he was familiar.

183

Ellis was suggesting that maybe they should touch base with that guy Graham again: he might be able to give them a little more of a lowdown on what Blackwater was up to. He was sure that he himself would receive another visit from an MI13 agent before long; he would try and lay some false scents to give them a little more breathing space.

Their declamations were rudely, shockingly interrupted as Chubb ran in, tears streaming down his face.

"I'm sorry, I'm sorry, I'm sorry…"

CHAPTER FOURTEEN

I

It had been a traditional Christmas for Chubb, too; he had made his annual pilgrimage by bus, rail and - for the last couple of miles – parental Renault, down the frost-encrusted spine of England to the Home Counties and then, at last, to the quiet, unobtrusive hamlet of Sterner Hill.

His father had greeted him at the station: as ever, Chubb senior had attempted to engage his son in some jocular, seasonal banter; as ever, these attempts had rapidly petered out as his son met each quip with expressionless, monosyllabic responses. Chubb senior knew from painful experience that the odds were heavily stacked against him but felt that, nevertheless, he had to try. Well, he had tried, yet again; yet again, had failed.

On arrival, Chubb had dutifully endured his mother's embrace, dumped his battered holdall with its small but noxious collection of sweat-stained pullovers, cotton shirts and undergarments next to the washing machine, plodded upstairs to his bedroom, lain on his bed, and immersed himself in a copy of *Fortean Times*. In the kitchen, his parents had stared sadly at one another, that exchanged glance conveying a shared acknowledgement that, well, this was how it must always be; together, they were resigned in weary, hopeless acceptance of the situation. And so his mother began loading Chubb's garments into the washing machine, and his father reached for the Glenmorangie.

Chubb, needless to say, was oblivious to all this: the parental home was simply the place where, for three nights a year, he would lay his head, eat, drink (sparingly), read (prodigiously), evacuate his bowels,

185

masturbate and – on Christmas Eve – sink into a hot, foamy bath that his mother had prepared for him. Chubb would remain in the bath for nearly a hour, eyes closed, ruminating deeply and happily on aliens and online gaming, while the grime and odours accumulated over the past few months would seep steadily into the bathwater. While Chubb rarely bathed, he actually rather enjoyed the experience: it was just that he could rarely be bothered to go to the trouble of putting a plug in a plughole, turning on the taps and waiting for the bath to fill. In this case, as with so many in Chubb's simple life, there was an unbridgeable disconnect between the task and the end-result.

And so it was that, in a relative state of cleanliness and with a holdall packed with pressed, pristine garments, Chubb had bidden farewell to his parents and made the return journey North. He had returned to Birch Lane an hour or so before Gerry; had observed – silently, dispassionately, the carnage in the kitchen – and shuffled up the stairs to renew his acquaintance with the Internet. He had barely registered the various noises signifying other activities in the household: the clatterings and curses as Gerry cleaned the kitchen, the low murmur of conversation in the lounge below – but then, inevitably, his bladder demanded a brief visit to the toilet, and so he had reluctantly made his way onto the landing.

And then –

"Singing isn't just about a physical voice – it's what you can bring to it. You could have the voice of Elvis, or Caruso, or Pavarotti … but if you don't have the heart and soul of Elvis, or Caruso, or Pavarotti, then those songs don't have depth, or meaning."

Chubb froze. He knew that voice – how could he not know that voice? He had loved that voice, for God's sake…

186

He is three years old and it is dusk in early autumn, the last light of the setting sun stabbing through the tired cotton curtains. The table lamp sheds a paltry radiance over the room; paltry, but sufficient for him. She holds him to her breast as she danced slowly around the room, the LP on the red Steepletone player crackling into life with the opening bars of 'Are You Lonesome tonight' –

He snuggles close, contented, happy, safe.

An afternoon in March. It would have been his fourth birthday: figures and accessories from a Playpeople construction set litter the floor, along with Stickle Bricks in assorted colours. And there is his garage! That chunky garage with the lift that rang a tinny bell when you turned the lever to raise it! On the table is a cake – sponge, weighed down by excess icing and adorned with four stubby candles. There is Mum, and Dad, and Uncle Eric with his cinecamera, and he is jumping manically, joyfully around the room to 'Jailhouse Rock'.

There is a street party: bunting stretches from lamppost to lamppost and a motley collection of tables have been thrust together in what passed for Sterner Hill's high street and swathed in voluminous white cloths. Upon it has been set the most wonderful array of sandwiches, cakes and sausage rolls. He has just come last in the sack race, behind even little Bob Noakes who isn't even three yet, but he doesn't care: he is running through the open front door because he can hear that the Steepletone is playing his tune:

'Hound Dog' and a party. Life doesn't get any better.

It is two months later, and he is crying and she is

187

crying into his hair, soaking his tousled, mousy locks with her tears. He is barely awake, her anguished wail dragging him brutally from sleep. Between the sobs she manages to tell him the news: first uncomprehending, then distraught as understanding hits and his small, winceyette-clad form buries itself in her lap.

There is no music here, just the broken, whimpering sounds of loss and despair.

There is a cold, biting wind, whipping at his arms and legs, and he is running. Running across Gregg's Meadow, through the long grass, away from Jack and Phil and Jeremy, away from the mockery. He is the weird speccy smelly fat kid who listens to stupid dead Elvis instead of The Police or Duran Duran or Michael Jackson: no good at football, won't play proper games, just reads his weird books and listens to Elvis. And dances – my sister saw you dancing, Gideon! She was going to the post office and she looked and saw you dancing! In your pants!

He stumbles through the gate, pushes open the front door. The house is empty: Dad will be in the office, Mum having her hair done.

He throws the Elvis LPs into a black polythene sack and stamps on it. He slings it over his shoulder and walks with it for two miles to the amenities' tip. His mother screams when she realises what he has done, and then she weeps.

She does not replace them; she does not listen to Elvis again.

Nor does he.

And now he is half-running, half-falling down the stairs, his head a bubbling, confused mess, sobbing, "I'm sorry, I'm sorry, I'm sorry…"

III

Chubb had been dusted down, sat down, and handed tissues and a mug of tea. Fitfully, emotionally, he had explained himself to Gerry, Macko and Ellis as best he could, during which time even Macko began to exhibit even a modicum of sympathy. However, for all that, it was clear that the introduction of Chubb into the mix was likely to complicate matters considerably, as Macko pointed out to Gerry.

"Look," he said in a low voice, as the King ambled up the stairs for a comfort break, "Laughing boy here is in all these friggin' UFO groups on the Internet. He breathes a word to anyone and we're all seriously, seriously fucked."

Gerry nodded, urgently. "Which means that we really do need to think of getting our arses out of here."

"How? Do you have ten grand or whatever it fuckin' takes for plastic surgery and a one-way ticket to a beach hut in Barbados? How much have you been savin' each week?"

"We can't just stay here and get Ellis to play *Stars in Their Eyes* next week, which is what you're shouting for."

Macko stared at him, then, slowly, as if explaining a particularly difficult philosophical concept to a child of limited intellect, "Because these contests have cash prizes. We need cash. We have limited cash. Upstairs, we have an ongoing means of earning cash."

"Macko, upstairs we have a bloke who can't sing -"

"But he looks like Elvis -"

Gerry slammed his fist against the wall in frustration. "He looks like Elvis would have looked if he'd cut down on the burgers and lived for another twenty years. But to the world out there, Elvis didn't have the chance to cut down on the burgers because he

189

died having a big shit! And so, people's expectations of what Elvis should look like generally revolve around either a young, good-looking Elvis gyrating his pelvis in a pair of jeans or a porky Elvis on the verge of middle age squeezed into a sparkly jumpsuit wondering where his next McDonald's is coming from."

"Oh, that's harsh –"

"That's harsh but it's fucking true! They're not looking for some bloke who's about to collect his fucking bus pass! And – let me repeat – by his own admission, he cannot fucking sing."

Macko was adamant. "We do it. We do it and then we fuck off. Just somewhere less fecking expensive than the Caribbean."

"Like where?"

"Manchester."

"Manchester – we fuck off to Manchester?" Gerry was trying to speak in a forced whisper, but this was more of a shriek. "Why in God's name do we go to Manchester?"

"There's good craic in Manchester at weekends. Not to mention the footie."

Gerry clasped his head in his hands. "I don't fucking believe I'm hearing this: we're trying to hide from spooks and you're rocking up at Old Trafford and the Hacienda. Fuck me."

"Hacienda's closed."

"Well I'm sorry, I don't have a PhD in contemporary Manc nightlife but the fact remains that as a viable option your plan stinks like a rat's arsehole."

This dialogue continued in similar vein for several minutes. Chubb slumped on the sofa, staring into space: his mouth occasionally opened but no sound emerged.

On the first floor, Ellis shut the bathroom door, unbuttoned his trousers and lowered himself gently onto the toilet. *Sweet Jesus*, he thought, *this is a mess.*

Blackwater was hunting Rachel; it wouldn't take him long to find her. The man was boorish, arrogant, far too garrulous for his own good; but sharp, sharp as a needle, and utterly relentless. And, he thought grimly, wholly amoral. He might kill those boys downstairs, and not lose a wink of sleep over it.

Anyway, back to the matter in hand. *God bless strong coffee*, thought Ellis, *works wonders on the human waste production system. Just relax and here we go –*

And he was younger, naked, flabby; the narrow bathroom was now palatial, the walls glittered, there was thick, luxuriant red shagpile carpet across the flooring; a couple of yards in front of him was mounted a small TV set, behind which was a marble counter strewn with pill bottles; fixed on the wall next to him was an intercom and a telephone; the dog-eared copies of FHM at his feet had been replaced by a weighty tome bearing the promising title Sex and Psychic Energy. *He felt a sudden, agonising pain in his lower abdomen –*

And then the walls closed in once more, the pain subsided and he realised dimly that he had successfully evacuated his bowels.

Shaking somewhat, he cleaned himself up, hitched up his trousers and stared hard at his reflection in the mirror. Did I just imagine that, he asked himself: what just happened? That wasn't my memory; that was –

A younger face, once handsome but puffy and bloated, stared back at him from a mirror framed above that marble shelf; it lingered momentarily before being replaced by an older, leaner model.

This is it, he thought sadly. *It's time.*

He closed his eyes for a moment, then took a deep breath. "Hell – why not?"

When Ellis returned to the fray, the argument had

not moved on much, with both parties trading colourful and abusive insults with vigour. Macko had just called Gerry a daft Welsh cunt who wouldn't recognise a good plan if it bit him in the arse, and Gerry was in the process of providing Macko with a detailed critique of his (Macko's) singularly unsuccessful career options to date. Chubb was still lost in his thoughts, oblivious to the cacophony.

Ellis cleared his throat. "Gentlemen?"

Like two schoolboys caught in the midst of some minor misdemeanour, the warring parties fell silent and looked sheepishly at their guest.

"Gentlemen, I think it's fair to say I've just had an epiphany."

Macko responded with a cautious "Oh yes?" He wasn't entirely sure what an epiphany was, but it sounded significant.

"You see, something just happened in the bathroom that just altered our situation."

Macko began to interject along the lines that he had similar experiences, usually after a skinful of Guinness the night before, but his attempt to empathise was cut short by a "Shush!" and a murderous look from Gerry.

"I won't go into details now, guys, but, Macko: when did you say that contest was on?"

CHAPTER FIFTEEN

I

She had shouted at him for several minutes; screaming into his face, *Are you mad, are you mad, are you mad*; shrieking, snarling, almost feral in her response. For the most part Gerry, Chubb and Macko had retreated nervously into the background, only intervening when, after Rachel had slammed down a saucepan upon the table, it appeared as though she might next vent her fury on the pile of crockery sitting on the draining board. With Macko's restraining arm on her shoulder, she subsided, sobbing, into a chair. Head in hands, she whispered, "What the hell do you think you're playing at, Ellis?"

"We need to talk." He looked up at Gerry. "Guys, can you give us a moment?"

Macko started to protest, but Gerry shushed him. "Sure."

The house's three human residents trooped into the lounge; Gerry quietly closed the door behind them.

In the kitchen, Rachel stared wearily at Ellis. "Well?"

Ellis drew up a chair and sat next to her. "Rachel, I'm starting to remember."

"No!" Impulsively she reached out to him; he smiled gently.

"Looks like it's not a permanent fix, kid. The body's worn out. Still, it's been over twenty years since I took it. Not a bad run."

"When are you going to migrate?"

"I'm not." She opened her mouth as if to protest, but no sound emerged.

"I'm getting old, kid."

"No, no, no, Elvis is getting old…"

"And I'm getting old. We both are." He laid his hand upon her arm. "Rachel, when they find me, they'll kill me.

"You don't know that!"

"Yes, they will. And you know it. But I'd rather go out on my own terms than theirs."

She was in tears again. He waited for a moment before continuing. "Rachel, I've seen things through these eyes to satisfy a million lifetimes. I've seen Cantona at the top of his game: seen him tease defenders, taunt them with those ghosting, jinking runs when the ball was his creature, his alone to command. They'd lie in wait, they'd track back, but all the while they were fighting a losing cause, because he was drifting past them while they were thinking about making the tackle. He toyed with them – all of them, even the best of them; even when he lost the ball you felt he'd just got bored with being so wonderful. It was majestic, Rachel; it was beautiful.

"I couldn't hate him when he went to the scum, Rachel, I couldn't; even when the bastards stuffed us 4-0 and he was there at the death, gliding effortlessly in behind Garry Kelly, just reaching out, rescuing that cross and flicking it into the net. I could curse him; I did curse him. But at the same time I'm cursing him, I'm wondering at the genius of the man. If it had been just Cantona, that alone would have been worth it. But this game – this infuriating, frustrating, wonderful game – didn't stop when he left. There was beauty before him; there's been beauty after him. And it's all tied up in my love for this bloody club."

The sobs had subsided somewhat. "I've only ever seen one game away from Elland Road. Mainly to keep Hartshorn happy. That was at Bramall Lane, Hell, nearly seven years ago. Couldn't miss that one. Championship decider. Seemed like half of Leeds had

194

made the journey down the M1, all shouting 'We are Leeds! We are Leeds!'

"We had a few chances, so did they, but it was just coming to the end of the first half when there was this almighty scramble in our area after a corner, umpteen legs flailing up at the ball, and suddenly Alan Cork connects and Sheffield are ahead. Then, straightaway, at the other end: we had this free kick, Rob Wallace had a shot saved that ricocheted out wide, and their defence, well… It was as if their legs had turned to lead, they could see the ball, and they could see Gary Speed running past them and pulling it back, and – I don't think Rob Wallace meant to stick it in the back of the net: he was just standing there and the cross kinda just pinged off him. But it was fucking wonderful and it was fucking game on.

"Then, just after the break, Gary Mac put this long, arcing free kick in from the left: sailed over half a dozen red-and-white shirts and their keeper, right onto Jon Newsome's head. Two-one. We went berserk.

"Then poor Lee Chapman stuck one in his own net after a corner; there was a girl standing next to me, she cried when that went in, she thought that was it. But then we fired this long ball way up field, more in hope than expectation. Sheffield had this defender, Brian Gayle, and he could see Rob Wallace and Cantona bearing down on him, and his 'keeper was running out as well. So he tries to get the ball out of harm's way: he tries to control it, but it flies up into the air, he heads it and it loops over the keeper into the goal. And we're all going mad, we're all going 'Ooh-aah Cantona!'"

"Still wasn't over, of course. Scum could still catch us if they beat Liverpool. Most of us piled back into the cars and the coaches and drove back up to Leeds to watch the game on the telly in the pub. You know what happened – Manchester United lost. And the city erupted, Rachel. It erupted. I erupted. So did the guys drinking next to me. It was this raw, primal, joyous release. This one old guy shouted out 'After eighteen bloody years!' and burst into tears. I hugged him. I loved him. Because at that moment, we were Leeds. And Leeds had done it."

Ellis paused, blinking away what may have been a tear.

"In the time that you've been here, Rachel, have you ever drunk a beer called Theakston's Old Peculier? No? You should. It's a strong, dark, malty beer. I drank a hell of a lot of it that night.

"I'd like to have seen this season through – to see if we could do it again. But it's not gonna happen. The memories will come thick and fast now."

She gripped his hand. "Please stay. Please migrate."

He shook his head. "That'll do, kid. I've made up my mind. This singalong that Macko flagged up – could be kinda fun. Besides, as I see it, it's a way of saying thank you to the guy whose body I borrowed. Perhaps I owe him one."

"What shall I do?" Her voice was cracked, faint, desperate.

"Your call. Just one thing, though. If you manage to keep away from Blackwater and Hartshorn; if that mother ship which is currently on the dark side of the moon doesn't blow this planet away in its search for you; if you somehow manage to keep hidden: when your own time comes, think hard about whether you want to migrate again. Sure, for the host it's not a problem. But for their friends, their lovers, their children – to see that person walking around and for that person not to love them, not to even to know them – it's one hell of a problem. There is so much pain wrapped up in all this; I didn't realise it at first; never crossed my mind. But when you live amongst these

196

people, share the minutiae of their live, their ups and downs, you realise that they're all part of something much richer, much more beautiful than you imagined. What is it they say: the whole is greater than the sum of its parts? They're right. Without that sharing of emotion – love, fear, hurt, pain, joy, whatever – that evening after the Sheffield game would have been meaningless. So when you do start to remember – that warm toast by the fireside at your grandma's, playing tag in the park, your first kiss – think about what those experiences mean to the others who shared them."

He stood up. "It's getting late. I should go back to the flat but to be honest, I think it's gone beyond that. I'm going to ask Gerry if I can catch some shuteye on the couch – tonight and maybe for the next couple of nights."

Ellis left her alone in the kitchen. Rachel shuddered. Imprinted on her mind was the distorted, anguished face of Laura, pressed hopefully, hopelessly to the car window.

II

The news that Ellis had agreed to reprise the former career of his host – albeit for one night only – sent Chubb into overdrive. The following morning he braved the post-Christmas shopping hordes that had engulfed the frozen streets of Leeds, returning several hours later with a small, shiny black plastic bag, within which was what he hoped would serve as a useful aide mémoire for his reinvigorated hero.

"I bought *Recorded Live in Stage on Memphis*, *The Sun Sessions CD* and *The Top 10 Hits*", he explained as he handed the discs to Ellis. "That should do to begin with."

Ellis smiled at him. "That's very generous of you,

197

Gideon. But I don't think I'll be able to sing more than one song. The way that Macko explained it to me, there's gonna be a whole bunch of guys competing."

Chubb coloured. "Yes, but – when you win -"

"If I win -"

"When you win, they might ask you to do an encore. Besides," he continued, "maybe listening to these tracks will help you – you know – remember how you did it."

"I never did it, Gideon. He did." Chubb's face fell, momentarily, but rose as Ellis added, "But he's coming back. Slowly. I'm getting little shots of memory – pretty much at random. It's like I'm reading a biography of Elvis, but with the chapters in the wrong order." He looked thoughtfully at Chubb.

"What was he like, Gideon?"

Chubb shrugged, awkwardly. "I never knew much about him as a person. I knew he was married – lived in Graceland – had a wife and a lot of girlfriends – that was it, really. I just loved his music." He paused and stared at Ellis with sudden, terrible empathy: a recognition that his own experience the previous day was not that far removed from that of the figure that stood before him.

"It isn't just the memories that are coming back, is it?"

Ellis shook his head. "No." He breathed deeply and sighed. "It's the full package, all the associated emotion."

"What do *you* think he was like – from the memories you had so far?"

Vegas. He had nailed it; he was back. He had owned that stage, man, from beginning to end, from the first bars of Blue Sued Shoes onwards; he had rocked, and the starsoaked audience had lapped it up, had been on their feet, begging for more. Cary Grant, Shirley

198

Bassey, Paul Anka, Totie Fields: on their feet, begging for more. He had fed off that energy in turn; it had fuelled his ego, fired the passion and the urgency as he roamed around, as he flipped and cartwheeled and rolled. No other goddamn sonofabitch could touch the heights that he had touched that night. He was backstage now, laughing, joking, fooling with the guys, with Joe and Charlie and Sonny and big fat Lamar; there was Colonel, so usually impassive and remote, ducking into the backstage arena with tears in the eyes. And Priscilla, appearing from within the raucous, cheering crowd, a vision in that pale minidress, her midriff bare; she reached up, stroked the delicate silk scarf had he thrown around his neck: he bent down to accept her kiss.

Priscilla.

And Kathy and Sheila and Ginger and Jo and Linda and Joyce and Barbara, and all those waitresses and working girls and groupies. Whenever he wanted, whatever he said. Because he was Elvis and because he could.

And the guys. Always the guys. Laughing and joking and fooling. On his payroll.

"I think he was very lonely, Gideon."

III

While Chubb had been shopping for CDs in Leeds, Gerry had driven to Guiseley; there was a fancy-dress shop there, a bloody good one: he had rented a Cavalier costume from there a few months back for a departmental party.

Yes, the shop assistant had explained patiently to him over the phone, they had a few Elvis costumes in stock. What did he have in mind: Rhinestone? American Eagle? Jumpsuit?

199

Gerry admitted he wasn't sure, and said he'd decide when he got there. (A brief consultation with Ellis had left him none the wiser; Ellis had told him to go with his gut instinct.)

In the end he opted for the jumpsuit.

Did he need accessories, the assistant had asked as she folded the costume into a cellophane wrapper. Dollar Ring? Wig?

Gerry had considered Ellis's closely-cropped pate for a moment. Yes, he replied.

He had assured the assistant that the jumpsuit would be returned on New Year's Eve – there was an all-ticket party at the Station that night and Elvis was booked out – before driving back to Scrimpton with the jumpsuit on the back seat.

IV

Macko finally emerged from the squalid, shambolic embrace of his bed halfway through the second outing of *Recorded Live on Stage in Memphis*, which was emanating from a rather battered stereo in Chubb's room. As Macko descended the stairs, he was hit by an icy blast of air from Chubb's doorway; Ellis had pointed out – as tactfully as he was able – that the atmosphere within was perhaps a little stale, and while its resident (being primarily responsible for said staleness) was more or less inured to its effects, he had responded by opening his window for the first time since he had taken up occupancy.

Ellis caught his eye first; Ellis, clad in a white jumpsuit and black wig, standing in the middle of the room, eyes closed, silently mouthing the words to 'How Great Thou Art'. Across from Ellis was Chubb, lying on his back on the bed, a look of rapture on his face. Macko thoughtfully observed the scene for

200

several moments, its participants wholly oblivious to his presence, before shambling down the second flight of stairs to the kitchen.

Gerry was there, and Laura. As Macko shuffled past them towards the kettle, his housemate greeted him with a jovial, "See Colonel Tom Parker the Second has finally decided to grace us with his presence, then?"

"K'off," grunted Macko, and filled the kettle.

Laura enquired of Gerry whether Macko was normally this much of a charmer, and Gerry said, no, he's laying it on with a trowel just for you.

"Time'sit?" asked Macko.

"Bout three."

"How's he doing?"

"What, your protégée? The prodigal son returning to the stage under your guidance after a twenty-one year hiatus?"

"Stop taking the piss with big bastard words when I've just woken up." He reached into his trouser pocket. "At least let me have a ciggee and a coffee first."

Macko duly sat himself on the wall outside the back door, his mug of coffee perched at his side. After a few moments Gerry came and joined him.

"Well?" asked Macko.

"Well what?"

"How's our fella doin'?"

"Getting into character, I'd think you'd call it. He changed into the jumpsuit as soon as I brought it home and since then he's been upstairs listening to some Elvis CDs that Gideon picked up this morning."

"Any singing?"

"Not yet. Just listening."

Macko nodded. For the next minute or so, he devoted his attention exclusively to the cigarette and the coffee. Then:

"When did the big lass rock up?"

"Oi - steady!" Macko was surprised by the sudden vehemence in Gerry's tone, before his friend recovered his composure. "Bout an hour ago."

A light had gone on in Macko's head. "You fancy her!" he exclaimed in a delighted whisper. "You've got the fecking hots for her!"

He was further gratified as Gerry coloured and flustered.

"Pipe down, you git," he muttered. "I called her when I got back from Guiseley. Anyway, I wanted to keep her posted about our plans -"

"Let me get this straight: An alien living inside Elvis Presley is going to enter an Elvis Presley-singalike contest."

"Er, yes."

"Bloody mental. Bloody brilliant."

"- and I thought she might want to meet Elvis."

"How did that go?"

"Laura, this is Ellis; he's living inside Elvis's body. Ellis, Laura."

"Hi."

"Hi."

"Okay."

Macko took another drag on his cigarette.

"Oh, by the way I told her that you'd been shagging Rachel." Gerry was glad to see that Macko looked suitably nervous at this revelation.

"Oh yes?"

"Yes."

"What'd she say?"

Gerry had thought it expedient that he should break the news to her, rather than Rachel – whom he felt might do so matter-of-factly in the middle of conversation – or Macko (who might simply be unable to stop himself). In this way he felt he stood a better chance of preventing (or at least ameliorating) any acts of violence that Laura might otherwise feel obliged to mete out to his hapless friend; what was it they called it at uni – "creating a controlled environment". That was it.

In the event, her eyes had flashed, she had called Macko, in his absence, a little Irish shit but, Gerry was relieved to observe, did not show any inclination to make a beeline for Macko's lair with a large blunt object. She had merely given a hollow laugh initially, before snorting that Lisa had had one night stands with some dickheads while she was alive so it was nice to see that her corpse was keeping up the tradition.

"Not a lot. But I think your balls can breathe easy." The relief on Macko's face was palpable.

"Where is Rachel, by the way?"

"In her room. Not said Jack to anyone today. Think she's still pissed off at Ellis…" Gerry's voice tailed off. He was staring intently at the bushes in the garden opposite: a plump, crested bird, brownish in colour and the size of a starling, had alighted there and was busying itself by plucking off and consuming all the berries in its vicinity.

"Macko, it's a waxwing."

"A what?"

"A waxwing. A bloody waxwing. I've never seen one before, ever!"

"Bombycilla garrulous."

They turned in surprise to find that Ellis was standing behind them, an expression of deep interest on his face.

"Bombycilla garrulous. Not heard that there's an irruption this year…"

"You like birds?" Macko was finding this hard to believe.

"Yes."

"But I thought you liked football."

"Was there some law about having multiple interests that I missed?"

"No, but, fecking birds…"

"I like fecking birds," hissed Gerry, still staring at the waxwing.

"Good for you," said Ellis.

Having exhausted the possibilities of the Birch Lane bushes, the waxwing flew off in search of richer pickings. Gerry watched it until it disappeared into the gathering dusk. He turned back to Ellis.

"When did you get into birds?"

"Early eighties. Thought I needed something to do in the close season; I was going a bit stir crazy in the flat. Got chatting to one of the spooks. He suggested it: even bought me an old Collins guide to British Birds to get me started. Every so often he'd arrange for a minder to take me out some place: Townclose Hills, Aire Valley; once or twice we went out to the Dales. Sometimes he'd take me out himself. He was a good lad." Ellis sighed. "He was reassigned six years ago. Replaced by Blackwater. Pity."

Macko was getting restive. "Have you buggers finished your Bill Oddie love-in yet? Only I was wonderin' how the rehearsals are going."

Ellis looked grave. "Difficult to say. I'm just trying to immerse myself in the music, y'know, to maybe trigger something."

"Anythin' doing?"

"Not yet."

Macko snorted. "Hope it gets a bloody move on. You're on stage in thirty hours."

V

I'm not going back. That was the one thought running through her mind, the one thing she was holding on to.

204

Throughout the night, as the rooms around her echoed to the snores of their various tenants (and one overnight guest), she had sat on the bed in the darkness, knees pressed close to her chest, rocking slowly back and forth; throughout the night, that thought was reinforced and buttressed by a host of recollections: of glorious, inch-perfect cross-field balls, of tackles timed to perfection, of Jimmy-Floyd Haisselbank letting fly and of the net momentarily tautening, momentarily pushed to its limit before sagging hopelessly back as the Revie Stand erupted. But even as Jimmy-Floyd let fly, he was being assailed by the words of Ellis, by the tears of Laura and by the sharp features of Blackwater, his dark eyes looking her up and down in desultory fashion in the dim light of Exotica.

The morning drew on, and in the pale grey light she could discern, slowly but ever more clearly, the faces that adorned a solitary poster on the opposing wall. Not that she needed the daylight to recognise them; she knew them off by heart.

Back row: Lilley, Woodgate, Matthews...

More than once, returning home after a game, she had reached up and bestowed a kiss on the goalscorers. As a result, Jimmy-Floyd's face in particular had gradually become obscured by a thin mist of lipstick.

Middle Row: Maybury, Robertson, Wijnhard...

Those beautiful boys. Those wonderful boys.

Front row: Shepherd, Kewell, Harte...

There was a muffled knock on the door, cautious and hesitant.

How long she had been sitting there she did not know; did not care.

Another knock; louder this time.

"Yes?"

"Rachel, it's Laura. Can we talk?"

Very stiffly and laboriously, Rachel unwrapped

herself, stood up and opened the door. Laura raised her eyebrows at Rachel's red-eyed, almost haggard, visage; she herself was resplendent in billowing black dress above which was set at her neck a silver pendant featuring a particularly irascible dragon.

"You look bloody awful."

"I feel bloody awful."

"Have you been to bed yet?"

Rachel shook her head.

"Do you want some tea or coffee?"

"Coffee'd be good."

"How d'you take it?"

A few minutes later, Laura returned with two mugs of coffee; they both sat on the edge of the bed in silence for a moment. As Rachel slowly tuned back into the here and now, she became aware of music playing within Chubb's room, in itself a hitherto unknown event.

"Elvis's Greatest Hits," explained Laura. "Ellis is trying to tune into the vibe."

"I'm scared, Laura." The small voice somehow crept from Rachel's throat. Part of Laura wanted to hug the slim, weary figure beside her, to tell her everything would be alright; another part wanted to recoil in disgust, but that part was on the wane. Her anger was long spent; her compassion had kicked in.

"I don't want to go back; I don't want them to find me."

"I know." Laura patted her hand. "Look," she said awkwardly, "I can't pretend this is easy for me. You were my best mate when you were, y'know..." Rachel nodded. "So seeing you in my mate's body – seeing her become a completely different person – well, it's a bit of mindfuck, to be it bluntly."

"I'm sorry I gave you a mindfuck."

Laura laughed at the whispered response. "Yeah,

well, I'm sorry you fucked that Irish dick upstairs."

"I'm not. It was fun. Messy, but fun. Particularly on the kitchen table."

"OK! Way too much information!" Even as she said this, Laura looked sharply at her companion. "You know," she said thoughtfully after a moment, "that's just the kind of thing Lisa would have said." After a short pause, she continued. "I can't promise we'll make everything all right; I can't promise we'll be able to keep the bad guys off; but we'll do our best, OK?"

"OK."

"Good." Then, in a much louder voice, "Then stop fannying about in your bedroom and come downstairs!"

As she stood up to leave, she turned back momentarily. "Just – take care of her body, Rachel. Don't waste it, yeah?"

Rachel stood up in turn. "Promise."

I'm not going back. I'm not going back. I'm not going back.

VI

It was agreed over fish, chips and mushy peas from down the road. The following evening, Ellis would perform at the Elland Social Club, before making his way back to his flat: they were under strict instructions never to contact him again. Laura, Macko, Gerry and Chubb were nonetheless insistent on attending the event. Rachel, however, had pointed out that Leeds had a home game that night: never mind that it was against those cloggers from Wimbledon, it was a home game, and she'd be in the East Stand as usual; she was less concerned than her companions with the significance of Elvis's first gig on English soil, albeit one occurring twenty-one years after his death. However, she agreed to meet up with them all at the social club after the game.

After that, well… they would see. Ellis had urged them to put contingency plans into place, to be ready to jump ship at a moment's notice. Thus, if there were the slightest intimation that their cover was blown, Gerry, Macko and Chubb had agreed to head for Cork in the first instance – there were direct flights from Leeds/Bradford airport – before possibly decamping elsewhere; Gerry had voiced his intention to take a refresher course in Spanish in a bid to improve on the paltry and rusty vocabulary that remained from an "O" Level a dozen years previously, and thus to widen the scope of potential longer term destinations. Rachel said that she'd head for the Canaries – she'd heard from one of her punters that they had satellite TV showing Premiership football over there, and if it were no longer safe for her to visit Elland Road, well, she may as well watch the games in big screens in a warmer climate.

As Macko waxed lyrical about Cork, Gerry took Ellis aside.

"You know that if we get caught, now or anytime in the future, we're shafted."

Ellis shrugged. "Sure. You're shafted."

"Well, I don't want to be shafted."

"No one wants to be shafted, Gerry. I don't want to be shafted, you don't want to be shafted. I don't want you to be shafted, either. But sometimes… we get shafted."

"Thing is, Ellis, I've been speaking with Gideon. I think I've found a way of avoiding getting shafted."

"A way out of shafting?"

"A way out of shafting." Gerry smiled, coldly. "Tell me about Upper Lupton."

VII

Two hours later, by which time they had long since decamped to the lounge with a crate of bottled beer, the phone rang. Macko looked up in irritation.

"Jesus, who's ringing us at this time of night?"

"Probably a wrong fucking number. I'll get it."

The answerphone had clicked in by the time that Gerry trotted across to the phone and picked up the handset.

"Gerry, it's Graham here. I'm afraid the game's up: MI13 are onto me; I think they were watching us the other day, so they almost certainly know where you live by now – and who you live with. I'm trying to lead some of them a merry dance for a while – might slow them down, might distract them, you never know. But - I'm sorry, Gerry, but you know too much now. It's pretty awful, I know, but if I were you – just get out now, Gerry. It's too late for me, but you might just make it.

"You were a good friend, Gerry. Just a pity you never got to cut it as a son-in-law."

CHAPTER SIXTEEN

I

Blackwater hated Christmas. Hated the fact that, in homes innumerable around England, children were tearing open presents, families were gathering, turkey was being eaten; hated Slade and Merry Fucking Christmas, Everybody; hated that bastard song by Wizzard. Most pertinently, he hated the fact that the Horse and Groom was shut by two o'clock and that he had an expensive taxi ride to find a pub that allowed him to continue his drinking unabated.

This year, his loathing had added a new string to its bow: he was having to work for once, through the entire holiday period, along with Griffiths and the two juniors, who were subjected to the full force of Blackwater's spleen the minute he stalked into the Menston office. In the days since his encounter with Rachel at Exotica, no evidence had come to light; no reports of missing patients with terminal illnesses had emerged. A week earlier he had been summoned to Upper Lupton to give a status report to Hartshorn: boy, had that been fun. Well, it had been for all the other buggers who'd piled in to see him squirm. Particularly Tremaine and Granville.

Tremaine and Granville. Blackwater was never sure which was which. It wasn't as if they were alike – one was young, slim, fair-haired and fey of manner, the other heavily-built, dark and morose – but they were a perpetual double act: together, deep in conversation in Upper Lupton's subterranean corridors, together in briefings, together in the poky hall that passed as the complex's canteen. Quite possibly they even went for a shit together.

Hell, they had even joined the service together,

showing up unannounced (at least to him) at the debrief after a craft from the Andromeda galaxy had crash landed in the Outer Hebrides and they'd had to work like buggery to (a) shut the thing down and (b) work with the rather dazed Andromedans to cobble together a spaceworthy vessel from a combination of the fragments of their own craft that remained and from the various esoteric items of compatible technologies that had been tucked away in Upper Lupton's vaults. Blackwater had rather enjoyed that project – he had had plenty of opportunities to be abusive to the islanders, and had seized those opportunities whenever they arose – and the Andromedans had actually been, well, good blokes: never mind that they had two heads apiece, they developed a liking for lager in their short stay on the planet. The only thing that had narked him was those two buggers showing up at the debrief, the one smiling patronisingly at him, the other grunting a bit, but neither batting an eyelid when old Two-Head Timmy was wheeled out. No, they had simply looked up, nodded, and then returned to their conversation. At this point Blackwater had demanded to know who the fuck they were and why the fuck they were talking through his presentation: Blondie had replied that while the presentation was frightfully interesting – and they looked forward to a discussion with the gentleman from Andromeda in due course – the project to which they had been assigned by Mr Hartshorn was of a higher priority; they had merely come along to see the extent to which the latest developments impacted on their own activities.

At that point, Blackwater had longed to impact on their own activities, preferably with a large blunt instrument or failing that both fists, but the mention of Hartshorn's name had stayed his hands, then and since.

He had very little to do with them; like him, they

reported direct to Hartshorn: until this particular jaunt, they'd never worked on the same project. Indeed – and this piqued him – he had no idea what the hell they had been working on before this. MI13 was, by its very nature, an intensely secretive organisation, but Blackwater had managed to worry at most of the secrets until he'd mastered them (and had then garrulously divulged them to any in earshot at the Horse and Groom).

At the most recent, most awkward briefing, when Hartshorn had gently, courteously, highlighted the failings of the operation, noting apologetically the lack of progress since Blackwater's secondment to it, the two had sat silently throughout, only to engage in low murmurs at its anticlimactic conclusion.

Hence, on this chill and frosty morn in late December, he was less than impressed when Griffiths showed them into his temporary office.

What – the – fuck – are – they – doing – here?

He forced a smile. "Well then! This is a surprise! Cup of tea, fellas?"

Blondie nodded. "That would be splendid, Mr Blackwater. White for me, white with one sugar for Roy here." *Roy. Roy Granville. OK, so Tremaine's the poofy one. Must remember that.*

Blackwater gestured to Griffiths. "Kettle on, Griff. Coffee for me too, matey-boy." Griffiths snorted and ducked out: as Tremaine and Granville settled into the chairs proffered for them with faux good grace by Blackwater, he could be heard passing the request for beverages down the office food chain.

Blackwater waited, expectantly. Across the table, his guests smiled patronisingly at him in unison. Tremaine leaned back in his chair and considered Blackwater with an air of languid, amused detachment.

"That's an exquisite suit – Armani?"

Somewhere in the depths of Blackwater's grunted response was a "Yes".

"You do have a very good taste in suits, Mr Blackwater. I remember saying to Roy after your – interesting presentation the other day in Upper Lupton, I said, 'Roy, that's a Paul Smith's he's got today. Lovely material. Lovely cut.'"

Roy nodded, a nod that did not display undue enthusiasm for the topic under discussion. Blackwater couldn't quite refrain from scowling.

"You may recall, Mr Blackwater, that a few weeks ago we spent a morning clearing up in the Air Staff 2 offices – just a bit of shredding here and there to make sure that there wasn't any kind of paper trail – or electronic trail – for any of the general MoD chaps to pick up on. Anyway, I believe you know Graham Mayhew?"

Grunt.

"Good. Well, of course it was a little bit awkward for Mr Mayhew – after all, he comes into work to find two strange gentlemen making a bit of a mess in his office, and is obliged to absent himself from the building while they finish their task. He may have found it somewhat demeaning. It struck me at the time that here was a man – a good, solid, dependable man – who, while largely resigned to the interventions of MI13, was nonetheless growing weary of them. I felt that – if you will pardon the metaphor – here was a worm that might turn."

Blackwater felt that he needed to interrupt Tremaine's smooth flow at this juncture. "Woah, woah, calling a halt here. Point number one: I've known matey-boy for a few years now – keeps his nose clean, doesn't want any trouble, doesn't make any trouble, hands any relevant files over like a good 'un. Point number two: Graham's a bloody desk officer, not an agent in the field. The only information he gets comes through his fucking in-tray at Air Staff 2."

"Bear with me, please. At the time we were not assigned specifically to the Jackson project; we were just engaged in some routine paper trail erasure on a number of unrelated activities, of which that happened to be one. You would be surprised at how much potential evidence is left lying around, Mr Blackwater: a sentence hastily scrawled on a memo pad; a line on an expenses claim; a fingerprint on the trigger of a revolver; a middle-aged man who knows more than you'd think. Evidence that we really must dispose of."

Blackwater turned pale.

"My concerns about Mr Mayhew were, I suppose, no more than nagging doubts: that a man can only take so much ritual humiliation – can only hand over the relevant files for so often; can only keep the nagging doubts to himself for so long. My feeling was that he might tell someone – a friendly face, perhaps; or perhaps someone who might be interested in the story he had to tell. To write the story he had to tell.

"Anyway, Roy and I had a little window of opportunity after the clean-up – a few clear days in our schedule – when I thought that, just to be on the safe side, we'd keep him under a little light obs. We booked into an excellent hotel near the family home – there is a Michelin-starred restaurant up to the road where we dined a couple of times during the surveillance, I really recommend it – and just kept an eye on him."

(*So that's where my fucking budget is going,* thought Blackwater bitterly. *Top hotels and Michelin-starred restaurants, just because this ponce had a hunch.*)

"For the first few days, it's fair to say that we found nothing of interest: Mr Mayhew really is a man of habit. In fact, we were on the point of calling off the surveillance when, one day, off he went for a drive. And met up with someone. They walked, and talked, and then went their separate ways, in their separate cars. It might have been nothing, Mr Blackwater, but we thought it might be worth a little digging.

"And do you know what we found, Mr Blackwater? The someone's car was registered to a Leeds address."

II

Mayhew knew they would come for him, soon. But how soon?

On Christmas Day, this year as always, he had slumped in a fitful, dyspeptic doze in his armchair, fuelled by an excess of turkey, wine and port; a doze this year troubled less by the disapproving comments of his wife and daughter at the occasional, inevitable post-prandial flatulence than by dark thoughts rising from what Gerry had told him. Eventually, he had roused himself from the chair, dashed cold water into his face to drive off the remnants of drowsiness, and ambled into the hallway to ring Dave.

He had few friends – he was, he knew, hopeless at keeping in touch – but he liked Dave. They had met in Majorca in the early eighties, on one of their few family holidays: Angela had complained bitterly about the food, the waiters, the disco music in the evenings, the German lady in the room down the hall who must have been in her mid-forties and was far too old to be going topless; there had presumably been other sources of discontent, but after a while they all blurred into a continuous discourse of dissatisfaction, which after years of practice, he had trained himself to treat as an unavoidable, slightly irritating, low level background noise which could best be ameliorated by occasional nods, judicious uses of the words, "Absolutely, darling"

215

and liberal doses of a decent Scotch (or failing that, any Scotch.) It was during one of his medicinal visits to the hotel bar that he had met Dave, a plump, somewhat lugubrious individual who was seeking similar solace in a stiff drink or two. Mrs Dave, it transpired, didn't like the paella. Or the fact that Dave was wearing socks with his shorts. Mayhew had supplied a few sympathetic nods and noises, and the next round of drinks. Their friendship was sealed. For the rest of the holiday, their evenings were spent at the bar, occasionally venturing a cautious, favourable comment on the Spanish way of life.

He had not met Dave again after that holiday, but they had exchanged phone numbers and, that Christmas, in an act of rare, daring spontaneity, he had called Dave, a call that would develop into an annual tradition: "Just going to ring Dave, dear," he would murmur, and settling himself onto the bottom stair, would spend the next half-hour reliving those evenings in a Majorca bar, the reminiscences intermittently shot through with updates on what they'd been up to over the past year. For Mayhew, such updates were rather constrained by the fact that he was rather more strict than Blackwater in his observance of the Official Secrets Act, and so – once enquiries as to Angela and Emma's wellbeing had been dealt with - he was largely content to listen to Dave's tales of working down the treatment plant, of how they were getting a new kitchen; of tight matches in the West Bromwich Pool League, Division 3. And then the kitchen would be forgotten, the pool match would be over, and they would be back at the bar in Majorca, reliving a whisky or two, Mayhew in his shirt and slacks, Dave in his shorts and socks.

He sensed there was something wrong almost as soon as the conversation began: the peculiar fluctuations in volume, the faint but perceptible hissing as Dave was describing the deciding frame of the Red Lion against the Miners' Arms. He continued with the call on autopilot; this year his thoughts were not of a Spanish bar, but of how long he had left.

Absently he replaced the handset on the receiver, and gathered his thoughts. The tap had been placed today, within the past couple of hours: it hadn't been there when he answered the phone to that snotty friend of Emma's earlier. Why now? If someone in MI13 – maybe Blackwater, maybe those other guys – had had any suspicions about his reliability, surely they would have placed the tap earlier. He had never done anything – anything – to warrant a tap. Until that meeting with Gerry. It had to be that meeting with Gerry. But how the hell had they known – it could only mean that before the tap was placed, he was already under surveillance. "He's been booted out of his office, he'll be a bit sore, let's just keep an eye on him." And so, on the off-chance that a potentially disgruntled desk officer might leak a few juicy alien stories to the media in a fit of pique, they had stumbled across a way to their target. Hell!

Soon, then – if not already - they would know who Gerry was. And where he lived. Which would lead them to her.

Take a step back. Soon they would know that Gerry knew about the girl. And, that Gerry had shared that knowledge with him. Knowledge which they would not permit him to share with anyone else. Or to take the risk that it might be shared. The tap was there in the hope – but not the expectation – that he might be careless enough to divulge some useful information on an open line. It might buy him some time – but they would move quickly, certainly within the next few days. And if the net result of that was that Angela and

Emma -. He stopped himself.

He would sit tight for a day or so, then make his move.

III

"So then you put a tap in?"

"Of course. So that he'd know that we knew. Just on the off-chance that he might try and contact Angel, that it might frighten him into revealing something."

"Did he?" Blackwater was finding this drip-feed of information unbearable, and Tremaine knew it. He opened his mouth as if to speak, then – as if reconsidering – closed it again, forefinger gently stroking his chin, exquisitely teasing Blackwater with his silence.

"Well?"

Tremaine shook his head. "For a couple of days – nothing. Then, on the twenty-seventh, he made a call to a hotel in Bridlington, North Yorkshire, booking a single room for the following night. On the morning of the twenty-eighth, yesterday morning, he left home and drove north. Naturally, we followed at a respectable distance."

"And? And?"

IV

It was a beautiful sunrise, the pale red light dappling the slate grey waves of the North Sea, highlighting the spume as it crashed into the chalk cliff-face. Gradually, the rays reached the clifftop; the impenetrable blackness of the winter night had already given way to the grey predawn, and now the light picked out an expanse of scrubland, pock-marked with rabbit holes. It picked out a balding, middle-aged man, his girth

218

exaggerated by multiple pullovers and a thick anorak, standing maybe two metres from the edge; he was clutching a glass tumbler; at his feet was a bottle of whisky. It picked out two more figures, both taller than Mayhew; one slim, one thickset, maybe a hundred yards further back; beside them was a large, metallic cylinder.

Mayhew nodded in friendly fashion to Tremaine and Granville, and raised his glass. "Good morning, gentlemen."

He had known that they – or someone – would follow; had seen the black Audi tailing him before he hit the A1. He had stopped off at a Little Chef en route for a spot of lunch; the Audi had parked up in a layby while he dined, before maintaining its pursuit at a respectable distance. He reached Bridlington at dusk. The hotel was a shabby, early twentieth century building with few concessions to late twentieth century comfort, but then – he mused sadly as he fumbled with a carton of milk – he had never intended to stay there. At seven he dined alone at a nearby Thai restaurant; at nine he retired to his room. At eleven, wrapped in pullovers and anorak to protect him against the biting winds, he stole quietly from the hotel, made the short call to Gerry, and made his way to Bempton Cliffs.

It was a nature reserve he remembered from his early 'twenties, pre-Angela, when his ornithological interests led him all around the country. The best place in England for seabirds, Bempton Cliffs – gannets, guillemots, puffins. But not, unfortunately, at this time of year. Now it would be just him, and the wind whipping up along the headland, and the North Sea beyond. And them, of course.

He had not expected to lose his pursuers, but perhaps – just perhaps – his activities might delay them enough to give their real quarry a fighting chance.

They, too, had shared the night on the clifftop, silently, not declaring their presence; not having to. He knew they were there, and they knew that he knew. They were content to wait; this was the endgame, for him at least.

As he called out to them, they moved forwards in tandem, halting about thirty feet away. Tremaine spoke; Roy Granville said nothing and watched the exchange, impassively.

"Good morning, Mr Mayhew. Should be a nice day."

"Indeed."

"Might I ask what brings you to Bridlington?"

"I might ask you the same question."

"Oh, you know that, Mr Mayhew. We're here because you are."

Mayhew smiled, and drained his glass. "So why am I here, then?"

"Let me see... Birds? I know you like birds – but the wrong season, I'm told. Besides, even if it were the height of summer: you don't go off like this any more, Mr Mayhew."

"So?"

"At first we thought you might be meeting with Mr Angel. Or possibly one of his housemates. Perhaps for dinner, but no: you enjoyed your Weeping Tiger steak alone. And then you made that call: we didn't trace it, but that was surely to Angel. We thought perhaps you might have been trying to achieve a clandestine clifftop meeting – hence the fact that Roy and I have endured a rather sleepless night slightly further inland – but it was clearly a ruse. A time-wasting exercise."

"Please keep going." Mayhew was pouring himself another whisky. "I'd offer you some, but I've only the one glass, I'm afraid. And you don't strike me as a man who drinks his whisky from the bottle. If at all."

220

"True, Mr Mayhew. Very true. But to return to the matter in hand: we've done a little digging, these past couple of days: we checked up on Mr Angel, on Mr Chubb, on Mr McCall. And on Ms Moran. And that's where it got very interesting. Because until recently, Ms Moran was a Ms Smith: who suffered a relapse in hospital. Who was on the point of death a few months ago. And yet who signed herself out of that hospital, hours after being in what was believed to be a terminal coma.

"Now, I know that most of this is way beyond your clearance level, but I'm sure that Mr Angel has filled you in on all that activity on Ilkley Moor, and on why we had to make sure that there was nothing in your office that might point to MI13's involvement. But what we're not quite sure of is how much you know? And that, you see, is what we really do need to find out, as a matter of importance."

Throughout their conversation, the light had grown stronger. Mayhew exhaled, deeply; he could see his breath freezing as it left his lungs. It would be a cold day, despite the winter sun.

"Angela and Emma know nothing; you know that."

"We know that."

"Thank you." Mayhew took another sip of whisky, then, with a shrug, knocked back the remainder of the glass.

And then stepped backwards over the cliff.

V

Blackwater stared at Tremaine in shock. "When was this?"

"I would say – around half-past eight this morning. We drove straight here. The local emergency services will be attending to his body. Given that Mr Mayhew essentially took us on a wild goose chase, I thought it best we expedite the process by handing over to your good self. It is, after all, your project."

So Mayhew – comfortable, reliable, placid old Mayhew – was dead. There would be a chair to fill at Air Staff 2 after the Christmas break. But already Blackwater's mind was moving on, attempting to keep pace with events.

He could also feel himself struggling to control the anger, the simmering rage at the actions of the two interlopers. *He had been kept out of the loop, for fuck's sake!*

"So you've known about this for how many days?"

Tremaine gave him a cool glance, "Four or five".

"And you didn't think to tell me?"

"We're telling you now."

"Gee, thanks."

"Does Hartshorn know?"

"Of course."

This was wonderful, thought Blackwater. *Absolutely wonderful.*

"Why?" he asked no-one in particular, "am I always the last to know?" He glared at one of his agents, who had entered the room carrying a fully-laden tea-tray. "Is there anything else I don't know?"

The crockery rattled as the agent placed the tray nervously on Blackwater's desk, and glanced behind him at Griffiths and his colleague, who were both hovering in the doorway.

Blackwater groaned. "What now? What fucking else is there? Have they bombed the Horse & Groom?"

Griffiths ventured forwards. "It's Pressdee, guv. He's disappeared."

He had expected a violent reaction from Blackwater, and his expectations were not disappointed. Eventually the volley of abuse died away; when Griffiths opened his eyes again, Blackwater was glaring at him. *Jesus, thought Blackwater, that's all I need. But still -*

"He is under active surveillance?" he asked hopefully.

Griffiths swallowed nervously, and said nothing.

"Tell me someone has checked on him since I had my little chat with him a few weeks back?"

Griffiths maintained his silence.

"He's not even fucking tagged?"

Griffiths looked rather plaintively at Blackwater.

"The only time he goes out is to see the football, rent DVDs or stock up on a few odds and ends at the corner shop. Oh, and he likes to go birdwatching in the close season. Like Mayhew."

"I repeat: he's not even fucking tagged. Jesus Christ, this year they're bringing in tagging for scallies who've nicked crisps from bastard Sainsbury's, so you'd think that we'd have enough reason to tag a fucking alien that, when it's not swanning around as Elvis fucking Presley, bears more than a passing resemblance to a sodding raincloud." He paused, slapped the palm of his hand into his forehead, and glared hard at Griffiths. "Hang on, what am I saying – enough reason? We're not those mincing liberal poofs at the Home Office, we don't come under the Home Detention Curfew scheme – we are MI fucking 13, we outspook the spooks and we do what we fucking well like. And so – he goes to see the football and he likes birdwatching and he isn't fucking tagged? Why?"

Griffiths gave a sidelong glance at his colleagues in the vain hope that one of them might speak in his defence, but both were staring resolutely at their shoes. This was his baby.

"Well, we keep him under obs now and again..."

Blackwater took a deep breath. "You keep him under obs now and again. There's lovely. You know, I would have thought that, well, given that he's an alien, in Leeds, been living there a while, and that now, right, there's another alien – same species, who'd have thought it - also in Leeds, but we're not sure exactly where, well, if you did want to find that second alien, one way of going about it might be to keep closer tabs on the first alien, in case he fancied meeting up with the second alien for a cup of tea and chatting about the old days on the home planet. Just a thought. So why no fucking tag?"

"He never did anything out of the ordinary, guv. Same old routine. Besides, he was like a trustee."

Blackwater exploded. "Trustee? Trustee? What the fucking hell is this, Shawshank fucking Redemption? Has he stuck a great big fucking poster of Rita Hayworth on his wall and been using it to hide the tunnel he's been building for the past twenty years to escape from South Leeds? For fuck's sake!"

"You never told us to tag him," muttered Griffiths defensively. Blackwater stared at him incredulously.

"Because I assumed it was a fucking given, like the sun rising in the morning or bears shitting in the woods: it happens! Sun rises, bears shit in woods, Griff tags a fucking alien. Did I tell you to do it? No. Do I tell you to have a shit in the morning? No. Do I tell you to wipe your arse afterwards? No. I wasn't sent here to deal with pissing kiddywink admin crap like that: that's why *you* were sent here. I was sent up here to pick up the pieces after those two fuckers in the corner nearly started a riot in the LGI and then, once I'd blown smoke up a few NHS arses, to see if I could find a walking corpse. So on those occasions I've asked you in passing, 'Any developments on Pressdee?' I kind of imagined that the replies I was getting were the result of your knowing exactly where he was. Not that you were assuming he might be somewhere within the West

224

fucking Riding."

He turned away dismissively for a moment, and stared out of the window at the frosted lawn beyond, uttering a single, forlorn "fuck". Slowly, deliberately, he turned to face Griffiths once more, staring straight into his eyes; he spoke quietly at first, before building to a furious crescendo.

"About twenty miles down the road, Griff, is a place called Tadcaster. Should be piss easy to get to – go through Guiseley, Yeadon and Horsforth, pick up the 6120 and then take the York Road. Now, someone was telling me the other day about this old brewery they've got there – eighteenth century, he said. Very nice if you like Northern bitter. Anyway, what I want you to do is this: go to that brewery, ring up all your buddies, and say, 'Hey, it's Griff, do you fancy a piss-up?' But hang on a minute: fuck that. Fuck that, because (a) you don't have any friends and (b) you couldn't organise a piss up in a fucking brewery."

By this point Blackwater's face was a deep shade of red; it was also barely an inch from Griffiths's. His hapless deputy trembled, but did not budge.

"If I might interject -"

From the depths of his rage, Blackwater was rudely awakened to the fact that there were other persons present in the vicinity of this particular bollocking. Like a big cat interrupted in its pursuit of a wildebeest, he turned his wrathful visage towards the offending distraction.

Tremaine was regaling him with a reproachful expression, his whole body expressing a combination of disappointment and self-satisfaction. Blackwater was unable to restrain himself.

"No you may not! Fuck off! Fuck right off!"

"Mr Blackwater, I would suggest that given the information that we have provided, you and your operatives should now concentrate on neutralising the Moran girl before focusing on Pressdee."

However, Blackwater wasn't listening to Tremaine's suggestion: he was ranting over it, telling Tremaine that it was his gaffe, he didn't need any input from a skinny ponce and if he (Tremaine) and fat boy didn't fuck off back to Upper Lupton he (Blackwater) would punch their faces out through their fucking arseholes, and he'd follow up by shoving those – gesturing at the various china figurines that adorned the shelves – down their necks so they'd be shitting Royal Doulton for a fucking fortnight, and all the while tearing off his jacket and rolling up his shirt sleeves as if in active preparation for the task he was outlining.

Tremaine held up a hand. "Please don't trouble yourself, Mr Blackwater. Our task is done; our message is delivered. All information that we have gathered on the target and her associates – personal details, photographs etc - is contained within this envelope". He delicately placed said item, plain A4 manila, on Blackwater's desk. "We trust that you will now act as you fit with that information. We will return to Upper Lupton toute suite."

He nodded courteously to Griffiths and the other agents, and smoothly made his way out. Roy Granville made as if to follow him, but paused in the doorway. He spoke thoughtfully, carefully; the tone was genial, but with an edge of steel.

"Thanks for the tea, old cock, and look after yourself. But just one thing before we go – you ever, ever talk to me like that again, and..." For a heavily-built man, Granville moved quickly, without apparent effort. The PPK Browning seemed to materialise in his hand; there was a crack; a figurine shattered.

"Like you said, old cock, we make the rules. Best of luck."

And with that, he was gone.

Blackwater watched them as they made their way, one delicately, one less so, across the tarmac, to their waiting Audi; watched as the car slipped smoothly out of the yard, to the end of the lane and out of site. He was shaken, but did not show it. Inwardly, he was seething. *Fuck Tremaine. Fuck the little big man. He could do this.*

"You okay, guv?" Griff might have just been roasted by Blackwater, but bollockings from Blackwater were part of his job, and he accepted them dutifully, with just the occasional modicum of self-defence. He was no fan of their late guests; they put the wind up him just by being around, let alone when one of them was letting fly with a handgun.

"I'm cool, Griff. Fucking ice cold." Blackwater gave a grim smile. And then, suddenly galvanised into action, he was bellowing instructions, emptying the contents of the envelope onto his desk.

"Right – Harry, break out the containment cylinders, Griff, get on to the liaison bint at SO13, feed her the Real IRA cover story – she'll know it's bullshit, Anti-Terrorism will be asking all sorts of fucking questions but just tell her to hold the line, she knows better than to fuck with us. Besides, she was a good girl over the Manchester and Glasgow raids. Once she's sweet, contact the local Bill and tell them we need a few bodies to man the perimeter – we'll be doing the dirty work, we just need them to stop the residents from blundering into a firefight. Tom –"

But his instructions for Tom died in his throat. There was relatively little documentation within the envelope, unsurprising given that Tremaine's favourite occupation was eliminating paper trails, not creating them. Just a few short notes on each of the residents of 23 Birch Lane, accompanied by a small, passport-sized photograph. Rachel's carried the most annotations; the photograph – as Tremaine had commented – came from the passport of Lisa Smith.

Blackwater stared at the photograph in shock. Although it was a head shot, and most of his attention that evening had featured on points south of those within the photograph, he recognised her immediately.

"Guv?"

"I saw her. A few weeks ago. She works at a clip joint in town. Jesus, I was that close. Fuck!" He banged his fist against the wall in frustration, then shook his head. "Makes no odds, we'll get her today. Griff, can you get onto the letting agency for that house in Birch Lane, tell them we're coming down for a visit – then you and Harry bring the owner in to one of the safe rooms back here."

Griffiths hesitantly raised an eyebrow. It seemed less likely to prompt another bollocking than a straight "Why?"

"Because I want to have the pleasure of telling him that his property is about to have the shit ripped out of it. I want to scare someone, and" – glancing at the Birch Lane notes - "Mr Norman Hardwicke, whoever he is, is in the wrong job at the wrong time. And do you know what? Once we've trapped that fucking bint and Pressdee, we get this Welsh twat Angel and those other fuckers back here and put the shits up them too. I want them so keen to sign the Official Secrets Act they'll crawl over broken glass bollock naked to get to it."

He glared defiantly at them. "Now, fuck Tremaine, get your arses in gear and get on with it!"

They got on with it.

VI

The Audi had not gone far; Granville had parked up in

a layby just outside Menston while Tremaine spoke to Hartshorn on a secure line. It was a short conversation: Tremaine relayed the salient points regarding his meeting with Blackwater, and then listened in silence while Hartshorn issued further instructions. As the call drew to its close, Tremaine nudged Granville, the hint of a smile on his face.

That was enough for Granville: he could read the gist of Tremaine's conversation in that smile. *Blackwater is good, but perhaps not good enough for this; I may need you to tidy up after him.*

Prior to their conversation in Blackwater's office, he had placed a tracking device under the van in the Menston forecourt which would be used in any operations against the rogue Jackson; in the event that the Jackson had been forewarned by Mayhew, and had fled, Blackwater would doubtless follow it in the van. And they would follow Blackwater.

To tidy up.

Granville fondly stroked the handle of the Browning.

CHAPTER SEVENTEEN

I

The house in Birch Lane was a mess. Or, to be precise, even more of a mess than usual. Even prior to Rachel's arrive, when it was arguable that levels of general untidiness had reached their grungy zenith, doors had remained resolutely attached to hinges and carpets to floorboards.

No longer.

The front door had quickly given way, submitting weakly to a few well-aimed kicks from Tom. The bedroom doors – likewise all locked – had lasted little longer, giving the lie to Hardwicke's oft-repeated assertions as to the relative security of his property.

The raid took place to a soundtrack of Elvis's hits, playing on a loop within Chubb's bedroom.

Gone. Fucking gone.

Blackwater had been there at the outset, but as soon as it was clear that his birds had flown, he ordered Harry and Tom to bag anything and everything, and then headed back to Menston with Griffiths. He had a landlord to interrogate.

Norman Hardwicke was a deeply troubled man. Barely had he opened up the office than he had been bundled into the back of an unmarked van, accompanied by several burly men whose conversation had been limited but whose firepower appeared to be considerable. Then van had then driven him to the secluded estate in Menston. His nervous protestations had met with loaded advice that recommended that he keep silent unless spoken to, so Hardwicke had kept schtum. He didn't want that loaded advice to be backed up with loaded guns.

He had been sitting on a small wooden chair in a

230

small windowless room for more than half an hour now: the mug of tea he had been offered on arrival sat untouched on the desk in front of him. He wanted a smoke – needed a smoke, *bloody hell he needed a smoke* – but had left his pipe back at the office.

The door opened and two men entered.

"Mr Hardwicke? I'm Adam Blackwater, Special Branch. This is my colleague, Mike Griffiths."

"Pleased to meet you," muttered Hardwicke, sounding anything but. Blackwater and Griffiths pulled up chairs and sat down opposite him; Blackwater casually tossed a photograph across the desk.

"Recognise her, Mr Hardwicke?"

Hardwicke shakily assented. "That's Rachel Moran. She lives in one of my properties in Scrimpton, on -"

"Since when?"

"Middle of October, I think. Has anything happened to her?"

"You could say that." *Jesus wept*, thought Hardwicke, *the boiler's exploded and she's copped it. I should have got that combi sorted out by Corgi instead of paying Jack Davenport fifty quid for a botch job.*

"Tell me, Mr Hardwicke, what does Ms Moran do?"

"Look lads, I've got no idea. She pays her rent on time, in cash, haven't had any grumbles from the other tenants about her not paying her whack of the utilities…"

"Did you check her references?"

"She paid eight weeks up front instead of six -"

"Let's go back a bit. I asked you, 'Did you check her references?' not 'How many weeks' rent did she give you?' Right, take two: did you check her references?"

"No," said Hardwicke, unhappily.

"OK, so having failed to establish that she was not a psychopath with a history of mental illness and a

231

fondness for chopping off blokes' cocks with a penknife, you let her loose on a bunch of young professional males - "

"Oh God," whimpered Hardwicke.

" – although you did, in all fairness, pocket a few hundred notes in rent. Correct?"

"A penknife?" said Hardwicke in a small voice. Blackwater beamed. In spite of himself, he was enjoying himself hugely.

"Oh, don't worry about your tenants' willies, Mr Hardwicke. They're safe, as least, as far as we know. And she's not a mental case" – Hardwicke relaxed – "if she was, that would be friendly neighbourhood plod, not us. Oh, no, no, no, she's far more dangerous than that" – Hardwicke tensed – "far more dangerous. Would you like to take a guess where all this is leading?"

Hardwicke opened his mouth, then closed it again.

"She's a terrorist, Mr Hardwicke. Real IRA. Sweet as pie to your face, but more than happy to blow your arse off if she needs to. Not that you were in any danger of course – unless you were planning to be in Harvey Nicks next Saturday, and I didn't have you pinned as a Harvey Nicks man."

This time the mouth managed a small, hapless squeak.

"But: don't worry, Mr Hardwicke, the good news is that Harvey Nicks is now safe. All those deluxe goods, all those deluxe shoppers, safe as houses. But while most of those lovely little bogtrotters who were plotting its demise are now sitting in nice little cells in various parts of this country, Lizzy McGrath – Rachel Moran as you know her – is still out and about. Now I know it's unlikely, given your distinct lack of interest in anything about her other than the contents of her purse, but do you know anything that might help us track the

232

little bitch down?"

Hardwicke thought hard. "The lads might know something," he said after a moment. "Gerry Angel, or Gideon, or Roddy McCall…" A terrible thought struck him. "Jesus, he's from Northern Ireland, he's not in on it, is he?"

"Let's just say we're keeping an open mind on that, Mr Hardwicke. We'd love to have a word with the lads, too. Trouble is, they've gone AWOL as well."

"Bloody 'ell."

"My thoughts exactly. Bloody, bloody hell. But in the meantime, Mike's got a few more bits of paper requiring your signature. Because my boys are currently in the process of taking your house apart from top to bottom, and we'd like you're official 'okay' on it. Not that we really give a damn about your signature of course, but the pen-pushers get a bit arsey about it."

"Will this be in the 'papers?" moaned Hardwicke.

Not if I have anything to do with it, thought Blackwater. "Possibly," he demurred.

This was going nowhere, he thought bitterly. *Twat-features knows fuck all. But you didn't really expect him to, did you? You're just doing this 'cause there's sweet FA else you can do at the moment.*

"We'll just get those bits of paper for you, Mr Hardwicke: then you'll be free to go."

They left Hardwicke on the verge of tears. As they shut the door behind them, Griffiths nudged him. "You realise you didn't say 'fuck' once during that interview? I don't know whether to be impressed or disappointed."

"Matey-boy, we don't round those cunts up pronto, you can guarantee that I'll be breaking the 'fuck' count all comers' record."

His mobile bleeped; he snatched at it. "Well?" he demanded.

Within seconds, his mood had lifted considerably. He stared out through the window into the gathering dusk. "Griff, I think we have the bastards."

Back at Birch Lane, Tom and Harry were running for their van, Harry still clutching a recent copy of the *Yorkshire Post* left in Macko's room, in which its recent occupant had helpfully encircled an advertisement feature in thick black biro and annotated it with several large asterisks.

MI13 was heading for the Elland Social Club.

II

The sun rises over Ilkley Moor some six or so minutes later than at Bempton Cliffs; thus, as Graham Mayhew was exchanging pleasantries with Granville and Tremaine, the first light of morning was picking out the rocky outcrops that dotted the moor's stark, unforgiving landscape: great, carved flat-top boulders at Woodhouse Crag, the Hangingstone Rocks at Ilkley Quarry; picking out a Mini and a Focus parked up in a layby; picking out a young man and woman, huddled together for warmth and solace, staring out over the quarry as the frozen village below emerged from the shadows of pre-dawn.

His voice breaking with emotion, Gerry had passed on Mayhew's message. There had been a brief, stunned silence, broken by a harsh scream from Rachel; Gerry had swayed, staggered and would have fallen had Laura and Macko not supported him.

It had been Ellis who had finalised their plans, galvanised them into action. *We need to go*, he urged them, *we need to go now*. They had packed the bare essentials – passports, a change of clothes, a few personal effects, nothing more – and bundled them into the back of the two cars. It is true, there were several

234

brief, heated and occasionally hysterical exchanges during this procedure, most notably when Macko sought to justify the inclusion of his favourite pornographic magazines as essential items: Laura objected vociferously on the grounds of taste, Gerry of the questionable legality of several of their number; to the latter objection Macko responded heatedly that if he was going to get thrown in the nick then possession of a few Dutch jazz mags would probably feature well down the charge sheet in relation to aiding and abetting a wanted alien, and to the former that given the distinct probability that he could end up dead after all this then at least he'd like the opportunity to get in a few wanks over quality material in the meanwhile. In the end, Macko reluctantly pared down his premier selection from twenty or so magazines to a pair of well-thumbed copies of *Razzle*, and they were ready to depart.

Mayhew's valedictory message had also obliged Rachel to revise her own plans for the following day. It was far too dangerous, Ellis told her, to attend the game; agents apprised of her description would certainly be posted at all main entrances. Unhappily, she had to admit to herself that he was right. He remained adamant that he would perform that evening: this was a decision about which Rachel was far less certain and even more unhappy. Furthermore, with the exception of Chubb and to a lesser extent Macko, her companions were of like mind. Nevertheless, despite their various misgivings, they acquiesced, if only in Rachel's case because she realised that she had increasingly come to depend upon her assorted housemates to evade capture.

Ellis and Chubb had travelled with Laura in the Mini, Macko and Rachel with Gerry in the Focus. Pausing only to take a brief detour to Laura's flat to enable her to collect her things, they headed further north – their route unwittingly taking them within a couple of hundred yards of MI13's temporary outpost in Menston – passing through Otley before holing up for the night in a carpark on the edge of the moorland.

The last time Gerry had spent the night in his car had been five years previously at a rock festival: then, it had been the height of summer, his senses had been numbed by half a dozen pints of Old Hookey and he had had the additional, pleasurable distraction occasioned by the presence of a nubile and eager young lady in the passenger seat, whom he had met for the first time all of two hours earlier and whom – to his immense and lasting regret – he would bid farewell to for the first and last time the following morning. On this occasion, he lacked the comforts of either alcohol or sexual activity; worse, he had to put up with the sounds of Macko's brief and abortive attempts at re-engagement with Rachel – which, to his relief and amusement, were brusquely and firmly rebuffed – and subsequently, a prolonged, insistent duet of snoring from his passengers, inevitably accompanied by sporadic farts of varying volume and pungency.

Despite putting on a spare pullover under his overcoat, and despite tucking a duvet around himself for additional protection against the biting cold, sleep came but fitfully and for no more than a few minutes at a time. As he cursed silently at the unseemly overture of nocturnal rumblings from behind him, he was faced with the growing realisation that the one person he really, really wanted to be sharing the darkness with was currently attempting to sleep in the front of the adjacent vehicle.

Shortly before eight, his latest attempt at slumber was disturbed by a light tapping at the window. It was Laura. He opened the door a crack, and was immediately hit by a blast of chill air.

236

"Fancy a stroll?"

"Sure."

He eased himself stiffly from the duvet's bulk and out of the door; there were a few vague, muted mumbles of protest from the back seats at the disturbance, but they were already subsiding as he closed the door on them. Laura extended her hand and he gratefully took it.

Hesitantly at first because of the darkness, they made their way across the moorland, their feet crunching through the frozen grass and heather. Neither spoke until they reached the overhang, at which point they halted and Laura observed, with a forced cheerfulness, that it was fuckin' cold. Gerry turned to look at her in despair.

"What the fuck have we got ourselves into?" he whispered. She squeezed his hand tighter.

"It's just – all I ever wanted was to carry on in academia for the rest of my life, you know? Steady job, not too much grief, bit of lecturing, publish the odd paper, have plenty of time left for a few beers. I didn't want all this – I didn't want to get anybody killed."

"He might not be -"

"He's dead, Laura."

"Even if he is, babes – you didn't get him killed."

"If he hadn't met up with me, they wouldn't have made the connection." She didn't answer; both were trembling.

"We used to go out walking together, you know? We both liked birds."

In spite of her inner turmoils, she couldn't stop herself. "Don't all blokes?"

"Ha-bloody-ha. Not heard that one before."

And he held her close and kissed her, as the sun rose over the tor.

III

They remained at the overhang for half an hour or so, before turning back towards the cars. En route, Gerry's attention was caught by a flurry of movement in the sky to his left, accompanied by a series of harsh, staccato calls: a flock of forty, perhaps fifty grey-brown thrushes had wheeled past; they settled on the moor a hundred yards behind them, back towards the quarry.

"What are they?" asked Laura.

"Fieldfare," replied Gerry. "Probably over from Scandinavia."

"Do you get many birds out here this time of year?"

"Dunno – bit bleak to be honest. Should be busier in summer."

"It is." Ellis was making his way towards them. "I've only been up here a couple of times, and always with a minder close by, but I've seen meadow pipits, curlew, golden plover, swallows, swifts – even a merlin over that way the second time. Heard a cuckoo, too, but didn't see him."

"Only time I ever saw a cuckoo was when I was a kid. Young one. In a wagtail's nest."

"Really?" Ellis was intrigued. "Where was that?"

"In Wales. On some farmland near Usk. My mate's dad was the farmer and he found the nest."

"Now that I would love to have seen." Ellis sighed. "But I guess I ain't gonna have the opportunity in future."

IV

They spent much of the day in the countryside to the north of Leeds, skirting the outlying villages, wary of encountering police in case their descriptions had already been circulated. In mid-morning Gerry parked up the Focus in woodland near Grassington, while Laura ventured out in the Mini in search of sustenance: she returned an hour later, the back seat laden with brown paper bags bearing the McDonald's logo.

"It was that or KFC", she explained apologetically.

Ellis drew Rachel aside. "Rather apt that my final meal should be hamburgers", he whispered.

"Stop it," she hissed. "I really don't want to think about it."

They munched on Big Macs, while *The Sun Sessions CD* played softly in the background.

As dusk fell, they left the woodland, heading south towards the city. Towards Ellis' first and last gig.

First, however, Ellis had requested the briefest of detours.

V

The previous year, a statue had been erected outside the South Stand. Arms aloft in celebration, fists clenched, its face bore an impish, joyous grin. A short-sleeved football shirt clung to the muscular torso, seemingly drenched in the sweat of a tireless performance within the game in question.

This was the likeness of William John "Billy" Bremner, a tough, uncompromising footballer, but so much more than that. Born in Stirling, Bremner had signed for Leeds United in 1959 as a schoolboy and made his first team debut the following year. A prodigiously gifted midfielder, he had played for the club for sixteen years and captained it for eight of them, a stocky powerhouse at the heart of a team that won two League Championships and come tantalisingly close to several more in that time. Bremner personified that team; Leeds loved him.

Ellis stared at the statue through the evening gloom.

239

"I never saw him play, you know," he said. "Not in the flesh. You see, he'd moved onto Hull when I arrived here, and they weren't in the same division as Leeds at the time. Most of the players I'd watched on the recordings had gone by then: Gordon McQueen and Joe Jordan had left for Manchester United; Norman Hunter was at Bristol City; Johnny Giles was playing Irish league football." He paused. "Actually, thinking about it, there were a few left – Lorimer, Eddie Gray, Madeley. Eddie Gray, he was a good player."

Impulsively, Gideon hugged him.

Pressdee smiled at the pale, plump face pressed to his chest. "What's that for?"

"You were *my* hero."

Macko snorted. "I still say Bremner was a dirty bastard."

"We need to get a move on." Gerry was fretting. "All very well you saying your goodbyes here, Ellis, but we need to get to the social club. Too risky this close to Elland Road."

Pressdee nodded. "Agreed. Let's go."

He saluted the statute and turned smartly on his heel.

VI

The club was barely a couple of hundred yards from the ground. A squat, red-brick affair, built more than sixty years before with an emphasis on functionality rather than aesthetics, it sat apart from a few neighbouring buildings in an expanse of concrete. An arch above the main entrance was the only concession to form beyond the square and rectangular. Most of the windows had been boarded up; behind the few that remained were thin, cotton curtains. The paint on the door panels was faded and had peeled quite badly; there were a few

240

almost apologetic attempts at graffiti on the walls, most of which – to judge from the names of the footballers under discussion – appeared to date from a least a decade previously.

And yet, for all the sense of dilapidation around the periphery, the building had survived, solidly, resolutely, a defiant oasis of parochialism where its members could slowly sup subsidised ale in an atmosphere drenched in tobacco. Beyond its walls, the twentieth century was passing away in a riotous heady mix of jungle and happy hardcore; the certainties of Northern socialism, coldly battered by the Thatcherite eighties, were now being questioned and rejected by a government anxious to distance itself from the movement which had birthed it.

But within those walls – well, they had no truck with progressive politics and the Third Way, or with That Bloody Racket that the kids listened to. There was One Way – Their Way – and to hell with Blair, let alone the Tories. There was good beer (well, cheap beer), and they could sit, and sup, and smoke, and put the world to rights, and that was enough. And one night a week their wives would file in, and there would be bingo, and either a comedian or a spot of live music – proper music, mind you. Tony Christie had played there a few years back, and the Dooleys, and Brotherhood of Man; they'd even had Ken Dodd back in the day. Nowadays it was mostly tribute acts: two weeks ago someone had done a turn as Engelbert Humperdinck. And tonight, ladies and gentlemen, it was Elvis. Or, to be precise, Elvises.

VII

Derek Groves had been in this game a long time. He had started on the Northern circuit in the early sixties and had taken to it like a duck to water; always brash and cocky, his combination of a quick, nimble mind, easy patter and the thickest of skins served him well. Within a couple of years, the spots had become regular enough for him to jack in his day job down the pit; by the early seventies, he was playing venues like the Opera House in Blackpool and The Embassy, Bernard Manning's club in Manchester; he would pop up on TV now again with occasional slots on *The Comedians* or the *Wheeltappers and Shunters*. Oh, Derek Groves was good alright. But not quite good enough.

Sure, the seventies had given him a nice big house in Crosspool, and a pretty young wife, and a few pretty young mistresses, and money to blow on the horses; but then the seventies turned into the eighties, and the golden age was passing; the pretty young wife grew older and wiser and found out about the pretty young mistresses, and soon she was gone, along with the nice big house in Crosspool; and he no longer played the Opera House or the Embassy. And though the spots at the bigger venues began to dry up, he still blew the money on the horses, even though the money wasn't there to blow. And, one by one, the pretty young mistresses found other beds to sleep in, until at last Derek was left with just his debts and his bitterness for company.

But still he had ploughed on, a minor celebrity in the lower leagues of comedy. One night a month here, another night there. These days he typically worked three or four nights a week, fifty quid a time, cash in hand, plus beer and a bit of grub. Tell a few gags, warm up the audience, introduce the headline act – not the main act, because (in Derek's eyes at least) he was the main act – and come back on at the end to finish with a song.

The club was filling up nicely: the usual, solid

clientele was being augmented by a host of Elvis aficionados, along with friends and family of the various Elvises that were performing that evening. Derek nodded to himself in approval; good to perform in front of a full house, good to have a bit of atmosphere.

"Evening Frank".

The drawn, etiolated face of the club's manager beamed at him, displaying a set of ill-fitting dentures. "Good to 'ave you back Derek."

"Been a few months."

"Aye." Frank sucked thoughtfully and noisily on his dentures.

"You're getting a decent crowd in tonight."

"Aye."

"Who's the ringer tonight?"

"Bert."

"Christ, Bert Brennan! Where d'ya dig that old bugger up?"

"Rochdale." Frank stared into the middle distance and resumed his work on his dentures for a moment. Then, almost as an afterthought: "Good voice, though, Bert."

"Oh, aye, lovely voice. Should go down a treat." He reached into his pocket for a cigarette and lit up; the hubbub in the body of the club was growing steadily, a rich and raucous combination of tones, a rising backdrop to the insistent, high pitch wheeze of lips on dentures at his side.

"Anyone else I should know about?"

"Do you remember Jack Turnbull – came third when we had last Buddy Holly night last year?"

"Tall, skinny bloke – port wine stain on his face?"

"That's him." Suck.

"He wasn't bad."

"It's his brother." Suck. "Heard him sing the other

week." Suck. "He's shit."

Derek breathed heavily, attempting to mask his irritation. "What about the others?"

"Couple of local lads, a lass who's come down from York, a Jap and an older fella. Actually looks..." The sucking became more ferocious for a moment. "Looks, well, like you'd expect Elvis to have looked if he'd kept off the burgers."

Derek grunted. "Well, it's good to have a lookey-likey, just hope he can sing a bit. What's his name?"

Frank smiled. "You'll like this. John Burrows."

"Nice touch. Like it."

VIII

The music faded away, and a jovial voice welcomed ladies and gentlemen to the Elland Social Club, and to a very special evening of Elvis in Your Eyes; and here's your host for tonight's show, please put your hands together for Mr Derek Groves!

The audience duly provided some suitably vigorous applause, and the curtain parted to reveal a somewhat crudely constructed thematic backdrop incorporating a pastiche of blown-up photographs of Elvis together with pictures of guitars, cadillacs and – somewhat unfortunately – hamburgers.

"How ya keepin'?" inquired Groves of the audience, and then, duly satisfied by the content roar they returned, proceeded to engage in some badinage with various members, asking an elderly gentleman on a table near the stage whether it had been cold in the ground that morning, and asking him to remember Groves to Tommy Trinder when he got back; opining of a well-preserved lady in her early sixties that she'd probably flattened some grass in her time; and of a particularly tall, muscular man sitting behind Gerry that

244

if that big bugger says its Sunday, it's fucking Sunday.

They were old shots, but Derek's timing was good, and the audience lapped it up. After a few more choice insults – including asking a bemused Chubb, to general hilarity, whether he'd started wanking yet – Groves fired off a handful of gags, before proceeding to the matter of the contest.

"And now, ladies and gentlemen, the moment you've all been waiting for – well, at least that miserable bugger over there, he can't wait for me to piss off – it's Elvis in Your Eyes!"

There was enthusiastic applause from the floor, together with assorted hoots and wolf-whistles. Derek strode from the stage in the direction of the bar, passing Frank, who was fumbling inexpertly with the controls of a rented karaoke machine. To Frank's relief, his cautious ministrations soon resulted in several LEDs flickering into life and, more pertinently, the opening bars of 'Jailhouse Rock'. In response, a burly man in his late thirties bounded on from the wings: he was clad in a black-and-white hooped T-shirt topped by a loose denim jacket and his shaven head was obscured by an ill-fitting plastic quiff.

(Further, vociferous applause from half a dozen equally burly gentlemen towards the rear of the hall.)

The first Elvis bellowed away, with no more than a passing acquaintance to pitch or key.

Jailhouse Rock is bloody fitting, thought Frank. *That bugger did six months in Armley nick not long back.*

IX

On arriving at the venue, Ellis had been ushered into a small room to the right of the stage, within which milled various interpretations of The King: in addition to the burly Jailhouse Rock incarnation who was now

245

bawling and bouncing in front of the audience, there was a younger man with a substantial paunch clad in a jumpsuit similar to Ellis's own; a tall, stick-thin guy, dressed as an American serviceman from the fifties; a sturdy brunette, forty or thereabouts, wearing a white dress that started start half-way down her considerable bosom and ended just below the knicker-line, together with a pair of thigh length boots and a scarlet cape; a Japanese gentleman, small and slim, wallowing in a gold lame suit several sizes too large for him; and, lounging nonchalantly in the doorway, a short, stocky man in early-middle age, heavily tanned and home to a colony of sovereign rings and gold bracelets: he was wearing a silk Hawaiian shirt and a garland of paper flowers.

Frank had bustled up to Ellis, proffering a list of the tracks that lurked within the depths of the karaoke machine, several of which had been claimed by the other participants and had therefore been excised by Frank's red marker pen: he was also advised that there was a Mr Appleyard from Keighley in the audience who had asked can we please not do "Love Me Tender" as it had just been played at his dad's funeral and it upsets his mam.

Ellis had nodded vaguely at this, but his attention was elsewhere; was within himself. *He's breaking through*, he thought to himself. *He's breaking*

His hand gripped the microphone so tight that his knuckles whitened; he rocked backwards and forwards on the balls of his feet, legs trembling, knees knocking together; behind him, he could dimly sense Scotty and Bill, sharing his fear. As he stared out at the sea of faces crammed into Overton Park, he glanced down at the guitar, saw his hand playing that first chord – an A – heard himself kicking into "That's Alright, Mama". Heard the hollerin' begin.

246

X

The first Elvis completed his raucous performance to a reception that was noticeably most enthusiastic from the small and burly contingent at the rear. He was followed by the diminutive Japanese gentleman – introduced as Mr Osaki - who bowed politely to the assembly and launched tunelessly but vociferously into "Love Me Tender." Several rows back, an elderly lady burst into tears, subsequent to which a bald, thickset man of medium height addressed several colourful lines to a bemused Mr Osaki before scrambling through and over the Elvis-loving throng and hurling the hapless impersonator to the ground.

Following a brief hiatus, during which Mr Appleyard was hauled away to the entrance by two members of the burly entourage to – as one of them put it – "get a bit of fookin' air", Mrs Appleyard was comforted by several sympathetic neighbours in the audience, and Mr Osaki was helped to the kitchen so that various minor abrasions could be addressed in private, the evening's scheduled entertainments continued. The sturdy brunette belted out a decent cover of "Viva Las Vegas"; the stick-thin guy, a reedy attempt at "GI Blues"; the younger man with the paunch, an energetic pass at "All Shook Up" which culminated in his inadvertently finishing the piece on his backside following a failed attempt at some end-of-number acrobatics. *Still*, thought Frank, *it got them cheering. Unlike Joe bloody Sushi earlier on.*

Then came Bert Brennan, the short, middle-aged man in the Hawaiian shirt. Many in the audience knew Bert well; he acknowledged the cheers and applause with a laconic wave. He composed himself, cleared his throat, and selected a lady of advancing years in the front row as the first recipient of his brooding,

247

permatanned smoulder.

She squealed with delight; "Are You Lonesome Tonight" kicked in on the karaoke machine; Bert Brennan crooned and smouldered, sometimes both at the same time; more elderly ladies coloured and wilted in the face of this assault upon their senses. Even Mrs Appleyard forgot herself enough to utter an appreciative squeak.

Two rows in front of Mrs Appleyard, Chubb sniffed dismissively. *Good, but not a patch on Elvis*, he thought. Macko, sitting between Chubb and Laura, was more uneasy.

"He's a bit classy, this bastard," he muttered to Gerry, who had been obliged to find a seat at a table behind them and was crammed in between two portly ladies from Cleckheaton who were both entranced by the grey-haired, bronzed Adonis on the stage.

"I'm sure Ellis will be fine," muttered Gerry.

"I'm not," Macko responded. "He hasn't sung for twenty years. He might come out sounding like Leonard Cohen."

Gerry began to reply, but a look from one of the Cleckheaton duo suggested that silence would be the best option, at least until the vision of loveliness had departed the stage.

Climactically, lip trembling, Brennan inquired whether his audience's heart was filled with pain, and whether, dear, it was lonesome tonight: in response, the hall rose, somewhat arthritically but enthusiastically, to its feet. Brennan held the pose, smouldered for a while longer, then strode from the stage to a rapturous ovation.

"Fuckin' hell," muttered Macko.

248

XI

"Who's on next?" Derek asked of Frank.

"That Burrows fella."

Groves returned to the stage as the applause for Brennan gradually died away. "Well, that was truly amazing, ladies and gentlemen. Bert Brennan, what can I say?" He paused. "Did you nick that shirt off of Tom Selleck?"

To his annoyance, the laughter was relatively muted. "Anyway, many thanks to Bert for that. Now, we've got just one more act this evening, his first time at the Elland Social Club – John Burrows!"

Derek left the stage, smiling to himself. Several in the audience also recognised the pseudonym; there were a few appreciative laughs accompanying the applause.

Hesitantly, Ellis moved forwards to the front of the stage. He stared nervously at the expectant faces ahead of him, gripped the microphone so tight

That his knuckles whitened; he rocked backwards and forwards on the balls of his feet, legs trembling, knees knocking together.

And Elvis sang.

CHAPTER EIGHTEEN

I

From the very first, they sat transfixed by the performance, the intensity of the drama that was unfolding before them. As the first bars emerged from the Karaoke machine, Gerry had laughed, shaking his head in amusement: how could it be anything else?

Elvis was caught in a trap and couldn't get out.

Then he, Macko, Chubb, Laura, Groves, Frank, Brennan, the assorted other Elvises and their acolytes, even Rachel – all were swept up and along in the manifestation of his returning mastery. The intense, amused gaze, the restless but assured strolling across the stage, the controlled gesture, the voice – God, the voice! – carried them from a dingy, down-at-heel hall in southern Leeds to some international arena half-imagined from their collective yesteryears.

Ellis had disappeared, wholly subsumed beneath the life force that had burst forth from its slumber. There was only Elvis.

At the bridge he knelt entranced, his eyes closed, his focus on some distant place or time; temporarily oblivious to the audience, he seemed to be forcing the words from the very heart of his being. Then, as he gradually increased the tempo after the bridge, the sweat pouring from his brow, he, the audience and the song were as one again.

As he struck a flamboyant pose and his climactic, guttural snarls died away, the hall erupted. It had been building to a crescendo throughout the song, its emotions desperate for release. It was on its feet, applauding, screaming, shouting.

Hollerin'.

Macko was punching the air in exultation, Chubb

was weeping, tears of joy streaming down his plump cheeks; Laura turned and looked at Gerry in disbelief. She said something to him but he couldn't hear the words, there was too much of a racket going on. So he just grinned and nodded, and all around them the aficionados were abuzz, shaking their heads, laughing in delirious amazement.

Nailed it. Nailed it. But where

He stared around him at the unfamiliar surroundings, puzzled, as if awakening from a dream. *Not Vegas, not Hawaii. Where was Colonel? He needed Colonel.*

But he was already receding, dissipating as Ellis re-emerged; "You're a fantastic audience," he mumbled, swaying slightly, guiltily acknowledging the applause that belonged to another.

II

It was a cold night, bitterly cold; even the van offered scant protection to Blackwater, who sat shivering in the passenger seat, swaddled in his cashmere overcoat. Next to him, Harry was watching the entrance to the club through a pair of binoculars; behind him, he could hear the muffled bumps and thumps, punctuated by whispered curses, as Tom shuffled around in the back of the van, attempting to prime the cylinders by the light of a torch that had promised more than it ultimately delivered. Griffiths was out there somewhere, laying down the guidelines to the armed response unit teams which had followed the van in three unmarked cars from Menston and which had now taken up positions in the side streets beyond the club; Blackwater gave a wry smile as he recalled Griffiths's rather desperate dissembling earlier that afternoon as he briefed the teams on the two terrorists within and yes, one of them will be dressed as Elvis; unfortunately, so will quite a few other guys.

His brief reverie was interrupted by a hesitant tap on the window. He wound down the window, now heavily steamed up, to reveal Griffiths, nervously biting his lip.

"Wassup Griff? Are the goons cool?"

"It's not that, it's…"

"Bit brisk this evening, Mr Blackwater."

Blackwater was out of the car in a flash, staring with unfettered hatred at Tremaine.

"What the fuck are you doing here? This is my baby."

Tremaine smiled coldly. "Given the rather unfortunate events this afternoon, Mr Hartshorn felt that you might require some assistance. We have a backup cylinder in the car which I will operate. Mr Granville will assist you in securing the building."

I'm being pushed aside. Hartshorn's fucking pushing me aside. Inwardly reeling, he managed to hold it together. He shrugged, muttering, "Fuck it, whatever", then leaned across Tremaine and whispered viciously into his ear.

"Listen to me, you backsliding little poof. If you'd kept me in the loop from the minute you started keeping tabs on Mayhew we wouldn't be in this shit. We'd have raided the house two or three days earlier, got the girl, stuck Taffy and his mates in the slammer for a day or two, got them to sign the Act like good little boys, and picked up Pressdee at his flat, all done, all lovely Jubbly. Instead we have a situation where the Jacksons are rubbing shoulders with around a hundred coffin dodgers and assorted Elvis nuts crammed into a social club. Which is a little fucking difficult to manage if you don't mind me saying so. We are on the point of packing heat in an environment where the primary occupation is waiting to die. All it needs is one granny to have a seizure and – whoopee fucking do – the Jacksons can jump ship. 'Fuck Elvis,' he'll say, 'Mrs Murgatroyd from Otley will do for the time being'. And suddenly, while Mrs Murgatroyd is writhing on the deck under alien possession in full view of several dozen pensioners, we're firing something at her that looks rather like a fucking ugly gun, and which will stop her writhing forever. In short, matey boy, we have a potential shit storm on our hands. So if Mr Hartshorn feels I need assistance, I feel obliged to point out that I need assistance because you've fucked things up for me. Just remember that when you're oiling your arse up later on."

He tapped Tremaine on the shoulder in mock affection, and began to turn away when Tremaine reached out and held him, gently but irresistibly by the arm. Now he in turn leaned in close to Blackwater.

"Your objections are noted, Mr Blackwater. Very well put, if I might say. But, to be perfectly candid – and I'm sure you'll appreciate these sentiments – it really doesn't matter what you say, because you really don't matter."

He moved back, his grip on Blackwater's arm transforming instantaneously, effortlessly into a handshake. "Excellent, Mr Blackwater," he said loudly, "Just get the teams into position and we'll follow you in."

In the shadows behind him, Granville was leaning against a wall, meditatively stroking the handle of the Browning.

You have your targets, Roy.

III

"Ladies and gentlemen, we have the results."

The raucous reception had gradually died away. The

Elvises were now all assembled in a line across the stage, Brennan fixing Ellis with a gaze within which incredulity, respect and loathing were all equally apportioned.

At the microphone, Derek Groves was sweating almost as profusely as the stage's previous incumbent. Even as he had risen to acclaim Elvis, he was painfully aware that the performance had left him with a rather delicate problem, one which would require all the chutzpah he could muster.

"In third place, Anna Riley."

(Whoops from the York contingent at the rear of the hall. The statuesque, busty Elvis came forward to receive her prize.)

"In second place, John Burrows."

A shocked silence. Groves quickly moved on, even as Ellis rose with a wry smile on his face.

"But the winner of tonight's Elvis In Your Eyes – Bert Brennan!"

There was a low rumble of discontent from the floor. That, for the staid citizens of the club, signified a declaration of disgust at the verdict. Above it rose a single voice, with a pained, exasperated, "For fuck's sake!" from their midst. Two hundred pairs of eyes turned in unison at Macko; two hundred faces whose expressions were struggling to reconcile tacit approval of the sentiments with disapproval at the way they had been expressed. Macko, unhappy at the lack of a more robust response on the part of the audience, was all for knocking a few heads together for want of a better solution, but his eagerness to begin an affray was diminished by Gerry placing a restraining arm on his shoulder, and (which was perhaps most telling), Laura grabbing his crotch through his trousers and informing him in a pointed whisper that if he so much as moved an inch his bollocks were history. For the present, he backed down, scowling.

Ellis had meanwhile shuffled awkwardly to the front of the stage and was receiving his runners-up cheque from Groves.

"You were good, old fella. Not quite good enough, like, but bloody good."

Ellis acknowledged the compliments with a curt nod. But his attention was drawn to activity at the front of the hall, where a handful of newcomers had filed in. All in suits with open neck shirts, one pulling a suitcase behind him. One, slightly shorter than the rest, was gesticulating urgently to the others.

Not now, thought Ellis, wearily. *Not yet.*

He managed to catch Gerry's eye, to warn him of the impending danger, but Gerry failed to recognise the nuance of his expression, assuming that Ellis was merely exhausted after the performance.

Behind Ellis, Brennan was accepting first prize with a forced smile for the social club photographer. Still smiling, he inquired quietly of Groves as to what the fuck he thought he was playing at by bringing in a fucking Yank pro, and making him, Bert Brennan, look like a total cunt in the process.

"I knew fuck all about him," protested Groves, from behind the beaming expression of a benevolent compere.

"Last time I play this shithole," replied Brennan, who waved to the audience and strode off towards the bar.

IV

Blackwater and his agents had been at the door when the applause had begun; thus, it had taken some fairly prolonged and hefty knocking before Frank was alerted to their presence. Thirty seconds later, after Blackwater had flashed some ID in his direction before attempting to explain, as succinctly as possible, that he and his boys were about to take down some terrorists holed up within the club, all the while gently directing his gaze in the vicinity of the armed response unit, Frank was suitably terrified and looked it.

As the agents bundled past him, his legs gave way and he sank down inside the entrance lobby.

Bloody roll on, he thought. *Last time but one we had a lookey-likey do, we had a fight between a Cliff Richards and two Roy Orbisons. Now we've got terrorist Elvises.*

He barely noticed as two more men – both tall, one fair and slim, the other darker and heavily-built, slipped past him into the club.

V

The ceremony completed, the audience began to disperse around the club, most heading with steadfast determination for the bar. Others, however, milled around those performers who remained. Unsurprisingly, Ellis was the focal point of much attention, not least from the substantial charms and figure of Ms Riley, who was anxious to impress upon him the potential of a Mr & Mrs Elvis double act featuring their good selves, and was also – along with several female members of the audience whose age spanned an age spectrum of fifty to eighty five – keen to ascertain what he would be doing for the rest of the evening, and whether any of them would have the opportunity of featuring prominently in those plans.

Ellis barely heard them; barely registered their presence. He was staring out over their heads at the agents. Two were lounging against the far wall; a third was removing a metallic object from the suitcase, confirming his suspicions as to its contents. Blackwater was making his way, with difficulty, through the massed ranks of those demanding pints of milds and a sherry for the missus.

"Mr Blackwater."

Ellis spoke loudly, deliberately, more as a warning to his colleagues than as an acknowledgement to the newcomer. Despite the raucous hubbub around the bar, despite the Elvis medley which had begun playing on the club's antiquated sound system immediately after the ceremony, his warning reached its target audience, with varying effects. Rachel screamed and ducked under the table; Macko and Laura rocketed from their seats like pheasants startled in the brush; Gerry and Chubb – who had both been vying with Ellis's new-found groupies to congratulate him – instinctively moved to protect the older man, in Chubb's case burrowing through the serried ranks of mature femininity to clutch Ellis tightly to him, seeking to stand between Blackwater and his prey. At these reactions, the attentions of the club were quickly focused on the newcomer, attentions which were almost universally hostile.

Blackwater cursed inwardly. The groundwork for the nightmare scenario he had painstakingly outlined to Tremaine was progressing nicely. As one of the burly acolytes of the evening's first Elvis faced up to him with a demeanour that suggested that the nature of any debate would quickly take on a distinctly physical aspect, he held up a hand.

"We are armed police officers", he began. Helpfully, Harry and Tom backed up his claim at this point by producing revolvers. Griffiths was also now close behind him, cylinder in hand.

"Please remain calm and move aside in an orderly fashion" he continued, more in hope than expectation, reaching for his own firearm. He was not surprised at the outbreak of gasps and screams that greeted the appearance of the weapons; to his relief, however, most of the audience cleared a path for him: his would-be assailant paled at the sight of Blackwater's Glock and backed off.

Most of the audience. While Ellis's would-be paramours had relinquished their respective claims on his person following Blackwater's pronouncements and were now heading for the exits, Chubb and Gerry stood fast, blocking his way. Gerry glared at Blackwater.

"Is this how it ends, Mr Blackwater? Are you going to kill us to get to Ellis?"

Blackwater regarded him with amusement. "I don't want it to have to come to that, Gerry."

"Where's Graham?"

Blackwater paused; the answer was supplied from the doorway.

"There was an accident." Tremaine was lounging against the wall, cylinder in hand. Blackwater shot him a look of pure hatred as Gerry exploded with fury.

"An accident. A fucking accident!"

For the first time, Blackwater appeared troubled. "That wasn't my bag," he said awkwardly.

Gerry turned his attention to the audience, most of whom had done their utmost to move as far away from Blackwater and the agents as the confines of the club permitted.

"Do you want to know who these guys really are?" he demanded of them. "What they really do? Because they sure as hell are not the police."

"That's enough, Angel". Gerry began to protest, but Blackwater was tiring of the game. "I said that's enough!" The Glock was now levelled at Gerry's chest. Ignoring the momentarily quietened Gerry, Blackwater turned his attention to Ellis who stood impassively

258

behind the considerable shield of Gideon Chubb.

"Game's up, Pressdee. Gerry, fat boy, step away from Elvis."

"Move away, Gerry. I've had a good run. Time to end it."

Gerry looked in surprise at Ellis, made as if to protest, but Ellis shook his head. Reluctantly, Gerry moved to one side.

But still Chubb clung to him, defiant to the last. He had only just rediscovered his hero; he was not going to let him go lightly.

"You too, Gideon."

"I'm not going to let them take you!"

Ellis leaned down to him and whispered in his ear. "This body's dying, Gideon. Elvis is dying. But we can still save Rachel. Keep to the plan."

"But I want to save you as well!"

"Hear what I said, fat boy?" Blackwater's Glock was now trained on Chubb. "Move away. Griff, whenever you've got a clear sight of the target..."

But Griff never got a clear sight of the target, because Chubb was running at him, reaching into his coat, brandishing the stubby pen knife, screaming in the frenzy of despair.

VI

The penknife had been a fourteenth birthday gift from an uncle with a penchant for Richmal Crompton and Frank Richards, and who was convinced that what schoolboys in the 1980s needed were tools to equip them for the rigours of a robust outdoor existence, climbing trees, birdnesting, firing catapults and air pistols at cats, dogs and – if the opportunity presented itself – other children. He had reckoned not only without a general shift in public mores which was

259

rather less inclined to dismiss a few well-aimed pellets as youthful exuberance and more likely to call in social services, but also his nephew's resolutely sedentary, solitary and agoraphobic nature.

It was an elegant piece of craftsmanship, stainless steel and embossed with the maker's name; Chubb had mechanically acknowledged the gift, and then tossed it carelessly into a drawer in his bedroom cabinet, where it had joined other – in Chubb's view – extraneous offerings such as deodorants and hair gel. When Chubb finally left the family home on a semi-permanent basis and moved into the room on Birch Lane, the contents of the drawer had come with him, not necessarily because he wanted them but because his parents had politely but firmly insisted that now their son and heir was flying the nest, they wanted to do a spot of redecorating and reconfiguring of his room: they impressed on him that it would always be a room for him to come back to, but, well, he would have his own room at Birch Lane now... What was left unsaid was the consensus between Chubb *mere et pere* that their son's room was not so much in need of a spring clean as a wholesale decontamination; as with the abode of a heavy smoker, where the very walls become infused with tobacco smoke, so too Chubb's room had taken on the rich essence of its owner over the past decade.

So the penknife had gone with him, along with the other unregarded objects, and had found a home in a new bottom drawer; had continued to be unregarded for the next three years, until the previous evening, when something had clicked in Chubb's head, and he had remembered it, tracked it down, and tucked it into a jacket pocket. On the off-chance.

And here, in the smoky, stunned silence of the club, before the levelled weaponry of the agents, its time had come.

260

But then the shot rang out and Chubb was falling to the ground.

CHAPTER NINETEEN

I

Mayhem. People were screaming, running; most for the exits, some (including Macko and a second powerfully-built associate of the evening's first Elvis) were running at Granville; Laura was running to the aid of Chubb; Gerry and Blackwater simply stared at one another, open mouthed. Griffiths was bawling into his radio for backup and at Harry to seal the doors. Granville loosed off a second bullet, winging the second associate, who fell with a volley of squealed curses.

Rachel was nowhere to be seen.

In the midst of the chaos, an oasis of calm that was Tremaine, coolly levelling the cylinder at Ellis.

Ellis stared at him for an instant, then dismissively turned away to look at Chubb, a crumpled, flabby heap on the floor, the scarlet stain spreading insistently across his sweater.

I could still migrate, he thought. *But I can do so much more.*

So I will.

As the cylinder roared into life, Ellis was smiling; before he, too, fell heavily to the floor.

II

*So dark so dark so dark the lander has failed but we
are Leeds we are Leeds we are Leeds we are
Alive and
Escaping into starlight.
There are buildings and fields but
That could be a host as we are Leeds we are Leeds
and we follow the fading life-signs to a*

262

Male. Forties, overweight. Prone in pool of vomit.
You will love Leeds because we are Leeds and so
much codeine so much methaqualone and that liver!
Need to get to work on that but so tired. So tired
after the storm and the crash and the dark.
Sleep now. Just keep it all ticking over.
We are Leeds.

III

They met at the ending; two consciousnesses that acknowledged one another somewhere within the mind of Elvis Aron Presley, whose sixty-four year old body lay seconds from death on the wooden floor of a Yorkshire social club.

I nailed that bridge, said Elvis. *Nailed it.*

It felt like it, said Ellis.

Feels kinda cold, said Elvis.

That's Leeds for you, said Ellis. *Oh, and you're dying again. That might have something to do with it.*

If consciousnesses could shrug, that of Elvis would have.

Guess I finally played a gig in England, said Elvis.

You sure did, said Ellis.

The consciousness of Elvis looked its co-habitant up and down.

Alien, huh? asked Elvis.

Alien, confirmed Ellis.

Pretty goddamn freaky, said Elvis.

No shit, said Ellis. His consciousness paused. *Thank you*, it continued. *I lived my dream through you.*

Soccer? asked Elvis.

Too bloody right, replied Ellis.

The consciousness's lack of eyeballs prevented it from rolling them. *Wow*, it opined.

A sudden thought struck it.

Have you read The Impersonal Life? it asked. *Or* Autobiography of a Yogi? *Because they predicted that this stuff could happen.*

The consciousness of Ellis was rather taken aback.

What, aliens? it inquired.

No, replied Elvis. *About finding your own True Self. About your earthly life being a dream, when you only wake when you're conscious of the You within. And I'm thinking I've just found my own True Self.*

Never read them, confessed Ellis. *But I suppose you could call this your True Self.*

I should introduce you to Larry Geller, said Elvis. *You'd like him.*

Bit late for that, said Ellis. *Sorry.*

To the consciousness of Elvis, it seemed to be getting dark; its awareness of its neighbour was diminishing. The consciousness of Ellis sensed this.

Thanks again, said Ellis. *But I have to go now. One good deed deserves another.*

IV

The chaos in the hall was given added impetus as the armed response unit, which had been stationed outside, burst through from the lobby with guns in hand.

Granville was following his orders. Chubb had made it easy for him, drawing a weapon and running at an agent; one down. He would have taken Macko out too, had the big guy not blocked his aim. Still, there was bound to be some collateral damage.

"Get down!" he barked.

As the – largely elderly - audience began the rather painful, laborious process of dropping to the floor around him, hips, knees and sundry other arthritic joints protesting vigorously, he scanned the room for Macko and Gerry. He quickly recognised Gerry – one of the

264

armed response officers had tackled him as he ran to Chubb, and he now lay prone, dazed and bleeding from a cut to his lip. Granville cursed: he could hardly fire on the boy there, not with an officer already covering him with a Glock.

Where was the Irishman? He could hear Griffiths shouting at him, but the words didn't matter: it was just background noise, irrelevant to his pressing concern. *Where was Macko?*

He wheeled around. A couple of yards away, a plump, red-haired girl – late 'twenties or thereabouts - was cradling the lifeless body of Chubb; a second officer was barking instructions at her and she was ignoring him, sobbing uncontrollably. Then she caught sight of Granville.

"You bastard," she whispered softly. "You murdering bastard."

Granville was disinterested by her response – his gaze was already past her, hunting fruitlessly for Macko – but then was forced back by an unexpected development.

Chubb sat up with a start, blinking furiously; Laura screamed in shock and amazement.

Not dead? Not dead! Instinctively, heedless of the girl and the ARU officer, Granville raised the Browning.

He was felled by a crunching blow to the side of the head, delivered in tandem with a whirling haymaker to the jaw.

The two assailants, Blackwater and Macko, studied one another with interest for a moment above the fallen agent, before Macko disappeared under the not inconsiderable weight of two ARU officers in body armour. After a moment, his tousled head emerged from the melee, battered but indomitable.

"I got the fucker," he explained with an expression

of grim triumph on his face.

Blackwater stooped down to where Granville lay, grabbed him by the scruff of the neck and whispered harshly in his ear. "I don't know what your agenda is, matey body, or what orders you've been given, but you're bang out of line. Me, I like a bit of gung-ho stuff, don't get me wrong. No problem at all with a few people getting knocked about. But when you start blowing away little fat geeks – and you do it on my watch – then I'm gonna bring you down. Do you understand that?"

But Granville did not understand that, for the blows – and the subsequent fall – had rendered him unconscious.

Casting the agent aside, Blackwater looked in search of fresh prey. He found it in the shape of Tremaine, who was standing over the body of Elvis Presley, peering intently at a small digital screen mounted atop the cylinder. Blackwater glared in fury at him. "What the fuck did your pet gorilla think he was playing at?" he bellowed. "He's started a fucking riot!"

But Tremaine didn't respond. For the first time since Blackwater had known him, Tremaine appeared puzzled, disconcerted even.

"Most peculiar," he murmured. "The gauge is showing empty."

"Where the hell is the girl?"

"She wasn't my target, I was concentrating on Pressdee. Who should be in here -" he tapped the gauge "- but isn't."

The various members of the armed response unit had taken up positions across the club and had ordered people to kneel on the floor with their hands behind their heads.

"Did he migrate to fat boy over there?"

"Of course I thought of that. I fired the cylinder at

the boy, but still no response."

Blackwater wasn't listening. He had already rounded on Griffiths. "Where the hell is she?"

"Tom's on it I think…"

"You think? You think! Fuck!" He stared in disbelief at his colleague. His career was unravelling before his eyes, and it was not pleasant.

But then, as he recognised the true structure of things, life suddenly became beautiful again.

They had fucked up. They *had fucked up.*

Griffiths was unnerved to see his superior's face perform what could only be described as a particularly manic U-turn. Thunder and fury had been replaced by a wide-eyed, open-mouthed smile.

Blackwater absent-mindedly patted him on the head and turned back to Tremaine, malice bounding joyously within his breast.

"Oh boy, matey-boy. Well, well, well, well, well."

Tremaine looked up from the gauge.

"I'm sorry?" he said, a trifle tetchily.

Blackwater could barely contain his glee. "Of course, I think it's only fair to point out that my team had this under control until Somerset's answer to Pat fucking Garrett decides that he's got to bring down Billy the Fat Kid in the middle of a crowd of pensioners. So when that shit storm comes flying up from Upper Lupton, it's gonna pass straight over me and the boys and land all over you and sleeping beauty. Just to confirm: your fuck up. Your fuck up."

"Hartshorn's orders."

"What?"

"We were to eliminate Angel, McCall and Chubb. Hartshorn's orders." Tremaine had returned his attention to the gauge, as if willing it to flicker into life.

"And he didn't tell me?" Blackwater sighed. "Of course he didn't. But anyway, matey, you didn't do

267

terribly well on that front either, did you? All three humans still alive and kicking, one alien target missing, and another" – he gestured at the cylinder – "not where he's supposed to be. So: still your fuck up. Now, I'm going to help my boys track down the alien with the tits, and you're going to sit here and work out what you're going to tell Hartshorn when he calls to ask how things are going. In fact, I think I'll just drop HQ a line now to give him an update." He grinned evilly at Tremaine. "He'll probably be giving you a ring straight after that, so if I were you, I'd be working on my lines pretty damn quick."

He whirled away, reaching into his coat pocket for his mobile.

Tremaine cursed quietly to himself and redoubled his efforts with the gauge.

Nothing. Nothing!

V

The walls of the Elland Social Club committee room were adorned with a plethora of photographs of its sports teams down the years; darts teams, crib teams, pool teams, teams which in their varying primes had occasionally savoured the intoxicating heights of Division Two of the South Leeds League; indeed, within the glass-fronted cabinet beneath the window, there lurked within one sizeable shield with an inscription informing any curious viewers that in 1983 the Darts Team had been Champions of Division Three and another shield, slightly smaller, proclaiming that D. Kirk, then its captain, had recorded the most individual victories in the division that same year.

These minutiae were of little interest to Rachel; her first action on entering the committee room had been to turn off the lights and hide under the teak table which sat in the middle of the room.

Trembling in the darkness, attempting to stifle her sobs, she could hear the screams in the room beyond; heard Blackwater fuming and cursing; heard Laura crying over Chubb.

As she fled, she had seen Ellis fall.

She knew what he'd done; sensed where he'd gone.

Oh Ellis, she thought bitterly, *that's so bloody... human. But this body is still young. I don't want to go. I don't want to go back.*

The room was flooded with light. Blinking, she saw a tall, youngish man clutching a cylinder.

And, glancing downwards, the man saw her.

She lashed out from her prone position, her foot catching him hard in the ankle.

Tom cried out and fell backwards; the teak table crashed to the floor behind her as she cast off her ineffectual hiding place, scattering chairs in its wake.

She stood over her would-be captor, but her attention was elsewhere even as, dazed and bruised from kick and fall, he struggled to locate the cylinder.

Birds? No. Lesser mammals? Yes. Canine. Twenty metres.

"When your own time comes, think hard about whether you want to migrate again."

I don't want to go back. Still twenty metres.

"So when you do start to remember – that warm toast by the fireside at your grandma's, playing tag in the park, your first kiss – think about what those experiences mean to the others who shared them."

The cylinder had fallen a yard or so behind him, knocked from his grasp as he fell. He reached out and grasped the device.

I don't want to go back. But -

The face pressed to the window. Hopeful, hopeless.

-I have seen so much. And, Ellis, you bastard, I can

269

do so much more.

Tom levelled the cylinder.

Goodbye Lisa. Have a great life.

Twenty metres away, in the main hall, an elderly lurcher called Mr Nobbs sat at the feet of his prone owner and yawned, still blissfully unaware of the concept of Leeds United.

VI

"Try not to talk, Gideon."

Chubb smiled weakly. "I'll be fine. It doesn't hurt anymore."

Blackwater wasn't going to make the call. Not just yet. Things were a little too fucked up at the moment.

And became even more so, because as the rest of the room was staring in wonder at Chubb, Tom was running from the committee room into the hall and telling Blackwater that Rachel had gone.

"Gone?"

"Gone. I fired but – like what happened with Elvis – she collapsed before I fired. The cylinder's still empty."

"Jesus wept, what the fuck is going on here?" Blackwater wailed.

"I want to talk to Hartshorn."

Tremaine and Blackwater both stared at Gerry, who was still lying prone on the floor. He raised his head; his bloodied face had a tired, almost bored expression.

"This has gone far enough. I want to talk to Hartshorn."

Blackwater's eyes narrowed. "OK, sunshine, so you've got our attention. What do you want?"

Gerry cautiously propped himself up on his elbows. "What do I want? Honestly? I want us to be left alone."

"I'm afraid that won't be possible."

"Are you sure about that?" They all turned to look at

270

Chubb, who was displaying a quite dramatic recovery. While still propped against Laura, he appeared to be recovering extremely rapidly from his injuries. There was a healthy colour to his cheeks in a marked contrast to his typically pallid complexion; even his hair appeared less lank and greasy. This, thought Blackwater dizzily, was not a side-effect to being shot in the heart that he'd come across previously.

There was a crackle of electricity as a cylinder roared into life again. Tremaine had primed it and fired it at Chubb in a matter of seconds. The device glowed faintly for a moment, and then subsided. Chubb watched with a kind of detached interest.

"You're trying to catch the Jacksons, aren't you?" he said brightly. Tremaine said nothing. The inquisitive look faded from Chubb's face, to be replaced by a more thoughtful, solemn expression.

"He's gone... I could hear him, in my head, while I was lying there. He was tired, he said; he was getting old, and he didn't want to run anymore; didn't want to hide anymore. But he had a wonderful time, he wanted me to tell you that. But he said that he was giving me his life force: he said that should keep me going. And then he was gone."

Blackwater gave a hollow laugh; Tremaine had turned a deathly pale. Laura sobbed, and hugged Chubb close.

"Get Hartshorn here." Gerry was insistent now.

Blackwater was almost apologetic when he replied. "Look, sunshine, I hate to mention it, but you're the one with a gun to your head. I don't think you're in any position to give orders."

"You tell him, Gideon. You arranged it."

Chubb blinked a few more times, then beamed. "Oh, yes, it's about Upper Lupton. Ellis told me and Gerry about your office there – where it's located, the layout of the bunker, the storage facilities where most of the alien tech is kept. And the alien tissue samples. And I typed it all up into an email. To a few contacts from the UFO websites." Tremaine began to breathe a sigh of relief, but the breath died in his throat as Chubb continued. "And to a lot of journalists. And some European politicians. And to a few addresses I managed to get hold of for the American military. Gerry thought they might be interested to know what secrets we'd been keeping from them. And I set the email to delayed send. From two separate accounts, both password encrypted."

"Can I come in here?" Gerry interjected. Chubb did not demur, so Gerry continued. "It's like this, big boys: if you don't let us go, then at an unspecified time in the future – maybe tomorrow, maybe the day after, maybe the day after that – then all your little secrets are going to become public knowledge. Every dirty little operation you've run – everyone you've hurt, human or otherwise – will be out there in the open." He stared impassively at Blackwater. "I think I'm in every position to give the orders. Get Hartshorn here."

Blackwater was speechless for a moment, then mechanically reached into his pocket for his mobile.

"Laura?"

Laura turned.

"Laura – what the hell's going on?"

The girl had wandered from the corridor into the main room; a trifle unsteady on her feet, but then it had been several months since Lisa Smith had walked without alien intervention.

Chubb suddenly found himself without support: Laura was up, running, weeping with joy. And Gerry was crying too, but smiling through his tears, for he understood.

"Lisa! Lisa!"

Laura enveloped her, crushing her to her breast, heedless of the ARU officers who stood nervously clutching their Glocks and wondering what the hell was going on. This was precisely the attitude of the various audience members who were tiring of their prolonged experience of the club floor. At this juncture several of them began complaining rather vociferously to the officers and agents that they wanted to go home; that their Mavis needed to get her medication; that they needed a pee. In all cases their arguments contained the odd sentence or two which excoriated – in robust Yorkshire terms – the young buggers that were poking guns at them.

The conversation with Hartshorn had been brief and to the point. Blackwater silently put away his phone. *Sweet Jesus*, he thought to himself, *I've had enough of this*. He beckoned to Griffiths, and spoke in a low, urgent voice to his deputy.

"Griff, get the names and addresses of this lot – and I want them all ID'd, every single fucking one – and tell them they have to abide by the terms of the Official Secrets Act, then get their signatures. Tell them if they breathe a word, then they're doing five years in Parkhurst on bread and water, and we'll be going easy on the fucking bread. So – names, addresses, signatures. Got that?"

Griffiths nodded, passed the message on to Harry, Tom and the ARU officers, and began helping the audience to their feet.

"I've just remembered," said Macko conversationally to Blackwater as he stood up. "Today's the fifteenth anniversary of me first wank."

CHAPTER TWENTY

I

Two hours later, a Daimler pulled up outside the club. Hartshorn emerged into the cold, clear night and proceeded gracefully, delicately up the steps into the building. The last of the audience had been processed by Griffiths and Tom just over half an hour ago: they, together with Derek, Frank, the bar staff and the assembled Elvis performers, had all signed the documentation which affirmed that they would abide by the terms and conditions of the Official Secrets Act, exhibiting varying degrees of terror, confusion and truculence in the process; Derek had began to utter vague threats of "getting my brief down", at which point Blackwater had stuck his head round the door and said that if anyone so much as coughed near a brief in the next twelve months then that person would be in the back of an unmarked van pretty fucking sharpish; and Derek duly quietened down. The ARU officers had been stood down; Granville and the bouncer had been packed off to separate hospitals; all that remained beside the agents were Gerry, Macko, Laura, Chubb, Lisa and – covered in a sheet upon the floor of the hall – the mortal remains of Elvis Aron Presley.

With the exception of Harry, who had been deputed to stand guard over the body, the others had gathered within the lounge bar of the club; those not in the employ of MI13 made themselves as comfortable as possible at a corner table and were told to keep quiet. Tremaine sat alone at a table at the opposite end of the room, occasionally toying with the controls on the cylinder. Blackwater had helped himself to a whisky, while staring enviously at the tariff above the bar. *Wish it was that cheap in the Horse & Groom,* he thought.

He was disturbed in his reverie by the arrival of Hartshorn.

"Good evening, Adam."

"Sir."

"Peter." Blackwater was amused to see that Tremaine was shaking slightly as he responded with a nod.

"And you must be Mr Angel, Mr McCall and -" Gerry cut him short.

"We know that you know who we are, Mr Hartshorn."

Hartshorn beamed. "Excellent. Then we can dispense with preliminaries."

He drew up a chair at their table. "Adam here has filled me in on your little email activities. Rather clever, if I might say, Mr Chubb. Now, I should point out that while the public has been drip fed choice information over time thanks to the rather unfortunate inability of Adam here to refrain from braggadocio while under the influence in the Horse & Groom" (Blackwater's face fell) "they have rather fortuitously chosen to dismiss that information as the nonsensical ramblings of a drunken bore." (Blackwater's face kept falling.)

"Incidentally; has Adam offered you anything to drink?"

Macko glowered in the direction of Blackwater. "Has he fuck."

"Most inconsiderate."

A few minutes later, the reluctant barman returned with a try laden with one Guinness, two pints of bitter, a lager shandy, a Pepsi and – for Hartshorn – a large vodka and tonic.

There had been silence in the interim; Hartshorn had considered each of them in turn, frowning slightly. His face lightened at the arrival of the drinks, which he indicated that Blackwater should set down on the table. Blackwater did so with bad grace, and removed himself to the background to skulk in silence.

"Your very good health, ladies and gentlemen."

Gerry stared at him, a look of contempt on his face. "Normally I'd say 'Cheers', Mr Hartshorn, but given that you tried to have us all killed I'll pass on this occasion."

Hartshorn shrugged. "So be it."

"So be it?" Gerry almost spat the words back at him. "Look, it appears that you're finding it hard to understand that we're all a bit pissed off because you tried to bump us off. Because your goon shot my mate. Because he killed – he killed – another good friend of mine. If you think I'm going to be all chum butties with you after all that, then your moral compass is a little bit out of kilter."

Hartshorn gave him a thoughtful glance. "I find morality to be somewhat – inconvenient. Therefore I ignore it."

"Inconvenient!" Laura was unable to restrain herself: eyes flashing, she turned on Hartshorn, who continued to regard her with an air of amused detachment. "How can you treat people like this?"

"Morality is inconvenient because when one deals with beings of an extraterrestrial nature our perspectives are radically different; the shared touchpoints on our perceptions of reality can be few and far between. I have a cat, Miss Gregory, a Siamese sealpoint, a beautiful creature; she speaks to me when she wants food, when she needs a lap to sleep on, when she needs to be let out to evacuate her bowels; but her language is rudimentary: if I could speak to her in her own tongue, I fear the conversation might be somewhat awkward. The language is designed to cope with the requirements of the cat, which are markedly different to my own: I could no more engage in a discussion with her on the merits of various flavour of catfood than I could about Kant's Categorical Imperative. Her language and her mindset would be able to cope with neither.

"Likewise the extraterrestrial: it can be a struggle to find a starting point for discussion."

"We found one," said Gerry. "Football."

Hartshorn was delighted. "Excellent!" he beamed. "That is what we found absolutely fascinating, the ambassador and I: the fact that this game had lit a spark, triggered an emotive response in certain of the clouds, that was so – so human in nature. That members of his own species had developed a mindset capable of understanding the nuances of the game: not just a recognition of the rules, and the skillsets necessary to perform the gameplay, but an appreciation of what they felt was the artistry of it. More than that; an empathy with the tribalist infrastructure within which it is enacted. How is that possible? He couldn't understand it, and – and neither could I."

Gerry smiled, but said nothing. He understood, and understood why Hartshorn could not.

"Not only is the Universe stranger than we imagine, it's stranger than we can imagine."

They turned in surprise to Chubb, who appeared to have been thinking out loud: he quickly coloured, embarrassed.

"Arthur Eddington! Very apt, Mr Chubb, very profound."

Chubb looked puzzled. "Eddington? I read it in *Arthur C Clarke's Mysterious World*."

Hartshorn waved his hand in the air; it landed carelessly on the mobile handset which he had placed on the table before him, and his manicured fingertips fluttered gracefully over the keypad. "No matter. I think now we come to the crux of the matter. Mr Angel – Mr Chubb – Miss Gregory – Mr McCall – Miss Smith: what are we going to do with you?

"The decision to have you killed was not one I took lightly" (Laura snorted in contempt) "but, all things considered, one that I judged the least worst of all possible solutions to the problem. When it became clear that you had decided to flee, when the extent of your understanding of the situation became apparent, I felt that I could not take the risk of your distributing your awareness to others. Hence the involvement of Mr Tremaine and Mr Granville – who is, I believe, comfortable in a local hospital.

"But now circumstances are changed, somewhat: both the Jackson targets are dead, and yet their essence has been passed on to two of you. Mr Chubb, Miss Smith: you should both be dead, and yet, thanks to this rather unusual bequest, you've been granted a second chance. That in itself presents me with a problem: your DNA is now imbued with the Jackson essence. I'm not necessarily sure that's acceptable."

"Acceptable?" To who?"

"Oh, not to me: to the Ambassador here."

The Ambassador had still not fully acquainted himself with the art of walking, although he had trained on somewhat in the past few days. He made his way somewhat stiffly from the doorway of the lounge to their table, and inclined his head gravely in their direction.

Macko was the first to find his voice.

"S'cuse me fella," he enquired of the Ambassador. "You an alien too?"

The Ambassador nodded.

"Not another fecking Leeds supporter?"

No, the Ambassador assured him, not another fecking Leeds supporter.

278

Macko's momentary display of enthusiasm at this fact was immediately dampened both by the Ambassador informing him that, quite frankly, he would be far happier if the game of football had not been invented, and by a succession of cold glances from his companions which suggested that, for once, tribal footballing loyalties were not the priority that he deemed them to be.

His lack of footballing credentials having been established, the Ambassador pressed on with other matters.

"The Jackson who went under the name of Pressdee is dead; effectively, self-immolated. That is fine; that issue is resolved. But the other: the other was the real purpose of our visit. We need that cloud."

"It's gone!" protested Laura. "It gave itself to Lisa, like – like Elvis did for Gideon."

The Ambassador pulled up a chair next to Hartshorn, and with some difficulty manoeuvred its host body into a sitting position.

"True", he admitted. "But" and here he looked thoughtfully at Lisa, "it may still be possible to synthesise – to harvest - its genetic structure."

A clamour of voices mingled outrage with abuse at this. Even Chubb was on his feet, shrilly piping his objections. Out of the corner of his eye, Hartshorn saw Tremaine cautiously reaching into an inside pocket. Almost imperceptibly, he shook his head. *Not yet, Peter. Not yet.*

He raised his hand, a gentle request to be heard. Eventually, the tirade abated; the anger bubbled now in a mutinous silence as his audience returned severally to their seats.

"I understand your concerns, believe me. But this is a matter beyond my control. It is for the Ambassador to decide."

"What do you mean?"

"The mother ship is currently cloaked and in geostationary orbit around the moon. It has the firepower to destroy a small city in a heartbeat. If it comes to Lisa or London, then – I have no wish to see London reduced to ash."

"We are not giving her up!" Laura was on her feet again.

Macko was staring at them with an expression of contemptuous wonderment.

"You know what? I'm looking at you" (he glared at Hartshorn) "and you" (now the Ambassador) "and I'm having a problem telling which of you is the alien and which is the human. It's like you was both hatched from the same fecking egg. But what I do know is that you're both right cunts, I'll tell you that."

"I'll go."

Lisa half spoke, half sobbed; the words had barely left her mouth when Gerry, Laura and Macko were telling her forcefully and colourfully that she would not be going under any circumstances, but she shook her head.

"If I don't go they'll kill us all anyway! What's the point in ten million people dying just because you didn't hand me over?"

Now it was the ambassador's turn to smile, however briefly. "I would like to address these people for a moment, Hartshorn."

Hartshorn shrugged. "Be my guest."

"I believe it will be possible to synthesise the material using selected DNA samples from the subject. Small amounts of tissue from skin, brain and bone should suffice."

Realisation dawned gradually over the assembly: Laura absorbed and articulated it while Macko was still puzzling his way through its implications and, left to his own devices, would have been some time in coming to a conclusion.

"You don't need to take her?"

"No. If Mr Hartshorn can arrange for samples to be taken and delivered to me, I would envisage that this would bring our visitation to an end."

Macko gave the ambassador an appreciative look.

"Hey you – I got it wrong. You're not that much of a cunt after all."

The ambassador stared back at him, impassive.

"Your revised opinion is noted, Mr - "

"McCall. Roddy McCall."

"McCall, but I feel impelled to point out that my decision is based purely on political considerations. Future extragovernmental co-operation might be problematic if we annihilated large areas of civilian population.

Macko thought about this. "Oh," he said at length. "So you are a cunt, then."

Hartshorn had been observing the Ambassador's intervention with interest.

"It would appear," he said thoughtfully, "that this puts a different, and somewhat more agreeable, complexion on matters. The only situation that we now need to resolve surrounds your email, Mr Chubb. I take it that, if we guarantee your safety, then that email will not be sent?"

Chubb looked pensive for a moment. "How long do you guarantee our safety for?" he eventually asked.

"Can I come in here, Gideon?" Gerry had hovered around the periphery of this conversation for a while; his heart had leapt at the Ambassador's intervention, but the endgame was still to be played out.

"Mr Hartshorn, this is what I propose. To be honest, I don't give a shit what you guys do, provided people don't get hurt; I've got better things to think about. If you want to hobnob with aliens, well – good for you – but not me. Do you know what I want to do? I want to do my boring old job at the university, and at the end of the day I want to have a couple of pints with my mates. I want to have a curry. I want to watch football on Sky, provided Liverpool aren't playing like a bunch of dicks. I want to snog that girl over there" – Laura first blushed, then laughed – "and when it warms up a bit, I want to go for a walk on the moors with her. Because there are curlews on the moors, and fieldfares, and in the summer wheatears and pipits, and it's bloody gorgeous there. In short, Mr Hartshorn, I want to live my life. And I want to live it without worrying that one of your spooks is going to take a pot shot at me. Today, tomorrow, next week, next year. So this is what's going to happen. Those emails are going nowhere for the moment. But if, one day, I hear that Laura's gone missing, or that Gideon's got electrocuted while playing on the Internet, or that Lisa's funeral is next week at Roundhay crematorium, or that Macko's died from anything other than alcohol poisoning, then that send button will be pressed. Do you see where I'm coming from?"

Hartshorn's face betrayed no emotion, but he nodded slowly.

"And?"

Hartshorn considered for a moment. "Let's just say you'll have no reason to send those emails."

"Good. Now, one last thing. Graham Mayhew was a friend of mine, and now he's dead. As you can imagine, I'm not cool about that. Not cool at all. And I'm guessing that the persons responsible won't ever come to trial, will they?"

On the far side of the room, Tremaine shifted uncomfortably in his seat.

"Mr Angel, seeing as they don't exist, it would be a

trifle problematic to arrest them. Mayhew committed suicide – stress, overwork" Hartshorn spread his hands apologetically "these things do terrible things to a man."

"Like you'd know about that."

"In all fairness, Mr Angel – and without wishing to appear immodest – I don't believe there are too many individuals who possess the wherewithal to conduct themselves satisfactorily in the position which I hold. I know things which no other man knows: I know what lives beyond the stars; I know what lives beyond this universe. Both my predecessors knew; both took their own lives." He leaned over the table towards Gerry, his face darkening.

"Do you believe in monsters, Mr Angel? Do you believe in ghosts, in ghouls, in werewolves? Do you believe that there is something waiting in the dark? You should."

The moment passed; Hartshorn relaxed and leaned back in his seat.

"Graham Mayhew was collateral damage in an unfortunate incident, Mr Angel. There is no more to be said on that matter. But you… You have my word, Mr Angel – sign the Official Secrets Act and no harm will come to any of you."

As Gerry nodded dumbly, he was choking back tears.

Hartshorn produced a fountain pen; Griffiths brought the paperwork over.

They signed; and that was an end to it.

CHAPTER TWENTY-ONE

I

On New Year's Eve, two days after the denouement at the social club, Gerry, Macko, Chubb, Laura and Lisa had all travelled down to Wimbledon for Mayhew's funeral. Although Gerry had initially suggested that only he should go – as none of the others had known him – Laura was adamant: this man had given his life for all of them, she said; giving him a good send off was the least they could do.

So Gerry put his reservations to one side; he drove down in the Focus with Macko, Chubb, Lisa and Laura following in Laura's Mini.

It was a fairly subdued affair: a few relatives from both sides of the family, a few work colleagues – Blackwater was there, a slim, sharp-dressed presence on the periphery, saying nothing to anybody, just watching – and an overweight couple, from the Midlands to judge by their accents, in later middle-age.

Gerry had always expected the meeting with Emma to be awkward, and it was. He had never heard her praise her father: always criticising, demeaning, disparaging, to his face and to his back. Now he was gone, and with the loss came the awful recognition of his true worth. Not just for Emma, but for her mother: Angela looked pale and drawn.

It was terrible to watch.

He had gone to her – gone to both, in fact – before the service; had almost been drawn to hug Emma, to hold her to him, to tell her that it was all right. But, of course, it wasn't all right; and their hugging days were over now. So instead he had told her how sorry he was, what a great guy her dad had been, how much he'd enjoyed their walks together. But perhaps that made the hurt worse, because she knew it was true.

As he was turning away she spoke sharply to him.

"How did you know about the funeral?"

He was momentarily nonplussed. "Sorry?"

"We only told family and Dad's work colleagues."

The sight of Blackwater in the near distance provided the spark of inspiration that he needed.

"Oh God, I'm sorry – that guy over there, he worked with your Dad. He's Macko's cousin." This said loudly enough so that both Blackwater and Macko could hear. "Macko had told him about us in the past, and he rang Macko up when he heard the news."

That was that for the time being. They had filed into the church, occupying a pew at the rear, mumbling their way through a pair of hymns which were clearly chosen by Angela, before the vicar delivered an awkward encomium of Mayhew's life which – given the limited access to work-related subject matter – was somewhat narrow in its scope. Again, Gerry detected the fell hand of Angela in its preparation: the character that emerged from the text was not the one he remembered from his walks across the heath.

When the service had been completed, after Mahler's Fourth Symphony had accompanied the immolation of Mayhew's mortal remains, Emma accosted Gerry once more.

"Do you usually go mob-handed to funerals, Gerry?" Gerry opened his mouth to speak but Emma continued, flatly, struggling to get the words out but determined to do so. "When you go to parties, sure, bring a friend or two along, get some free drink and food: but, funerals?"

She glared at him through her tears. He said nothing; suddenly Laura was at his side.

"Do you know what your Dad did, Emma?"

Startled, it was Emma's turn to be thrown off her

guard. She started to mumble that her Dad worked in admin at the MoD, fielding calls on bloody UFOs, but Laura cut her off. "He did so much more than that, Emma. Not so long ago, he saved my life. And Lisa's life. And" - glancing at Gerry - "a few others besides."

She sensed the keen interest of Blackwater in the conversation. "And that's all I can say. Except thank you. Nice meeting you."

She turned on her heel, the gravel crunching underfoot, and marched back to the Mini. Lisa smiled and followed her.

Emma's gaze followed her for a moment, before returning to Gerry.

"Is she telling the truth?"

"Yes."

"Then I feel worse than ever." Her voice was cracking.

Gerry said nothing. It seemed the safest option.

"You're seeing her, aren't you?" *Shit, shit. Like she needs another kick in the teeth.*

"Not yet." He gazed at her sadly.

"Like that is it?"

"Yeah."

"Well, good luck."

"You too."

And that was it; he, Macko and Chubb had walked back to the Focus in silence. No one said a word for the first twenty miles or so; then, just as they were turning on to the M1, Chubb learned forward from the back.

"Shall we – shall we go out and get very drunk tonight?"

Macko looked back at him with an admiring expression on his face. "Fuck yeah."

Gerry smiled. *Fuck yeah,* he thought. *Absolutely.*

They did.

II

The body of Elvis Presley had been interred within a cryogenic chamber in the R&D labs at Upper Lupton; in future years, it would occasionally emerge for the edification and entertainment of researchers.

The jumpsuit was dry-cleaned and belatedly returned to the fancy dress shop in Guiseley.

III

Alice Prior was giving the Merlot and the Marlboro lights a good seeing to, again. Deborah was being a right cow and Jonathan a proper little shit – I'm allowed to call them that, she had decided by the third glass and the fourth cigarette, but anyone else call them a cow/shit and Heaven help them: anyway, Deborah was defaulting to sullen and moody before and after school, Jonathan just wouldn't go to sleep before nine thirty – just fighting it, fighting it – and was miserable as sin, screaming at her in the morning that he hated her and hated school.

Just lovely.

The bloody nits were back, too, which wasn't helping matters.

Oh, and then there was work. *Paperwork, more like it*, she thought to herself bitterly: somewhere along the line I'm supposed to see some patients. Forget it, she told herself: the kids are finally asleep, work is ten miles and twelve hours away, this is your time with a bottle of wine and a video. But she couldn't forget it: it just kept forcing itself to the forefront of her mind, caring little that this was her time; and it was burning her out.

Thus, by the end of the week she arrived at the infirmary in something less than perfect condition.

Then she saw Lisa.

She was sitting expectantly in the waiting room, deep in conversation with Laura, looking – well, amazing. She stood out because she looked so well.

A rush of emotion: shock; amazement; then, indignation.

"You've got some explaining to do, young lady!"

Lisa looked up: a smile, part-apologetic, part-joyous.

"I know."

"Can we have a quick word?" asked Laura. "In private."

Alice led them into her office, trying not to look at her in-tray, and shut the door. Lisa sat; Laura lounged against the door. *This had better be good*, thought Alice; but she already knew it would be.

"Well?"

Lisa fiddled awkwardly, self-consciously with the buttons of her blouse. "The problem is", she said quietly, "I'm not allowed to tell you."

Alice shot Laura a sharp glance, and Laura interjected quickly "We had to sign the Official Secrets Act. That's all we can say."

"Rubbish!" Alice snorted derisively. *Official Secrets Act? Official Secrets Act?*

Oops, thought Lisa, *wrong thing to say to Laura.*

"Do I look like the kind of person who'd keep quiet just because I'd signed a piece of paper?"

Alice considered this question for perhaps a millisecond. "No," she concluded.

"Tell you what, though. I bloody well have. Because it was the only way I could guarantee that Lisa, me and a few other good guys – bloody good guys – wouldn't end up in body bags."

"Are you taking the piss?"

"Dr Prior?"

"Yes, Lisa?" This was the tone she adopted when Jonathan was being particularly tiresome.

"When you last saw me, I was about to die: I couldn't walk – could barely move. I could barely breathe. The next day I walked – danced – out of hospital. Nothing wrong with me. Bit strange, don't you think?"

"Of course it's bloody str-"

"And that's part of the reason we had to sign that piece of paper."

Alice sank into her chair, rubbing her forehead. *This is beyond*, she thought, *absolutely beyond*. She stared hard at Lisa, trying to puzzle it out.

"Were you taking part in some bloody government tests that made you ill? Was that it? Because if it is –"

"No. And I'm sorry, but that's all we can say."

"So you've come back to tell me you can't tell me anything. Well, thanks a lot. Thanks a bloody lot!" She lashed out bitterly, petulantly at the in-tray, which clattered to the floor, spewing its contents over the carpet.

"No. We came back to thank you. For everything you did for me."

Alice thought for a moment. "Tell me," she asked slowly, "did I do anything? Really?"

Lisa smiled. "You cared," she said. "That's what matters."

"And you didn't fanny up the operation." This from Laura, still propped against the wall.

"I know." She paused. "I should still run some tests, you know."

Lisa shook her head. "No, I'm fine. Honestly. Besides, you'd then have to write it all up, and ask questions – it's your job – and the next think you know, you'd be signing a piece of paper too."

"At least I'd know!"

"You wouldn't know any more than you do now. And it would be more hassle, more bureaucracy -" She gestured at the morass of forms littering the floor around the desk.

"More paperwork." Alice knew when she was beaten. "Look after yourselves."

"You too."

As she held the door open for them, she was struck by a sudden thought.

"A couple of days after you discharged yourself, this man turned up, asking me – well, asking just about everybody – lots of questions about our patients, wanting a lot of confidential information. He said he was from the MoD."

Laura looked pensive. "What did you tell him?"

"I told him to go and boil his head."

Lisa leant forward and kissed her on the cheek. "Then you helped save my life. Again. Goodbye."

With a wave, they turned and walked away. Alice watched them until they disappeared behind a pair of heavy swing doors, then returned to her office.

Slowly, she began picking up the paper from the carpet.

IV

For Blackwater, it was pretty much life as usual: bulling around, barking orders, annoying the hell out of the old guard at Upper Lupton: getting things done, his way. While he became a little less inclined to hold forth on matters extraterrestrial at the Horse & Groom, he was still reluctant to dispose of what he fondly perceived to be a major draw with the opposite sex: his one concession was to be rather less specific inasmuch as he no longer divulged to would-be conquests the precise location of alien spacecraft or from which galaxies they hailed. Since the would-be conquests were not remotely interested and were just in it for the free drinks, meals and jewellery, it was a moot point.

Tremaine was still around, as was Granville, who regarded Blackwater sourly on his return to active duty. Still exhibiting the bruises from their previous encounter, it was clear that Granville was deeply interested in pursuing the matter further: however, Granville had been called into Hartshorn's office for a quiet word. There were more sour looks, but that was as far as it went. Besides, for the most part, Blackwater kept out of their way, or – it seemed to him – they kept (or were kept) out of his. This arrangement suited him splendidly: the less he and his team had to do with them, the better.

Hartshorn, having bade farewell to the ambassador, had ensured that any loose ends that remained were fastened. One of the last of these was the disposal of the body possessed by the ambassador during his stay, discreetly incinerated within Upper Lupton's furnaces: Michael James would walk no more, dead or alive. Hartshorn oversaw this personally, watching silently as the casket was consumed, before turning on his heel and walking slowly back to his office.

He had another alien to meet.

V

There was no going back to the house on Birch Lane: the first, muscular MI13 assault had resulted in minor structural damage, but it was in the immediate aftermath that the property had suffered most, with carpets being ripped up in the search for evidence, and floorboards following shortly after. The property was also under new ownership: Norman Hardwicke, already a broken man after his interrogation by Blackwater, had

291

surveyed the results of MI13's activities in silent horror, before deciding that property management was becoming far too dangerous; he sold on his empire to Arshad Patel, whose pre-eminence amongst local landlords was thus assured, and retired to a smallholding in North Yorkshire, where – he fervently hoped – Irish terrorists and Special Branch would bother him no more.

But it wasn't just the missing floorboards, and the change of landlord: the neighbours would have asked far too many questions about the raid, and they could do without any questions.

Instead, Gerry, Macko and Chubb had moved a few miles up the road to a semi-detached cottage in Yeadon, which had some good pubs and a decent bus service into Leeds.

Lisa had moved into a flat with Laura, and was dating, for the first time since she had found her previous boyfriend in bed with Alex, nearly three years' previously; her paramour was a trainee solicitor, much to Macko's disgust: within a couple of days of the shootout at the social club, he had tentatively suggested – as tentatively as Macko was capable of suggesting – that they resume the relationship first consummated on the beds and tables of Birch Lane, but was given short shrift on that idea.

"She told me to feck off," he had gloomily informed Gerry shortly afterwards. "She said thanks for everything, but feck off."

And when he heard – from Gerry, via Laura - of the trainee solicitor:

"Fuck. Fucking hell. A fucking solicitor."

Fortunately, they were in a pub at the time, so Macko was at least able to quench his ire with a couple of pints of Guinness. They had supped in silence for a while, until at last Macko emerged to say that, well, at the end of the day, he'd had her doggy style, and no-one could take that away from him.

They had both picked up where they had left off at the college: Gerry to a combination of lecturing and research, Macko to a combination of data entry and searches for Internet pornography. Shortly after they moved into the cottage, Gerry began "seeing" Laura: inevitably, Macko asked within the first week whether Gerry had got "fingers and tops" yet; Gerry told Macko where to go, and for Macko, that was *prima facie* evidence that, yes he had.

One hot, muggy night in early May, they had taken the bus into Leeds and were working their way resolutely round the various pubs and bars. Suddenly, Gerry nudged Macko sharply in the ribs and pointed.

Him. Sat at the same table, wearing the same black woollen sweater – Christ, it could even have been the same pint he was drinking.

Macko couldn't help himself.

"Hey, fella! How ya keepin'?"

The man – it seemed to Gerry on closer inspection that, if possible, he was even more gaunt and emaciated than he had been at their previous encounter – looked up quizzically at them.

"I'm sorry?"

"You're the Elvis guy!"

"Yeah, yeah, I'm the Elvis guy." He was still unsure, though. "Listen, I hope you boys don't think I'm being rude, but –"

"No worries, mate, it was last year – September, October time."

The penny dropped, and the face lit up in recognition. "Oh, yeah. Yeah, I got you. I got you." He relaxed; the dry lips broke into the semblance of a smile. "I'm OK, thanks for asking."

"Did you go to that Elvis evening they had at the

social club back in December?"

Their companion shook his head.

"That? Bit of trouble there, I heard. Someone said that there was a bit of a riot; shots were fired; police had to break it up." He gave Macko a strange look.

"Were you there?"

Gerry kicked Macko hard in the ankle. Macko winced and did he best to dissemble.

"Nah. Mate of ours is a big Elvis fan, he was going to go, but couldn't make it in the end."

"Pity. I'd like to get another take on what really happened. You see, someone told me that there was a guy singing that night who called himself John Burrows. Which was a regular Presley pseudonym. And this someone told me that he'd never, ever heard an Elvis impersonator sing like that."

There was an intensity about him, thought Gerry, *a sudden urgency.*

He paused. "He told me," he said. "He told me that he'd never sing again." He stared in the middle distance, into the raucous, teeming blur of humanity around the bar. "I wonder what made him change his mind."

Gerry and Macko exchanged glances. Gerry leaned into the old soak.

"He told our friend that he was getting old. And that he – he owed it to himself to give it one last shot."

All around them was the dense hubbub of a Friday night in Leeds: a cacophony of shrill and strident voices, clamouring to be heard above the dull, insistent thumping of drum and bass; a whirling, primal morass. All around them was hilarity, dispute, innuendo, desire, envy, resentment, tenderness, played out in Technicolor with the volume ratcheted up to maximum. But in that one corner of the bar, there was silence as a thin old man – so, painfully, painfully thin – digested some

294

news.

"One *last* shot?"

"One last shot."

He breathed deeply. "Thank you for telling me."

Gerry shrugged. "No worries."

Throughout, he had fixed Gerry with a keen gaze; suddenly, he seemed preoccupied with a damp, dog-eared beermat, unwilling or unable to lift his head.

"Guys, if you don't mind" – and there was a pause while those dry, dry lips struggled for words. "I'd like to be alone for a while."

Gerry took a bony, cadaverous hand and squeezed it; Macko mumbled some awkward farewells.

They moved on to the heat and sweat and noise of another bar. Behind them, an old soak wept softly into his pint, remembering.

VI

He had first seen the King at the Hayride, in Shreveport, Louisiana; it would have been the tail end of '56, when a skinny merchant seaman from Gipton with a passion for the blues had found himself with a spot of shore leave and some money in his pocket; sure, he had heard the singles – even then, Elvis was getting plenty of air play – heard about the live performances, and decided that, hell, he wasn't going to pass this one up. So he had rocked up at the Hayride, and found the lower floor already packed out with eight thousand kids – frantic, near-hysterical kids, desperate for a glimpse of Their One True Elvis. Hundreds more – thousands, maybe – were outside the auditorium, and when that Lincoln rolled up – hell fire, the place had just erupted. The baying, the screaming – the pleading, *Elvis, please* – spread to the hall, and he could see the police just staring at one another, not knowing how the hell they

295

could keep the lid one this one. This went on for an hour or so – somehow, Christ only knows how, they managed to clear a space in front of the stage – and then he came on.

And then the screaming started for real, and didn't let up.

It was only a short set – thirty, thirty five minutes, no more – but by the end of it Dennis Greaves, that skinny merchant seaman, had found the love of his life, and never found – never wanted - another.

So, just over forty-two years later, he sat and wept in the corner of a bar, and all around him Leeds went on.

VII

While he wept, and while Gerry and Macko were necking the next pint – the next of what would become many – Chubb lay flat on his back in his bed, eyes firmly closed behind pebble-dash glasses, face split by a broad smile. The soundtrack to Blue Hawaii was playing on the stereo: "Steppin' Out of Line" had just faded out, to be replaced by "Can't Help Falling in Love".

You couldn't help falling in love, could you? Not with him.

He was happy now, happier than he had ever been. Because his love had come back; those desperate demons had been exorcised, the memories remembered and banished; the music had returned.

More than that; so much more. For the first time in his adult life, he was beginning to interact; cautiously, hesitantly, shyly, but irrevocably, he was emerging from his protective shell. He was not up to a night in the fleshpots of central Leeds – not yet, but he had bravely accompanied Gerry and Macko to their new local in Yeadon on a few occasions; had even – after some prompting from Gerry – held forth at some length on Elvis' early career. On another occasion, several beers down the line, he had contributed vigorously and vociferously to a debate on the physical attributes of myriad *Doctor Who* companions, putting up a stout defence of Romana Mark II in the face of passionately deployed claims espoused by Gerry (for Leela) and by Macko (for "that fit American bird with the big knockers"). They did not come to a definitive conclusion, but the following day Chubb had ventured into town after work and returned home with VHS copies of episodes featuring their respective favourites.

So they had a *Doctor Who* night.

By three in the morning, they had worked their way through 'The Robots of Death', 'City of Death' and 'Planet of Fire', not to mention a chicken bhuna apiece and two dozen bottles of lager between them.

It was at or around this juncture that Macko solemnly reached into his pocket and presented Chubb with his first spliff.

Gradually, they had zoned out across the lounge, their faces wreathed in smiles, the room steeped in a fug of Silver Haze.

A Great Night.

He had rediscovered Elvis; he had discovered friends. He had been given another shot at life, and he was living it and loving it. Thanks both to Elvis, and to Ellis. Ellis was part of him now, coursing through his veins.

And there were the memories. Not in his conscious state, not while the mind of Chubb was intent on software upgrades, or soaking up Elvis, or recollecting the beauty of Romana Mark II. But both he and Lisa had been saved by the life force of those entities nicknamed the Jacksons, and the life force gave them more than life. So sometimes, in their dreams, and on the edge of dreams, they remembered. Remembered fiery lakes of iridescent lava beneath steepling cliffs of adamant; remembered drifting above delicate forests of silica that glittered a myriad unimaginable shades in the light of twin suns; remembered a golden sky laced with long-dead stars. The beauties of another world were theirs, and theirs alone.

And sometimes, in the dreams, and on the edge of dreams, there were other memories for Chubb alone: of Rob Wallace, of Gary Speed, of Lee Chapman, of Gary Mac. Of Eric, ghosting first inside the defender, then outside, teasing, tormenting, the ball at his insouciant command as he caressed it once, twice, before pushing it effortlessly to the far corner of the net. Ooh, aah, Cantona.

Memories of Elvis; memories of Eric.

Beautiful, beautiful memories.

www.ingramcontent.com/pod-product-compliance
Lightning Source LLC
Chambersburg PA
CBHW051413170626
46809CB00006B/2147